By Evil Means

By Evil Means

Sandra West Prowell

Walker and Company
New York

First published in the United States of America in 1992
by Walker Publishing Company, Inc.

Published simultaneously in Canada by Thomas Allen & Son
Canada, Limited, Markham, Ontario

Library of Congress Cataloging-in-Publication Data
Prowell, Sandra West.
By evil means / Sandra West Prowell.
p.   cm.
ISBN 0-8027-1248-7
I. Title.
PS3566.R77B9   1993
813'.54—dc20   92-558
CIP

Printed in the United States of America
2 4 6 8 10 9 7 5 3 1

This book is gratefully dedicated to the following people:
Bruce, who believed;
my children, who believed along with him;
my parents, who made me possible;
my friend-agent, Barb Puechner;
my editor, Michael Seidman;
my copyeditor, Susan M. S. Brown;
and last but not least,
Phoebe Siegel, wherever you are.
Keep talking to me, Phoebe!

By Evil Means

$\triangledown$

1

MARY KUNTZ SITS DIRECTLY across from me. She stares at me with dead, tearless eyes. I know she doesn't see me, nor does she hear the sound of her index finger as it taps a mindless, arrhythmic cadence on top of the tooled leather handbag she is clutching on her lap.

I feel hypnotized by the soft, steady pulse. My hands feel like lead weights as I try to raise them from my sides, where they have been hanging limply, encrusted in a brown mosaic of dried blood.

Her presence makes me uncomfortable. Two weeks ago I didn't know she existed, and now, in the screaming silence and oppressive heat of this office, we share a knowledge, a tale of terror, that has blistered both our souls. There's a sob crouching in my throat, hidden behind my disbelief and confusion, waiting to pounce.

Somewhere beyond my vision I hear people laughing. With great effort I turn toward the sound and see nothing except my own reflection in a glass door. The laughter has stopped. Only the tapping of Mary's finger on her purse remains audible.

I raise my hand in front of my face, and as I clench my fist I feel the dried blood crack and reveal, in small, fine-lined patterns, the color of my skin. My thoughts are wandering, desperately searching for some sane thread. What has happened has to make sense, only I know it never will.

I've got to hold my temples to keep my head from exploding. Perhaps I'm not here at all. Maybe I'm in the belly of the beast where there is no digestion, just confinement and foul, noxious darkness.

By the time the end of February rolled around, I started getting anxious. It wasn't always like that; then three years ago the Ides of March decided to desert Caesar and pound the shit out of me.

The first blow came at the beginning of March and was a double-edged sword. My father's twin sister, and my beloved mentor, Zelda, dropped dead, literally, on a beach in Jamaica. When I received the call from my mother, all she said over and over again was "Why would a woman that age want to para-sail?"

To me the answer was obvious. It was something she'd never done.

A few days later the prestigious law firm of Daget, Noble & Daget of New York City informed me that one and one half million dollars had been deposited in a Franklin Puerto Rico Tax-free Income Fund in my name. I would be allowed total access to the fortune Zelda had gleaned from three husbands, with two stipulations: the first was that I could not tell anyone, without exception, that I had inherited the estate; the second was that I live my life as free from inhibition as she had.

During the second week of March I drank one long Irish toast to my dearly departed Jewish aunt, who, by the way, never quite forgave my father for marrying Maggie Flannery in St. Patrick's Cathedral on V-E Day, May 8, 1945.

I was hung over and curious that third week, wondering how one and one half million dollars would change my life, which so far had been damn simple.

Two weeks after high school graduation, I married the boy next door, Lanny Wilson. Six years later, on a cold, windy day in March, we walked out of the Yellowstone County courthouse in Billings, Montana, divorced but pledging eternal friendship. I can honestly say I didn't feel one trace of pain or bitterness on that day. I could accept the fact that we just screwed up a good friendship by getting married. But when he remarried one month later, it really pissed me off. Figure that out.

I had worked as a dispatcher at the Billings Police Department and helped Lanny finish college while I took a few courses myself. He graduated and was accepted to the Police Academy. I stayed home, worked nights, and picked up a credit here and there.

When Lanny started with the PD, I started school full-time but kept my job. I think we both knew it was over at the same time. There was never a battle or hatchet job, just a cold acceptance that we had gone as far as we could. It always hurt a little to hear his voice over the radio knowing he'd be going home to someone else.

I finally graduated from college, was recruited by the FBI, and jumped at the chance to get the hell out of Billings and train at

Quantico. For a token female recruit, I did pretty damn good and placed near the top in almost every area.

On the twenty-second of March, I was qualifying for the last time on the firing range when the Ides delivered all it had to offer. My instructor, a big guy with no neck and a heart of gold, tapped me on the shoulder and said five little words, "Your brother Ben has died."

My only real memory of that moment is how my fingers melted into the grip of the 10-mm semiautomatic I was holding and of my own reflection in his mirrored sunglasses. It didn't look like me.

Ben, an eight-year veteran of the Billings Police Department, had been found dead in his car; a single gunshot to his right temple had guaranteed that he would not make it to age thirty-five.

The next morning I was on a plane home. I never went back to the academy. I was too busy wallowing in the slug trail of unanswered questions that suicide leaves. A death is tough enough for families to handle. Suicide is downright lethal.

On March twenty-sixth we buried Ben in the family plot next to my father, who had died ten years earlier; Zelda, who had insisted she be next to my father, and my older brother, Sam, a statistic of Vietnam. My brother Michael, a priest, officiated. On that day, I stopped crying and abolished March from the Gregorian calendar, and from my mind.

That's what I was doing the day Mary Kuntz walked into my office, ceremoniously ripping March, the first through the thirty-first, page by page, off my desk calendar. I'd never been caught in the act before, so I did what anyone would do. I covered my ass.

"Have a seat," I said and smiled. "Calendars aren't what they used to be. One misprint could throw a person off for a full year."

I bunched up the thirty-one days and successfully tossed them into a wastebasket a few feet from my desk. She said nothing as she sat down.

The first thing I noticed was an FFA patch on her green nylon windbreaker. My mind churned through a quick succession of applicable terms and settled on Future Farmers of America.

"I'm Mary Kuntz," she said as she reached over the desk to shake my hand. I caught a whiff of a heavy musk scent, the kind people sell door to door. It didn't fit the woman. She scanned my face as if anticipating some hint of recognition.

My mind flipped through my untidy mental files and tried to put a face with the name and connect it with a problem.

"Have we met before?"

She said nothing for a moment and just stared at me. "No, we've . . . I've never met you, Miss Siegel."

She sat there and continued to study me. I felt like a bug under a microscope.

"You did some work for one of my neighbors on an insurance claim. Jesse Bennett?"

"Right," I said slowly as my mind kicked into gear. "Doesn't she live out by Silesia? She was being harassed by someone," I said. I love to impress prospective clients with my retentive memory. It's good for business. "There were some kids involved, as I remember, who were vandalizing her farm equipment. Right?"

"Right," Mary answered as she stirred in her seat. She didn't look impressed.

"How's she doing?"

"Great, she's doing great." She set a paper shopping bag down on the floor beside the chair.

There's something intimidating about farm wives. Everything about them is in order, or at least organized. They exude a subtle strength that lets you know right away that they don't have time for crap. I respect that.

So there I was at 8:00 A.M., with the Ides bearing down on me, eight oral injections of caffeine winding their way to my nervous system, sitting across from a woman who probably had done enough work already that morning to put a healthy man in his grave, and I was already starting to experience those heavy March blues.

"I should tell you right off that, as of tomorrow, I won't be available for a month. If this is anything urgent, there are some good people I can refer you to locally."

"No," she said in a hushed tone of voice. "I need you, Miss Siegel. You are Phoebe Siegel, aren't you?"

Something about her was disquieting. Foreboding.

"Yes, I am," I answered.

"John Flannery's niece?"

"Right again. Do you know Uncle John?"

"I've had the occasion to speak with him on certain matters," she said as her mind seemed to drift backward. "He advised me against contacting you. I don't want you to think he referred me. I . . . I wore my welcome a little thin with him, Miss Siegel. I—"

"Call me Phoebe," I interrupted. "Miss Siegel sounds like I'm ready for those sensible shoes that have all those little holes on the side."

A smile appeared briefly at the corners of her mouth. It was gone in a flash and never reached her eyes.

"It has to be you."

"Like I told you, Mary," I said. Sometimes a first-name basis put them at ease. "I don't work in March. It's just how it is. Now, here are some names of some very good and very competent investigators that I am sure . . ."

I reached into the top left-hand drawer of my desk and pulled out a telephone list. "If I can read through these coffee stains, I think I can come up with someone that you'll find satisfactory."

"I just drove thirty miles. You've got to hear me out," she snapped. There was an edge in her voice that compelled me to listen.

For the three years that I've been in business, I've had an assortment of people, from politicians to drunks to paranoid—and not so paranoid—spouses, sit across from me.

After Ben's funeral, I shut down emotionally, so none of the people walking through my office doors have gotten to me. They talk. I listen. If it works out and we're both in agreement, they get me for twenty dollars an hour plus expenses. That's a real blue-light special, and it's not like I need the money. I'm damn good at what I do. But not in March.

I leaned back in my chair, less than enthusiastic. The story was all too familiar. A troubled kid, the apple of her parents' eye who started off playing with drugs in junior high school and was sucked into a pool of addiction deeper than the Atlantic Trench.

She started spending more and more nights away from home until she was finally busted for prostitution. Mary narrated the tale dry eyed. It was all a matter of fact. When she paused, I took my best shot at worming my way out of whatever it was she wanted before it went any further.

"This sounds like something Juvenile should handle. How about I give John a call and—"

"I was there yesterday. And every day before that for two weeks. They simply aren't interested."

"Have you tried counseling?"

"Yes. We've been through all of that."

"Look, Mrs. Kuntz, Mary, I don't do kids. They have agencies out there that do nothing but. I don't even get along with kids. I'm not a counselor."

"I want you to find out what he did to my daughter."

"He? He who?" As soon as I said it, I knew I sounded like a birthing instructor.

"We've been riding an emotional roller coaster for four years. Six months ago Jennifer ended up back in treatment. The third time."

"My little sister went to treatment a few years back . . ."

"Then you understand. The first time she went into treatment, four years ago, it was in Minnesota. Jennifer completed the required number of days but had some problems with . . . she just didn't do well. During family week we had a meeting with the resident physician, a Dr. Curtis as I recall. He told us at that time that Jennifer's drug and alcohol abuse was secondary to deeper emotional problems. He suggested that we get her intensive psychiatric counseling plus outpatient care for the drugs and alcohol."

"Sometimes the best treatment programs can't help these kids if they don't want it. I'd suggest—"

"We brought her home, contacted the psychiatrist that Dr. Curtis recommended, and Jennifer started with him almost immediately. His name was Dr. Drummond, and she did fine for a while. She was involved in a youth group aftercare program and wasn't doing drugs and she wasn't drinking."

"I wasn't aware that Dr. Drummond was still in town." Jim Drummond was as well known in Billings as the yellow pages were to Ma Bell.

"He isn't. Six months into Jennifer's therapy he left. Another doctor took over his practice."

"Is she using now?"

"No . . . no she isn't."

"Look, Mary. If all is well . . ." I knew that behind that facade of stability something had to be haywire. "I guess what I'm trying to say is that I think family counseling would be more appropriate." I stood and tried to glower at her. "Now, I have lots of things to take care of since I'll be closed this next month."

Tears flooded from her eyes, and I'm a sucker for tears. Maybe because I'm so damn glad they aren't my own.

"Could I interest you in a cup of coffee?"

"I think I could use one right about now," she answered as she reached into her purse, pulled out a minipackage of Kleenex, and dabbed at her eyes. "What you need to understand is that the girl that Jennifer used to be is gone. She's much worse. Worse than before she became involved with him. There's—" Her voice broke. "There's something wrong. Horribly wrong. She's a totally different person."

I turned my back to her, walked to the file cabinet that I had the coffee maker sitting on, and started filling two cups. I was fifteen hours away from March first, so anything could happen. I tried to retain my composure and lick the I-knew-it smile off my lips before I turned around.

"I'm sure you're confused by now. Why wouldn't you be?" she said.

I've always been an admirer of perception.

"Curious would be a better word for it," I said as I handed her a cup and sat back down. "Maybe it would help if I shared something with you. You're right. They aren't the same kids when they come out. My sister definitely wasn't. They can't afford to be."

"I understand all of that, Miss Siegel. The problem is that, since Dr. Drummond left, Jennifer has been on a spiral down. We're not allowed to participate in any part of her therapy. She's refused to talk to us about the center. And this last stint cost us close to six hundred dollars a day. I expected some progress, a change, anything—"

"You paid what?"

"In two and one half months we have a bill in excess of forty thousand dollars. It's not the money," she said and waved her hand in the air. "I can assure you of that. I haven't placed a price on my daughter. We have insurance that will pick up a large portion of the bill."

"Let's get specific here. What *is* the problem?"

"She's changed. Dramatically."

"I thought that's what you wanted." I looked at my watch and gave myself ten minutes to get her the hell out of my office.

She set the cup down on the desk and leaned forward in her chair. "What I'm trying to say is that she is sicker now than she was when we took her to Minnesota. Three weeks ago I woke up in the middle of the night and thought I heard Jennifer walking around the house. I went to her bedroom and found her in her closet surrounded by her dolls." Mary leaned back in her chair. Her face became wary, reflective. "Lord, I never knew she even had those dolls anymore. But there they were. Around her like a little army. She even had a couple that belonged to . . ." She waved the end of the sentence away and became quiet.

"Go on," I encouraged her and hated myself for doing it.

She snapped back from whatever memory had seized her attention. "I asked her what she was doing, but she wouldn't answer me. She just sat there, rocking back and forth, and stared into space. I got my husband, Frank, up, and he insisted we take her back up to the center."

"Did you do that?" I checked my watch again. She had two minutes left.

"Yes. She was there for a week."

"I'm having a hard time following what you're getting at."

"Six months ago, my daughter was arrested for prostitution." Her voice was low, raspy. A muscle twitched in her neck. "She's been in trouble consistently for the past four years. I just never expected . . ." She paused. "Not that, not my Jennifer."

Something kept my eyes riveted on her mouth as she formed her words carefully. Slowly.

"Before she was released the first time, in Minnesota, Dr. Curtis told us that Jennifer could be suffering from a drug-induced psychosis and that her behavior could become erratic. He also said that she could be prone to hallucinations, but that if she received adequate psychiatric help and abstained from drugs and alcohol, there would be a good chance that all these problems could be reversed."

"Well"—I stood and looked down at her—"there you have it. I'm sure the psychiatrist that she's working with now can—"

"Have you heard a word I've said?" Her voice cracked.

"I don't mean to be rude, but the more I hear, the more I feel you're on the wrong track. Maybe," I said and hesitated, "maybe you need to talk with someone yourself."

"There's more to this than meets the eye. She's become progressively worse."

"I'm starting to sound redundant."

"My daughter is deeply disturbed, Miss Siegel. A danger to herself and . . . anyway, Jennifer wanted help. She had hit bottom, or whatever they call it. The girl that is living under my roof is . . . she's . . ." Her voice trailed off again. "Something happened up there. Happened to her. I'm begging you to find out, Miss Siegel. You. It has to be you."

I was intrigued but didn't know exactly why. She reached down, picked up the shopping bag, and placed it on the desk.

"Before you decide not to help me, watch these slides. My projector is in the bottom of the bag. I didn't know if you had one or not. You need to watch these carefully. Please remember that."

She reached into her purse, pulled out a check, and handed it to me.

"As you see, I've made it out to you in the amount of two thousand dollars. I had no idea what kind of retainer you would require. If this isn't enough . . ."

I held the check in my hands, dumbfounded. "I've tried to be honest with you. I have no intention of . . . I don't think this is necessary."

"It is for me. Please, I beg you, watch the slides before you make up your mind. Will it cover your expenses or not?"

I was ready to say anything just to get her out of the office. "More than . . ." I hesitated. "I'll hang on to this until I decide which way I'm going to go, but this isn't a commitment. Understood?"

"I understand."

"What facility are we talking about? We have a few local ones that I'm familiar with—"

"Whispering Pines. It's north of the city."

I tried to match a place with the name and couldn't. "What was the director's name? I'm not sure I caught it." She was running over on time, and at that point I would have done anything to get her out of there.

"I didn't say his name. It's Dr. Stroud. Dr. Victor Stroud."

The words came out as acidic as bile. She shoved the sack closer to me and leaned down. This was not the face of the woman who had first entered my office. She reached over, picked up a pen from the desk, and hurriedly wrote something on the pad that was in front of me.

"Talk to him. He's got the answers, and I want them, Miss Siegel," she said, placing a pen back on the desk. Her eyes narrowed as she leaned toward me again. "There's something else you should know."

In this business there's always *something else you should know*. I didn't say a word. I just leaned back in my chair and watched her and waited for whatever it was she had saved for last. It was usually a helluva lot more shocking to them than it was to me.

"Three years ago, we were encouraged by Dr. Stroud to file a complaint against an officer on the Billings police force." She shifted uneasily in her chair and again searched my face for some reaction.

"And?"

"Our daughter was supposedly involved with this officer. Sexually involved."

"You could write volumes on complaints like that against the cops. The majority prove to be false and do nothing but take up everyone's—"

"We followed Dr. Stroud's advice." Her voice was shaking. Her face became ashen.

"You did the right thing," I said, hoping she wasn't going to go hysterical on me. Hysterical women and root canals both rate high on my stress meter. So I avoid them. "The police department is usually very cooperative in these matters. Listen." I stood up, glanced at my watch, and smiled at her. "I'll take a look at these pictures, and I'll see what I can find out about Stroud and this . . . this Whispering Pines. Call me in a couple days, leave a message on my machine, and I'll get back to—"

"Two days after we talked to his superior, the officer in question killed himself." The words shot from her mouth in rapid succession. "That officer was your brother. Benjamin Siegel."

I remember everything else within my range of vision disappearing. Only the outline of her mouth was left, magnified in my mind, a thousand times larger than life, moving grotesquely, forming the words that were ricocheting around the room. I could see the smile lines around her mouth, seeping areas of red where her lipstick was bleeding out beyond her lip line, and the tip of her tongue as it worked behind her teeth.

That . . . officer . . . Benjamin . . . Benjamin . . . was . . . Benjamin Siegel . . . Ben Siegel . . . SSSSSSssssssss . . . Her words coiled, hissed, and kept striking my mind over and over again.

I reached out for the desk and steadied myself. The tips of my fingers flattened under the pressure of my grip on the wood.

"Who the hell are you?" I asked. I was outside myself. My voice sounded throaty, gasping. "I want you out of here. Now."

"I knew this would be hard when I decided to come to you, Miss—"

"If you're not out of that chair by the time I walk around this desk, I'll throw you out. Have you got that?"

She stiffened but didn't move. "I didn't believe it then. I still don't. I need the truth about my daughter. It's all tied together. Please—"

"You have the gall to walk in here with some cock-and-bull story about a complaint against my brother and want my help? You must be nuts. I would have heard about—"

"Truth. That's all I want. The truth. Don't you?"

Time stopped. Now there were new words echoing through my mind. Assaulting my senses.

"Be careful, Miss Siegel, please be very careful. Stroud is a dangerous man." Her voice was barely above a whisper. "And please, pay attention to the slides. I'll wait to hear from you."

She stood. I watched her turn and leave. The door closed behind her. Something had just happened, and I wasn't sure what it was. Something in the room changed. I was breathing in chunks of heavy, stagnant air. A shadow raced through my mind like an ominous dark cloud on the horizon. Something gnawed, clawed inside me like a rabid cat trying to get free. And there was something more. It had no name, no description, just pain. Whatever it was, I was hooked.

$\bigtriangledown$

2

LOOKING BACK, I KNEW Mary Kuntz had gotten to me just as surely as if she had dumped a bucket of chum off a boat and started a feeding frenzy among sharks. I'd been swimming two inches below the surface for a long time, cruising around looking for someone to bite. Without anyone available, I did the next best thing. I fished March out of the wastebasket. Little did I know that, by doing that, I bit myself.

My mind kept telling me that Mary Kuntz was whacked out and desperate. Desperate people have been known to go to any length, and she had definitely gone the distance. She'd poured salt on a festering wound I had nurtured for three years: Ben's suicide. But the question remained. Where the hell did she come up with such incongruous information?

There were a few loose ends I needed to tie up before I could call it a day, one of which was to run down the realtor I had been dealing with on a ramshackle Georgian mansion that sits on twenty acres at the edge of town. It had been vacant for as long as I could remember and had recently come on the market.

I knew I had to have it the first time I stepped on the porch and my foot broke through a rotting board. Inside, it was done in early decay, something out of a horror movie. But God, it was loaded with character and unlimited potential.

Price wasn't a problem, and with a little wallpaper and paint I knew I could make it habitable. The deal was due to close any day now. I had fully intended to start renovations during my month off.

As usual, Jackie, the realtor, a woman in her early fifties who had the most extensive polyester wardrobe anyone could imagine, was unavailable. I left a message and sat in my chair, staring at Mary Kuntz's sack for a good fifteen minutes, before I decided to call my little sister, Kehly. What the hell? Maybe she knew something about this Stroud and his operation. Maybe she knew something about Mary's wild accusations, although I doubted that. And besides, I missed her.

I phoned the department store where she worked and asked for the cosmetics counter. After several rings, she answered.

"It's Phoebe. You're not close to having a break, are you?" I asked.

"Is something wrong with Mama?"

"No. I'd just like to spend a little time with you."

"Come on, Fee," she whispered. "It's me. Remember? What's on your mind?"

"We haven't touched base for a while, so I thought we could have dinner together."

"A while? We live in the same town and I haven't heard from you for two months."

"I'm trying to rectify that. Don't make it hard." I caught myself snapping. "How about the Rex at five?" All I got was silence for what seemed like an eternity. "Are you there?"

"I'm here, Fee. Sure, why not," she answered. "I'll have a red rose clenched between my teeth so you'll know who I am."

"Smart ass," I said. "See you then."

Kehly was right. We had lost touch. I felt a little guilty about my motives for wanting to see her, but what the hell? Families are like that.

I spent the rest of the day thinking about Mary and what she had dropped on me, while I called some contractors about the house I didn't even own yet. And, before I knew it, I was due in court to read a Jane Doe deposition for a prosecuting attorney.

PI's don't have the glamorous jobs that most people assume. A Jane Doe can be downright degrading. You read it as is, on the witness stand, verbatim. All the "duh's" and "uh's" have to be read as stated. Between that and serving subpoenas the job can get boring. Real boring.

Maybe that's what intrigued me with Mary Kuntz. She threw something at me that was outside the routine. Or maybe I was tired of living without conviction. Without emotion. Whatever it was, I couldn't get her off my mind as I left the courthouse and walked back to the office.

The wind had picked up and pushed bits of freezing rain against my face. By the time I reached my office, my head was aching. I grabbed a note that was taped to the door and tried to wrestle the key in the lock before the phone stopped ringing. I didn't make it.

I threw my briefcase on a chair and read the note. It was brief, legible, and to the point: "Your place or mine?" Signed Roger. Few things brought any grins or giggles into my life. Roger was one of them, even though the relationship was drawing to an end.

I'd met him at the cemetery a year after Ben had died. I had been there on a chilly afternoon right after Halloween to assess any damage vandals might have done to the stones in the Siegel plot. Halloween is notorious for that type of sickness, so I was relieved that we had been left untouched.

Armed with a thermos of coffee, I had plopped down on the ground nearest the mounds to have one of my frequent conversations with Zelda. There was something convenient about having Zelda where she was. You could have a conversation with her and get a word in edgewise. The same applied to Daddy, Ben, and Sam. They were always there when I needed them, a captive audience.

I had felt someone watching me, so I turned and saw a tall, good-looking guy about my age glaring at me from a few feet away. I didn't catch on right away and steeled myself to do battle with what could have been a flasher dressed up like an attorney.

Then a light came on in my head. I was sitting on someone's, *his* someone's, grave. It turned out to be his father's, and he didn't like my weight on his father's chest. I apologized, finding his nasty attitude a little silly, but struck up a conversation to redeem myself.

In the length of time that it would take someone to read the Cliff's Notes for *Wuthering Heights*, Roger fell in love. I fell in like. We went from cemetery buddies, during which time he got over my squatting on his father, to dinner partners, and the occasional sleep-overs. It turned out that Roger was an attorney. Now, two years into an on-again, off-again relationship, I was moving toward calling it quits on the sleep-overs and rendering the relationship platonic.

I called his office and got his secretary, who informed me he was in conference. My message was briefer than his. My place, eight o'clock. I looked at my watch and decided to hit the Rex early so I could get a table away from the dinner crowd. I'd started to leave when I remembered Mary's sack. I picked it up and left the office.

Billings has its share of new money, old money, some money, and no money. Some days, when the wind blows out of the west, the city is blanketed with the fecal smell of money emanating from feedlots crammed full of cattle, standing knee deep in their own urine, being fattened for slaughter. No one seems to mind.

Any city worthy of Montana has its share of pickup trucks. Billings, Magic City of the Big Sky Country, is no different. Cowboy trucks, fondly called rigs by the locals, are easy to spot. They sport bumper stickers that declare cute little things like LOOSE WOMEN TIGHTENED HERE or COWGIRLS RIDE BAREBACK, or my favorite, SAME SHIT—DIFFERENT DAY.

Indians, born too late to die in historic battles, in town from one of the two reservations in the area, are less subtle. Emblazoned on their chrome is the old standby: CUSTER HAD IT COMING. Billings, if nothing else, is a conflict of cultures on all levels.

The Rex, a converted flea-bitten, turn-of-the-century hotel that now houses a fine restaurant, rises four stories above the Yellowstone Valley, which cradles the city. Boasting a gourmet chef and catering to Billings's more elite, it's never been one of my favorite hangouts. But I knew I needed every edge with Kehly, and she was into that sort of atmosphere, so what the hell?

Kehly entered the restaurant twenty minutes later than agreed upon, as usual. And, as usual, every man in the place watched her walk to the table.

"Sorry I'm late," she said without much passion. "I had a woman who couldn't make her mind up between a forty-dollar jar of wrinkle cream or a twenty-seven-dollar box of imported bath beads."

"Which was it?" I asked, trying to sound interested.

"Neither, she didn't have any blank checks in her checkbook." She giggled. "So, what's new, Fee?"

"Same old same old. How about you?"

"Everything's great," she said as she smiled, picked up the menu, and started reading. "Shouldn't you be home boarding up the windows and locking the doors?"

"I don't get it. What do you mean?" I knew damn well what she meant but asked anyway.

"The Ides and all that crap?" She peeked over the edge of the menu and grinned.

"Let's not start off combative. It's bad for the digestion." I smiled back.

We got through dinner, making the usual uncomfortable small talk. We were sitting there, each sipping a large glass of New York Seltzer, when she reached over and touched my hand.

"Fee, uh . . . I mean Phoebe," she said softly. "I worry about you. All this stuff with March—"

"Don't start. Please, Kehly," I said. Something about her directness pissed me off and intimidated me at the same time.

"All I'm trying to say is that I can always count on hearing from you at the end of February. Then you go underground or something. It's not healthy."

"Look," I said, feeling edgy, "you don't understand."

"Phoebe, I do understand. I know what it's like to stuff and hide feelings. But, for God's sake, it's been three years. No one can grieve forever."

I looked up into those green eyes and saw them wide and full of understanding. It scared the hell out of me. The lump that was forming in my throat scared me more.

"Hey, how's that guy, what's his name? Rudy?" I swallowed and forced a smile.

"He's great. We're great." She laughed. "You're impossible, Phoebe. Really, you are."

"Have you seen her?" I asked.

A year ago Charlene had married another cop who just happened to be Ben's best friend. I resented the hell out of it and, therefore, justified my resenting the hell out of her. I didn't attend the wedding.

"As a matter of fact, I saw her last week. She always asks about you, Fee."

"Really," I said sarcastically. "I'm sure you'll fill her in. Right?"

Kehly stood, grabbed her purse, and pulled her wallet out. "I've got to take off. This one's on me, Phoebe. We'll have to do it again sometime. Okay?"

"Sit down and let's start over."

"With what? Something like, 'I like your shirt. Do you like mine?' "

"Is it that bad?" I asked.

"That bad," she answered. But she sat down.

I was more than five years older but always felt she had all the maturity and ability to deal with the shit that had slammed us.

"Kehly, when you had that little problem five or six years ago . . ."

"Do you mean when I went to treatment for drug addiction and alcoholism?" She laughed. "Call it like it is, Fee. If I'm okay with it, you should be."

"God, you're tough." I smiled.

"I get it from you. What do you need to know?"

"I've always been curious about a few things. What got you hooked?"

"I did. I made the choices."

"But why?" I leaned forward. She was so damn beautiful that it was hard now to remember back to the rough times, when she wore dog chains for bracelets. She'd been a real punk.

"Maybe I inherited a recessive Aunt Zelda gene. If it was there, I had to do it. I don't know," she said wistfully. "Just a lot of pain. They say you know you're on the road to recovery when you can't remember what tore your guts out and made things hurt so bad. I must be solid."

"I've always felt responsible, like I should have been there for you."

"Come on, Phoebe. We both know we can't save anyone. Look at Ben."

Something grabbed in my chest, so I steered the conversation away from him. "How'd it go for you when you got out? Was it tough?"

"Sure it was. But it was probably tougher on the people around me. I got help. None of you did." Kehly called the waitress over and asked for refills on our soda. "I felt bad for the rest of you, if you want the truth. I had the chance to deal with a lot of crap."

Her mood changed. Something warned me, but I asked anyway. "Like what?"

"Don't, Phoebe. We're just starting to enjoy each other."

We both dropped into silence when the waitress showed up at the table and filled our glasses.

I took a long, hard look at Kehly. She was a knockout. Tall and willowy, she prided herself on dressing to the teeth. Her mahogany hair hung down to the middle of her back in wave after wave. Her moss-green eyes, deep set and wide, overflowed with a mischievous sense of humor. A smattering of freckles bridged her nose, a constant reminder of the little girl within. It was hard to imagine that she had come so close to chucking it all. I wondered what Jennifer Kuntz looked like. When the waitress left, I bulldozed on.

"I'm serious. I want to know. I mean, after all, how many problems could a girl have growing up with a Jewish father, an Irish Catholic mother, and five siblings, all of whom were older and practically perfect?" I said and laughed. She didn't.

"You just answered your own question. It was a hard act to follow. Mom had Dad, for what that was worth. Aaron left for back east when I was two. I've seen him three times since then, and each time he's more of a stranger. Sam left for Vietnam and never came back. I was five years old, and I can't remember a damn thing about him."

Something started crawling around in my stomach. I didn't like it, but I didn't interrupt her. I just sat, stared at her, and listened.

"Do you want me to go on?"

"Why not?" I answered quietly. "Go for it."

"Ben was . . . what can I say about Ben? I adored him. Worshiped him. Even now I think sometimes *he* should have been the priest. God, he was good. Loving." She shook her head and wiped a tear out of her eye. "I guess I'm not as solid as I pretend to be."

"We don't really have to . . ." I tried to offer her a way out. She didn't take it.

"Maybe we do, Fee. Maybe we do. Anyway, for me, following in Michael's footprints, or should I say the 'Good Fathers?' Has he been canonized yet?" She looked at me and smiled. A hint of bitterness hung on her words.

"That's not fair." It was all I could come up with, and it sounded pretty weak.

"I said that same thing over and over for years, *that's not fair*. I bet I said it twenty times a day until I went to treatment. Life was tragic, never fair, just tragic."

"Christ . . ." I was at my intellectual best under pressure.

"Mama and Dad were worn out by the time I came along. They had spent all their fun, and I suspect their energy, on you five. There wasn't much left for me, Phoebe." Kehly lowered her eyes only for a moment. "So, I thought that if I could be like one of you, or all of you, I'd have what I thought all of you had. Does that make sense?"

"I never knew, Kehly. I would have done something, I swear to God, or whoever listens in, I would have been there for you."

"It wouldn't have mattered if you had been. When I finally figured it all out, in my delusion, I had to accept the fact that Aunt Zelda wasn't going to take me on all those trips . . ."

"Zelda loved you, Kehly. You were just too young . . ."

"No, Phoebe. She only wanted you. And that Daddy was never going to be the same after Sam died, and that Michael and Mama had some special imprint from God himself, and that Ben was so involved with being a cop that his little sister was just another name on the street. I discovered something that helped the pain: drugs, booze, and sex. It just made sense at the time."

Kehly put her lips around the straw in her glass and sipped the soda out in one slurping suck. When she was through, she looked at me, eyes innocent, smile demure, and blinked a couple of times.

"Aren't you glad you asked?" She grinned.

I just looked at her. What could I say? "Well . . ." I tried. It didn't come out too intelligently, so I did what I do best. I avoided. "How did you first feel when you got out, Kehly? Apprehensive?"

"You bet. I had thirty days without any outside pressure. All I had to do was concentrate on myself. The thought of going back out into the world scared me to death, but it was more than that . . ."

"How?"

"I don't know, uh . . . I guess I was excited, scared, challenged, hopeful. The list could go on."

"What do you know about Whispering Pines?"

She looked at me curiously.

"It's a treatment center or something, north of town," I said. "Do you know it?"

She looked away from me for a minute and then back again.

"Isn't it one of those treatment centers that lean a little toward alternate realities or something?"

"Could be. Tell me what you know."

"God, it's been so long. But I think we did try a meeting up there. Seems to me, they were real light on AA and were more into some kind of sister love and brother love. That crap. Pseudosixties. Maybe that's unfair . . ."

"No, go ahead."

"They concentrated more on intellectual fluff," she said and twirled her index finger by her temple. "Two of us went up, and I remember feeling pretty out of place and awkward. Class act though; the place is plush."

"Nothing else?"

"Why? Are you thinking of signing yourself in?"

I laughed but felt a twinge of fear at the thought of it. "Not today. I'm just trying to get a line on the place."

"Come on, Fee. What are you snooping around about? You and I both know it has to be hot if you're going to take something on in March," she said and leaned closer. "Share. Please?"

"Just a case I think I've decided to turn down. No big deal, just a neurotic mother. Listen, I have to meet Roger. Can we do this again?"

I just couldn't bring myself to ask her if she knew anything, had heard anything about an allegation against Ben. Later. I'd have to wait until later.

"You mean to tell me that you're in a committed relationship?" she asked with her hand over her heart, eyes wide, and mouth open.

"Nothing more obnoxious than a smart-mouth kid," I said as I stood and picked up the check. "Next time you pay."

I'd been home about an hour, wondering where my cat was, half-hoping he had run away from home, when Roger called and said he'd be late. I was sitting at the kitchen table with my Smith-Corona portable plugged in and had just finished typing Mary Kuntz a letter of refusal. It was tougher than I'd thought. I even surprised myself with how gentle I was with my thanks but no thanks. The woman was obviously Loony Tunes. The thing about Ben was ludicrous at the very least. But, then again, life is a little ludicrous. I'd heard about dwarf throwing, where a dwarf wearing a crash helmet is thrown like a shot put toward a mattress in some bar in France. It'd be tough to figure what Mary Kuntz was throwing at me and why. At least the dwarf made $1,800 a night.

I folded the letter and stuffed it in an envelope. Just to make myself feel less guilty for turning her down, I made a mental note to mention her to Uncle John. Maybe he could do something. The conversation I'd had with her was still sitting in the back of my mind, so I tried to think of other things. Like Roger.

For an instant, I felt relief that he was coming over. There was so much crap rolling around in my head, I figured a little human companionship might do me some good. Good old Roger. He was mellow, level, and I had a personality that was either up or down. He was one of those males who was a born Ernie, a nerd, the guy who took the brunt of all the adolescent cruelty life had to offer. But the worm turned. When all those male hormones finally kicked in, Roger developed into a hunk.

We had settled into a comfortable, undemanding relationship. If we had any one problem, it was finding the time and the right situation for any attempt at unbridled passion. On those odd occasions we got it together, we had foreplay and fondling down to a science. Our relationship had never been based just on sex. He was not that sexually experienced, but what he lacked in that department, he made up for with eagerness. I guess we had an odd kind of balance. He was logical, organized, and goal oriented. I didn't give a shit about any of that. He verged on innocence, and I had none left.

Roger was an assistant prosecutor with the Montana Investigation Bureau. It was a big outfit and the self-proclaimed elite of law enforcement for the state. A lot of what he was involved with he couldn't talk about. I hated it. Not that I've ever been much of a talker, but the mere fact that he couldn't talk in detail about most of his work made it all the more challenging to eke information out of him.

I threw the letter on the table and spent the rest of the evening puttering around, reading magazines on restorations to keep my mind off Mary Kuntz. I went to bed early that night and slipped into a deep, dreamless sleep. I didn't look at the clock when I felt the mattress sink as Roger crawled into bed beside me. The next thing I knew, his hand was searching for my ultimate erogenous zone. We'd never really pinpointed it, but the search was definitely fun. I turned toward him.

"What time is it?" I asked as I snuggled close.

"It doesn't matter. This has been a bitch of a night," he answered as he pulled me closer.

"What happened?"

He shook his head and said nothing.

"That bad, huh?" My voice was getting husky. Arousal for us was never a problem.

"I need this tonight, Phoebe. God . . . I need you," he whispered.

"Goddess," I whispered back.

We accelerated our foreplay and moved right into the last act. It was one of those times when you're transported off the planet, and aware of nothing but wonderful, sensual passion. The phone rang. I doubt if Roger even heard it.

I tried to keep my mind on what was happening, but ten rings later my brain split in two, with half of me soaring to heights never before reached while the other half just had to answer that phone. I rolled away from him and sat on the edge of the bed. For a moment he didn't know what was happening.

"Phoebe, what the hell . . ."

"The phone's ringing."

He attempted to reach out and lock me in a half nelson. "Let the damn thing ring. They'll call back."

"It's the middle of the night. It could be Mama," I said as I turned and warned him off with a look.

By this time I had found the lamp and turned it on. Roger shielded his eyes from the light and threw himself back on the bed. I really felt sorry for the guy. I stood, looked at the clock, and saw it was a little after two. Roger made one more feeble attempt at grabbing my hand as I moved away from the bed.

"Phoebe," he said with desperation in his voice. I pulled away and started for the door. "Phoebe," he yelled. I could tell he was beating on a pillow. "Fuck!" he screamed in frustration.

Slowly I turned around, put my hands on my hips, and looked at him. The phone kept on ringing.

"Is that anything like 'Phoebe, sit' or 'Phoebe, heel'?"

He looked at me. Confusion and torment covered his face. I tossed my hair, as much as you can toss hair that has the texture of a Brillo pad, walked out of the room, and answered the phone.

"I'm sorry I'm calling this late."

"Why are you whispering, Kehly?"

"Rudy's sleeping. Phoebe, something has been bothering me since we talked earlier."

It was hard to be enthused at that hour. "What's that?"

"It took me a while to put my finger on it. When I did, it was like déjà vu."

"I'm glad our conversation was some metaphysical experience for you, but I'm going back to bed."

"Phoebe . . . wait! Don't hang up. I don't know why you were asking about Whispering Pines, but Ben and I had the same conversation shortly before he . . ."

"And?" I stopped midyawn and felt myself becoming alert.

"Phoebe, he was real uptight and wanted to know everything I knew about the place. He asked me about a group, the Children of Lite, and even mentioned a couple of names, and, for the life of me, I can't remember them." Her voice was rising. It made me listen. "I guess what I'm trying to say is that when I finally put it together, that the both of you had asked about the place, I got this knot in my stomach. Not long after he asked me those questions, he was dead. Now you're asking the same questions."

"What's with these Children of Light? Who are they?"

"It stands for something. The L-I-T-E part is an acronym for something. Living in . . ."

"Tents?" I groped for anything to ease the tension in her voice.

"Damn it, Phoebe. Get serious. True . . . true something. That's it. Living in True Enlightenment. As far as I know, they don't exist anymore. What's going on?" she asked. "Why was he asking about it, Phoebe?"

"I don't know. Ben's interest was probably just some silly coincidence. Don't worry about it." I tried to sound as casual as possible and dismiss the connection. "Thanks for calling. Sleep well." I hung up and leaned against the wall.

"Phoebe," Roger called from the bedroom. "Come back to bed."

"In a minute," I said, walking to the kitchen table. I picked up the envelope and looked at it. A cool breeze floated through a partially open window smelling fresh, caressing me in the dark. Goose bumps covered my moist skin. I walked to the window and looked out into the night. A dog was barking somewhere in the neighborhood. I tore the envelope in half.

▽

3

IN 1968, BEN TRADED his way into a 1949 Chevrolet pickup truck. I was nine years old at the time. That truck was the center of his life and mine as I grew up. A few days after his funeral, Charlene had called me late one night at Mama's and told me she had to see me right away.

Even though we were dealing with inconsolable grief, things were better between her and me then. Much better. It was around midnight when I arrived at their house. I stepped out of the car and into a biting March mist. It had been storming all day long. The rain had let up, but the cloud cover hung low in the night sky and kept a bone-chilling dampness in the air.

I could tell she had been crying as soon as I saw her. She said nothing as I entered the house but instead simply reached out, took my hand, and led me through the kitchen, the laundry room, and down the stairs into the garage. She flipped on a fluorescent light strip that hung overhead and walked over to where a canvas tarp covered the truck.

Her hands grabbed at the heavy material and tugged. The old '49 stood gleaming in the light and mocked my entire life. She turned toward me. I could tell she was having a hard time keeping it together.

"He loved you, Phoebe. I know he would want you to have it."

She spoke slowly and swallowed several times before she got the words out. I just stood there feeling like I had witnessed grief unveiled.

"Please, I beg you, don't say anything. This is hard enough. Just get it out of here, okay?" Her voice quivered, racked with pain.

I walked to the truck and placed both my hands on one of the fenders. Even in the warmth of the garage it was metal cold, dead cold, just like Ben. I couldn't say anything.

"He . . . he just got it out of the paint shop. He was so proud of it, Phoebe. He was waiting for the weather to clear up because he didn't want to get it wet. Now . . ." She walked over to me and put her hand on my shoulder. It felt like someone hit me with a bull prod. "I want it out."

"I don't know, Charlene." I struggled for words. "Give it a while . . ."

She turned, walked to the bottom of the stairs, totally ignoring the sound of my voice.

"He'd been having problems with the fuel line. He never had the gas tank recoated, so when the rust shakes loose . . . anyway, you'll have to take it easy. I'll bring your mother's car over tomorrow. The keys are in the ignition."

She walked over to the garage door, raised her hand to a switch, and flipped it on. The door whined behind me and rose. Not once did she look back. The stairs groaned under her as she climbed them and disappeared into the house.

The rain had started up again. The wind pummeled the windshield with sheets of water so hard that I had to pull off to the side of the road. My vision out the windows was completely obliterated. All I could hear was the wind howling like the Banshees, clawing, screaming, outside the truck. Maybe they were coming after Ben. Maybe they were coming after me, knowing I felt dead inside. I started shaking violently, but I couldn't cry.

Now I was sitting in the truck along Interstate 90, thinking about Ben. And, three years later, I was still having problems with the fuel line. I got out and opened the hood. I emptied the sediment bowl, got back in, and cranked it up. It took a few more times of cranking and emptying before I could slam the hood down and take off.

I knew an older gal who worked in Records at the Billings PD. I'd done a couple of freebies for her tracking down her runaway husband; she, in turn, was a real asset when I needed background information. If anyone had any contact with law enforcement, anytime, anyplace, Grace had access to that information, almost instantaneously.

The academy had instilled a constant state of distrust in me, so the natural course was to run a check on Mary and Frank Kuntz. Mary had two moving violations that dated four years back. Frank had been ticketed by the Montana Highway Patrol for not having a permit to move a tractor on a state highway. Heavy stuff. Other than those shocking revelations, neither of them had anything going.

I'd also put my feelers out to Grace on Jennifer's juvenile file. It surprised me when she told me it would take a couple of days. Jennifer Kuntz was slowly but surely coming to dominate my thoughts.

Mary had given me detailed directions over the phone that morning, so their place was easy to find, even though it was remote. It was neat and tidy, just like I knew it would be. I wondered how anyone living in the country could keep the country so clean.

The house was bigger than I had expected and different from other homes in this German farming community. Most were practical to the point of being boring. This one had a full two and one-half stories, a wraparound porch, and lots of gingerbread fringing the eaves. It was immaculate in every sense.

I pulled up next to the gate and parked the truck. A man, in front of a shed, wearing a welder's helmet, looked up from his work when I slammed the truck door. He lifted his faceplate, stared at me for a moment, put it back down, and returned to his work.

He was big and burly. One of those types that if you ever came up against him, you wouldn't have much of a chance. I've always equated big with dumb and wondered if he'd fit my stereotype. I assumed he was Mary's husband.

"You're late. I thought maybe you had a hard time finding us," Mary called from the doorway of the house.

I've never been in the habit of explaining myself, so I just smiled and walked toward the door. She ushered me in, sat me down at the table, and placed a cup of coffee in front of me. I looked around and didn't find any surprises.

You can usually connect a woman with the type of kitchen she belongs in. With Mary, I was damn close. The aroma of fresh baked bread reached out and squeezed those little glands under my tongue and filled my mouth with expectation.

"Was that your husband I saw?" I asked as I let my eyes follow my nose around the kitchen.

She nodded, her expression changing. "He's against what I'm doing. We had a terrible row after you called and told me you'd take the job. I'm grateful. Very grateful," she said as she placed her hand on my shoulder.

"Look, Mary. I want to level with you. If you hadn't brought up my brother's name, I probably wouldn't have taken you on—"

"Have you watched the slides yet?" she interrupted.

"No, I haven't. As for your daughter, something tells me you're throwing your money away."

"Do you have children?"

"No." I began wondering who was in control.

"Someday you will, and when you do, you'll realize that there isn't enough money in the world . . ." She turned away from me.

"I'm going to give this a shot with the understanding that if at any time I think we're digging in sand, we bunch it. Agreed?"

"Certainly. I'll agree to that."

"Now." I reached into my attaché and pulled out a spiral notebook, a contract, and a pen. "Let's get this out of the way, and then I can get some information down."

I spent an hour with her—sitting at the kitchen table, drinking coffee that was strong enough to grow hair, eating hot, gooey cinnamon rolls dripping with butter—and tried to take notes.

She repeated what she had already told me in the office. It was in the same matter-of-fact tone she had used the day before. I listened.

"You had asked me if we had tried counseling as a family. We did. We were all seeing Dr. Drummond. Of course, Jennifer saw him weekly on her own, and then all of us met once a month. When Jennifer found out Dr. Drummond was leaving, she took it very hard. It was then that your brother and another policeman picked Jennifer up for curfew and possession one night and brought her home—"

"Possession of what?"

"They had open beers in the car."

"Who was the other cop?"

"I have no idea. Your brother introduced himself, the other one stayed outside—"

"How long ago was this?" She looked at me curiously, and I realized I was sounding like a KGB interrogator. I smiled, reached out, and patted her hand. "Sorry . . . it's just that . . ."

"I understand," she said softly. "Believe me I do. You'll have to bear with me. It was a long time ago, and a lot has happened since then."

"Okay, she was popped for possession and two cops brought her home. Did you talk with Ben?"

"Yes. I liked him. He was a polite young man and very concerned."

A lump formed in my throat. At the very least, Ben was polite and concerned, especially when it came to kids in trouble.

"I really believe this wasn't the first contact Jennifer had with him. I definitely got the impression that he had run into her before."

"How so?"

"He mentioned names. Names that they both seemed to know. There was no doubt in my mind that she knew both these policemen," she said as she rested her elbow on the table and rubbed her forehead with her hand. "Even after she came home from Minnesota, she kept running with the same bunch she had gotten in trouble with. Apparently your brother worked with some of these kids, and that's how she came to know him."

The lump in my throat thickened.

"What about the school? Didn't they get involved, Mary?"

"The school," Mary said and laughed cynically. "Jennifer had pretty much blown it when she was a freshman at the local high school in Joliet. We tried Laurel, that lasted a week. Eventually she ended up going into Billings, and it wasn't long before she was on the verge of blowing that too. She wasn't attending classes regularly, and when she did, she was so rude and disruptive they'd end up calling me and sending her home."

"No one ever intervened?" I asked.

"There was a counselor that Jennifer liked. Her name was ... jeez, what was her name? ... Jean, it was Jean Dillard. I talked to her myself a couple of times. Jean seemed to be turning Jennifer around. Her attendance even picked up, and I always thought it was because she didn't want to miss her sessions with this Jean."

"And?"

"It was the oddest thing. Miss Dillard called late one evening and told me it would be impossible for her to work with Jennifer anymore. I tried to question her, find out why, but she became agitated to the point of being rude and ended up hanging up on me."

"How long had she been seeing Jennifer?"

"All through Dr. Drummond and for about another three months after Dr. Stroud took over. It was shortly after she stopped seeing Jennifer that things really got bad. This all happened shortly before Jennifer went into Whispering Pines for the first time."

"This counselor never gave you any reasons why she was terminating her relationship with Jennifer?"

"None. I tried to contact her several times after that conversation, but she wouldn't return my calls."

"What was Jennifer's reaction to all of this?"

"She was stoic and just shrugged it off. Underneath I could tell it hurt her enormously."

"Wait a minute. Let's back up. Is Dr. Stroud and Whispering Pines the same or are we talking about two different things?"

"Dr. Stroud took over Dr. Drummond's practice. In the beginning he maintained the practice at Dr. Drummond's office on the West End. Six, maybe seven months later we were notified by mail that, starting immediately, all further appointments would be at Whispering Pines."

"Then Whispering Pines didn't exist until Stroud?"

"That's right."

"Meanwhile, what was Jennifer up to?"

"She was still running with the same crowd, withdrawn at times, and at other times belligerent and aggressive. It was during this time that Jennifer was arrested for prostitution and ended up in jail. Dr. Stroud told us that it was critical that Jennifer go into the resident program."

"Any boyfriends?"

Mary lowered her head and then looked back up at me. "Yes. One. A young Mexican man. That's who you need to talk to."

"Who is he?"

"Jimmy . . . Jimmy Padilla. Your brother had gotten him a couple of jobs. This information all came from Jennifer, of course, so you have to take it with a grain of salt. I guess I was impressed with how she talked about your brother. She liked him, trusted him, and, according to her, he was one of the good guys that they all . . ." Her voice trailed off. "You know these kids and the cops."

"What about this Padilla kid?"

"Phoebe, I put all the blame on him. I felt that he made her do drugs again. Now I feel sorry for him. It doesn't make sense, does it?"

"Was he, uh . . . involved with . . . arrested with her?"

"Are you asking me if he was her pimp?" she said with a wry smile. "No. I thought he was, but no; I'm convinced he was as appalled as we were."

"What convinced you?"

"He showed up out here last week. Jennifer wasn't home, but Frank was. They were out by the welding shop, and I couldn't hear what they were saying, but I could tell he was angry, real accusatory of Frank. I thought they were going to come to blows." She grimaced and continued. "I walked out there, and they both calmed down a little."

"But you don't know what they were arguing about?"

"No, I don't. Jimmy kept yelling, 'She told me.' He even had tears in his eyes. He was shaking, and when I looked into his face, I saw concern. Honest-to-goodness concern for Jennifer. I was willing to give him the benefit of the doubt."

"And?"

"I asked him what he was doing here and told him I didn't want him around Jennifer. I was shocked he'd showed up. I'm sure Jennifer told him how we felt about him. He told us that he was trying to clean his life up, that he loved Jennifer and wanted to marry her, take care of her. Frank flew into a rage," Mary said and looked out the kitchen window. "Jimmy just stood his ground."

"And then what happened?"

"Frank ordered him off the place. Jimmy started to leave. Just before he got into his car, he turned around and looked toward Frank and said, *'I'm going to find out, man. You watch your back because I'm going to find out if it's true.'* He looked so angry, but at the time I just couldn't feel much sympathy for him."

"You've changed your mind about that?" Under similar circumstances I would be less generous.

"I don't know. I do know that Jennifer would have defied God Himself to be with that boy. When she came out of the center this last time, I was worried sick that he'd be around again, and that everything would start all over," she said and looked reflective. "I just figured she'd sneak out to see him."

"I can understand that. Did he come around?"

"You bet. And, when he did, Jennifer degraded that boy so cruelly, I had a hard time believing she was my own child. As a matter of fact, he called her a couple of days ago. She still wants nothing to do with him."

"Were you involved with her treatment this last time?"

"Not really. We, or at least I, was willing to do whatever it took. Frank was nervous and seemed relieved when Dr. Stroud informed us that we wouldn't be in group sessions with Jennifer."

"What is it, Mary?" I asked, picking up on something.

"Probably nothing. My mind has been less than clear lately," she said as she waved her hand in the air. "But, if I didn't know better . . ."

"Look, Mary, we can't pull any punches with each other. I need all I can get from you."

"It was that day the Padilla boy was here. Frank was so angry, but still, he was scared, too. It was like Jimmy . . ."

"Go on," I urged.

"Never mind. I keep looking for things. Anything. It's just that Frank was angry, I've already told you that."

"Right. You have."

"But underneath, it was fear, honest-to-goodness fear."

It was hard to imagine the man standing in the doorway of the shed being afraid of much.

"If you didn't see any results, why did you continue with Stroud?"

"We tried. There weren't any beds at a couple of the other local treatment facilities. Then, my . . ." She paused. "We were encouraged to stay with Stroud." She paused again. "It doesn't really matter. Over the years we relied on so many people for solutions. We even had one counselor, supposedly reputable, suggest we tie her to her bed to keep her from sneaking out. Can you believe that?"

I believed the story about the dwarf, so why not this? Talk about an assault on human dignity. "Yeah, I do."

I looked out the kitchen window toward the building where I had seen Mary's husband. He was gone. He sure as hell wasn't making much of an effort to join this little conference.

"He won't be in to join us, Phoebe. Frank's a private man. He comes off as being a little grouchy and such, but it's just hard for him to deal with things like this. He works hard out here," she said.

"I'm sure those things are true, Mary, but—"

"This place is bigger than it looks. In our younger years it was a working ranch. There was always lots going on all the time. We ran cattle and even trained a few horses. Things changed. Something—" She stopped, looking troubled.

"It turned out for the best," she continued. "Frank wanted to work the land, that was always his first love, so we ended up leasing out a good portion of it, and what we have he puts in beets. We keep a couple of head of beef just for our own use, but it's enough to keep us busy. It isn't the easy life that everyone thinks it is. It takes your time and it takes your health."

She looked at me intently for a moment, like she wanted to say something but wasn't sure she should.

"What is it, Mary?"

"Oh, it's probably nothing. I was just thinking back, and I'm rambling on and on like some fool anyway."

"Let's hear it. I need every bit of information I can get right now."

"When Jennifer was arrested, it was Stroud that went down and talked with Jennifer at the jail. She refused to see me." Mary raised her hand and covered her heart. "It gave me a twinge of jealousy, right here," she said, patting her chest. "I was shocked. I'm her mother. And it bothered me more that somehow he knew she had been arrested before we did. I could never figure out how he knew what happened."

"Who can figure kids? She was probably feeling ashamed of herself and called him before she called you. Then what happened?"

"On this one night I had some church work to do at the nursing home. There was no way I could get out of it, and I figured it would get my mind off Jennifer sitting down at that place." Mary stood up and reached for a pile of yarn that was sitting on a large wicker basket. "We make lap robes for the residents."

She held up an exquisite unfinished afghan. Her face changed, started flowing, as she looked at me, waiting for a response.

"It's beautiful," I said. I was liking this simple woman more than I knew I should, but it was tough keeping her on track.

"Do you knit, Phoebe?" she asked as she folded the piece and placed it back on top of the basket.

"No, I don't. I tried once and almost impaled myself." The memory made me smile. "I decided not to live life on the edge and took up reading instead."

Mary looked at me, puzzled, and then laughed. It was a good sound. Sincere. She sat back down and became serious again.

"As I was saying, I got home, and there was Stroud sitting at the table. He and Frank had been talking. At first I thought something had happened to Jennifer."

"Why?"

"Frank had been crying." Her voice cracked.

Something about Frank crying didn't fit the sumo wrestler image I had of the guy. In fact, the gap between my observations of the man and Mary's picture was widening.

"And . . ."

"I didn't want to humiliate him, so I didn't say anything and just sat down. Frank was subdued, and surprisingly supportive. Dr. Stroud had us sign some papers . . ."

"Did you read them first?"

Mary pulled an indignant expression out from somewhere and just stared at me for an uncomfortable minute.

"I'm not a stupid woman."

"I didn't mean to imply . . ." I knew there was no way I could get out of this one. Thank God she let it ride.

"Dr. Stroud left a short time later, assuring us that this was for the best. He said he could help her build a new life," Mary said. A strange look passed through her eyes.

"A new life," she repeated softly. Her attention strayed to some hidden realm that masked her face with grief.

"Mary," I said to pull her back from wherever she was. "How did you feel about Stroud when you first met him? Any negatives?"

"None," she answered. In seconds, she had pulled herself together.

"Did you ever question his credentials or check into the center and its credentials?"

"Why would I?" She looked me straight in the eyes. I couldn't tell where the cutting edge of her voice was coming from. "Why would a man that works with children be allowed to operate in this state if he didn't have the credentials? Or, for that matter, operate a treatment facility?"

I couldn't argue with that one. I had the names down. Jimmy Padilla was at the top of my list. At least I had a place to start.

"By the way, Mary, what do you know about the Children of Lite?"

"It's the name the kids at the center call themselves. Why?"

"I just ran across it and wanted to know if you'd heard of it." I shrugged it off.

"There's something else I need to tell you. It was Dr. Stroud that told us about . . . I don't know how to say this to you."

"Just say it." I knew what was coming.

"Dr. Stroud called us in and told us that Jennifer told him she had been involved with . . . uh, that . . ."

"My brother?"

"Yes. He said she told him they were lovers."

I felt my fingers tighten around the pencil I was holding. "What did you do?"

"I was shocked. I didn't believe it. Then he showed us a letter she had written. It was all there."

"Where's this . . ." The lump was back, bigger than ever. "Do you have it?"

"No. We went down to the police station the next day and talked with your uncle. That's who I gave the letter to."

I looked up at her, my mouth dropped open, and my mind slammed shut. "John? You gave it to John?"

"Yes, at the same time we talked with him about filing the complaint. Two days later your brother was dead."

I left around noon, without meeting the elusive Frank, and pulled onto U.S. 212 right behind a one-ton pickup truck. It didn't take long to realize that for the next twelve miles, before I connected with I-90, I would be staring at the ass end of a black Angus bull.

There was a head wind that pushed against the '49, picked up bits of straw from the stock rack of the truck in front of me, and deposited them on my windshield. I could see the smokestack of the Cenex refinery up ahead and decided to pull around my bovine friend before we reached the narrow bridge that crossed the Yellowstone River.

I had a lot on my mind and didn't give much thought to the consequences. Just as I pulled out to pass, the great black bull emptied its bladder. The wind picked up the heavy amber specimen and delivered it right across my windshield. There was nothing much to do but turn on the wipers. So much for Big Sky Country.

It's twenty minutes from Laurel to Billings. I got back to my office without stopping once along the interstate to empty the sediment bowl. That, to me, was progress. I picked up the newspaper that was neatly rubber-banded in front of the office door and went in.

There were several Padillas in the phone book, so I decided to start at the top and work my way down. The first four didn't answer. Finally, on the fifth try and several rings, a strong male voice came through.

"Yeah?"

"I'm trying to reach Jimmy Padilla. Is he at this number?" The silence was irritating. "Hello?" I asked, not sure if anyone was still on the line.

"Look, man. If this is some kinda fuckin' joke, it ain't funny."

"I need to talk with Jimmy. I'm a friend of Jennifer Kuntz?"

Again silence and then a sneering, muffled laugh.

"You ain't no friend of Jenny's, 'cause she ain't got any friends, man."

"Look, I have a message for him. An urgent message. Could you just tell me where—"

"Don't you read the fuckin' paper?" His voice was low, menacing. The line went dead.

I looked at the receiver for a minute and then hung it back up. I reached for the paper that was lying on the desk. The rubber band broke before I could pull it off and snapped the tip of my fingers.

I was sucking on my finger as I unfolded the paper. The headline was there. Bold: DRUGGED INMATE HANGS HIMSELF IN JAIL CELL. I wouldn't be talking to Jimmy Padilla.

$\bigtriangledown$

4

AMYRIAD OF THOUGHTS tumbled in my mind as I paced back and forth in my uncle's office at the Billings PD. Nothing connected, but the apparent suicide of Jimmy Padilla had set something in motion. Long ago, I stopped believing in coincidence.

I sat down in John's chair and swung it around. On a low ledge, beneath the window, he had gathered, over the years, a collection of photos of our family. My eyes honed in on Charlene and Ben's wedding picture. I reached out and touched his face with my index finger. "Come on, Ben," I whispered. "Talk to me. What the hell is going on?" I swung back around when I heard the door open.

"Admiring my rogues' gallery?" John said as he entered. "You should be in there somewhere." His voice sounded stressed, tired, and the day wasn't half over.

"Do you have a couple of minutes?"

"For you, Phoebe? You bet. What's on your mind?"

I stood and turned my cheek toward him for the kiss that always came when we met. "Jimmy Padilla."

"Is that all?" He laughed sardonically. "Did you know him?"

"No, but his name came up this morning."

"In what way?" He looked up.

"Apparently Jennifer Kuntz was involved with him."

"You're not taking that on, for Christ's sake?" He shook his head. "Have you met the mother?"

"I met with her this morning. She thought Padilla was someone I should talk to. Too late, I guess."

"You got that right." John leaned forward and rested his head on his hands.

"Are you all right, John?"

He rubbed his brow hard. "Doesn't make any damned sense."

"What?"

"This kid hanging himself. I'd worked with him a lot when he came under Juvenile, and if there was ever a kid that I held out some hope for, it was Jimmy."

"How so?"

John reached out and buzzed his secretary. "Tillie? Bring us in a cup of coffee and couple of those hockey puck doughnuts if there are any left."

He shuffled a few papers around on his desk, lit up a cigarette, and looked me straight in the eye.

"When are you coming to work for the PD, Phoebe?"

"Come on, John. We've been through this before and you—"

"You're right. We have. But you can't blame a man for trying, now can you?"

"What's the story on him?"

"Same old routine. We've got a two-inch-thick juvenile record," he answered as he picked up a ragged-edged, thick folder and dropped it back to the desk. "He was in my office a couple of weeks ago and told me he was clean and under some job-training program. He was even thinking of getting married. Good-looking kid, Phoebe. Bright as hell."

"So what happened?"

"I have no idea. That was the last contact I had with him. Nine one one responded to a call last night on South Thirty-seventh. His mother called in and said he was strung out on something and tearing the house apart."

John leaned back in his chair. He looked tired. Troubled.

"Officers responded. They found him in the rear of the house, on his knees praying in front of one of those little home altars. When they approached him, he went crazy."

"What did they do with him?"

"They tried to restrain him. You know how they get when they're on that shit. He was holding a crucifix so tight they thought they'd have to break his fingers to get the cuffs on him." John sighed. "Shit. His mother was ranting and raving, the kid was whacked out and screaming about the devil, and there's these two cops . . ."

John stood, turned away from me toward the window, his arms folded across his chest.

"They finally got him under control and into the back of a cruiser. Detox was full. They even tried getting him into that other crap place, but they wouldn't take him because he didn't have insurance." He turned back around, a weary smile on his face. "Can you believe that one?"

"Unfortunately, yes." Little surprised me anymore.

"So, they booked him rather than put him on the street. All of this is off the record. Right?"

"Right," I answered, as I made mental notes for my own record. "Seems a little unbelievable that praying got this kid popped. There had to be—"

"Look, Phoebe, I've said a little more than I should already. I've got to get downstairs."

"John, call it a hunch or something, but I need to know if—"

"Sorry, Phoebe." He held one hand up. "Now, if this conversation was between myself and another officer—"

"You never quit, do you?"

"Never."

"Why didn't you ever tell me about the allegations Jennifer Kuntz made against Ben?" Nothing like a dropkick to get someone's attention.

"What the hell are you talking about?"

"You know damn well what I'm talking about. Why wasn't I told?"

John held his hands up in the air and rolled his eyes toward the ceiling. "Mother of God . . ."

"No, Phoebe. And I'm down here. Talk to me, John. There's no reason I should have found out this way."

"There was nothing to tell. Now drop it. This isn't something that needs to be dug up. Do you understand me?" He leaned forward and narrowed his eyes into nothing more than intimidating slits.

"Some young girl says she's been sexually involved with Ben and there's nothing to tell? I'm not some—"

His voice turned cold. "I told you to drop it. Now, I've got my hands full here, and I don't have time or room for any more bullshit."

"I'll find out on my own, then. Did Mama know? Charlene? Who, John?"

"God damn it, Phoebe. No one knew," he yelled. Then his voice dropped, sadness flooded his eyes, and he slumped back in his chair. "No one knew. I swear to God. Two days after the Kuntzes came in with that damn letter, all hell broke loose. Ben was dead. Hell, I thought I'd lose your mother, and Charlene was a mess. What did you think I'd do, lay it on them right then and there?"

"Did you talk to Ben?" I could feel tears stinging my eyes.

"Of course," he said and sighed. "Immediately. He was horrified that the kid even wrote the letter. I told him we had to follow through on it. He understood. He wasn't happy about it, but he understood. I also told him he should prepare Charlene. Whether he did or not," he said, sighing, "she's never brought it up."

"Why didn't you tell me about it, John? For God's sake, you should have said something."

"The mother came in the day it came out in the paper. She said she was uncomfortable about the letter and wanted it back."

"She's got it?"

"I couldn't find it. It got lost in the shuffle or—"

"You lost it?" I was incredulous. "You lost it?"

He shrugged. I stood and looked down at him. John was known to booze a little too much, and his Irish temper was a legend, but incompetent he wasn't. He was a detail man, organized, with a bear-trap mind. It was hard to believe that he would misplace a potentially damaging letter, particularly when it involved his own nephew. There had to be something more.

"Who else knew about this?"

"George Shanklin. Ben told me he was going to talk to George."

"Did George ever approach you about it?"

"No. Never." John stood and walked around the desk. When he was standing in front of me, he reached out and placed his bear-paw hands on my shoulders. "Leave it alone, honey. Your daddy would want that and so would your brother. Don't open old wounds, okay?"

I said nothing. Why lie? I stood on my tiptoes, kissed him on his cheek, and left the office knowing damn well I'd hit him up again. John was like that. A little bit here, a little bit there. I hung around the crowd of reporters downstairs in the lobby of City Hall, hoping to glean something, anything, from their conversations.

Not a lot happens in Billings. People like it that way. When something does happen, it's news. A death involving the cops on any level makes tongues wag with speculation. Sometimes that speculation can be riddled with facts. That's what I needed right now, facts. I didn't know where to start.

The crowd downstairs didn't have much to offer, so I ducked into the coffee shop directly across from City Hall, scooted into a booth, and waited for the waitress to come over. It wasn't long before I had a cup of coffee in front of me and breakfast on the way. My head was buried in a newspaper left on the seat when I heard someone sit down across from me.

"Reading the help-wanted column, Phoebe?"

I looked up and into Lanny Wilson's freckled face. His hair was the same disgusting shade of red that mine was. The kind that pulls a lot of head rubs and hey-there-carrot-top remarks when you're a kid.

"Lanny, Lanny, Lanny." I grinned and made as big a production out of his presence as I could. "You must have heard my prayers."

"I thought you weren't into that," he said and smiled.

"Right." I put the paper down on the table.

"I had a call over by your place last night," Lanny said as he motioned the waitress over and ordered a cup of coffee.

"It's a rough neighborhood."

"This one concerned you."

"You're kidding. My life is so quiet it's boring."

"Your neighbor called in and said that your cat attacked her poodle, pinned it down to the ground, and pissed all over it," he said as straight faced as possible.

He took off his cap and placed it on the table.

"I think I even wrote down the name of the alleged attacker." He flipped trough the spiral. "Yup, I sure did. It's right here. Does the name Stud ring a bell?"

"Never heard of it. Who the hell would name a cat Stud?"

"Your neighbor says she's heard you yelling 'Stud' out your back door on several different occasions," he said as he sipped his coffee and eyed me over his cup. His eyes were mischievous.

"I could have been looking for a man. A girl gets lonely."

"Could be heavy, Phoebe. Assault with a deadly weapon can get pretty sticky."

"Listen, she's a neurotic old bat that can't mind her own business. Did you see that poodle of hers? Christ! All it does is bark. The only thing it's good for is selling it for a Bass plug. It probably got on Stud's nerves, pushed him to the edge, and he flipped out." I threw my hands up in the air in mock surrender. "So arrest me."

"Next time." He grinned back. "I'd keep Stud locked up for a while and out of trouble, if I were you. God," he said as he started to laugh. "That poodle stank."

"I've been running into that sort of thing lately," I mumbled, thinking back to the bull.

"What?"

"Never mind. You would've had to have been there. On a lighter note, I was thinking about touching base with you. I just left John's office."

"He's had a rough morning."

"That Padilla kid?" I tried to sound casual.

"Did you know him?"

"I've heard the name around," I answered but didn't look him in the eyes.

We sat there for a moment and said nothing. I felt a flood of sadness, remembering a time when we knew each other, biblically and otherwise, so well. Now we had to struggle with conversation.

"How's things, Phoebe? Are you makin' a living?"

"I get by. How 'bout yourself?" I said and finally looked up straight into his face.

"Okay. Things are great. Fran has a hard time sometimes. The job and all. She's never gotten over the fear that some night I won't come home . . ." He stopped and cringed. "God, Phoebe, I didn't mean to . . ."

I picked up the cup of coffee in front of me and gulped some down. He touched me gently on my arm. It felt hauntingly familiar.

"Hey," I finally responded. "You know you don't have to walk on eggshells around me. Ben's . . ." I just couldn't say the word. "Ben's gone. We just have to live with it. Right?"

"Phoebe, if you ever need to talk, you know I'm out there. Right?"

"I appreciate the offer, Lanny. But let's face it, if Fran is having a hard time dealing with the job, I wouldn't put her in the position of dealing with the ex-wife." Besides, he was about three years late.

I just sat there for a minute, holding him with my mind, caressing myself with memories. It's a dangerous thing to do.

He pulled his hand away from my arm and smiled.

"I hear you have, what's the term they use now? A significant other?"

"Pretty old news, Lanny, and I wouldn't call it significant. It's been on and off for two years now."

"I hear he's some high-powered attorney with the MIB or something."

Lawyers and cops aren't a mutual admiration society. The thought that Roger was being touted as some high-powered anything was a little ridiculous, but hearing it did a lot for my pride, particularly with it coming from Lanny.

"He's one of the good guys," I said casually. "Listen, what's the story on that Padilla kid?"

"No story. Just the same old shit. A nine one one came in, two officers responded—"

"Who were they?" I knew that part.

"I don't know for sure; George Shanklin and . . ."

George was a tough guy. The kind of cop that I, personally, thought should never have been on the force. He'd never win a popularity contest, but the fact remained that you'd never find anyone who *wouldn't* want George as a backup if they were in a tight spot.

"Wouldn't ya know," I said sarcastically and sat up straight in my seat.

George's marrying Charlene had left a bitter taste in my mouth. George and Ben had been partners for as long as I could remember.

It started early, long before either had entered grade school, and continued all the way through the Police Academy. George had even been Ben's best man at the wedding. Now he had Ben's wife, Ben's house, and Ben's bed.

"Come on, Phoebe. George is an okay guy. He was right there for Charlene all the way, and he would have been there for you—"

"Who was his backup?"

"Sharon Webb. She's been on the force about a year now. She's young, but she's tough." He shook his head. "Why all the interest?"

It's funny how a cop's mind works. They're always on the lookout, always uptight, and they're damn sure used to asking all the questions.

I wasn't ready to talk about anything yet. None of it made sense, so what was the point? I stood, faked him out with a look of panic, and checked my watch.

"God," I exclaimed. "I almost missed an appointment. Gotta keep those dollars rolling in, ya know. Catch you later, Lanny." I leaned down, kissed him quickly on the cheek, and left. Not too obvious.

It was late Saturday afternoon when I finally ran the truck through the car wash and headed down Twenty-seventh Street. Billings, like most towns spawned by the railroad, was divided ethnically and economically by worn iron rails originating in Chicago and stretching all the way to the Pacific Coast.

I had just crossed Montana Avenue when a red-and-white railroad crossing arm dropped, signaling a train coming through, and traffic ground to a halt. The truck started to vibrate as the giant cars rolled past, shattering the air with a screaming whistle. When the train had passed and the arm had raised, I pulled on through and crossed over to the South Side.

Predominantly Hispanic, the South Side was the closest thing Billings had to a big-city borough. Passion and pride run deep through most of the community. This was Jimmy Padilla's turf, and somewhere, behind closed doors, Hispanic women were praying for his soul.

When I pulled up in front of Guadalupe Church, I turned off the truck engine, got out, and leaned against the fender. I'd spent most Sundays during my youth on my knees inside those walls.

Neither the neighborhood nor the church had changed much over the years. It still drew a kaleidoscope of backgrounds through its massive carved doors and into the fold.

I guess one thing did change. Now the keeper of the fold was my brother Michael. When I found it necessary to consult him on a professional level, I knew I could find him here.

In fact, it was the only time I walked through those doors now, never looking for a priest, just looking for what we all took for granted in Michael, a higher wisdom.

I pulled on the gleaming brass handle and opened the door. A small Hispanic woman passed me on the way out, a look of satisfaction, or maybe it was absolution, on her face. The heaviness of incense and past wax assaulted my senses.

The church's interior was dim, lit only by the last of the afternoon shafts of sunlight that filtered through the stained-glass windows and fell in supplication across the pews. I didn't bother to dip my hand in the font and anoint myself; I just walked in and headed straight for the confessional.

A rotund, milky-skinned woman was attempting to free her body from the oak grip of a pew, having wedged herself between the bench and the kneeler. I smiled, secretly wanting to laugh, knowing that laughing over those types of situations will send you straight to hell.

I opened the door to the confessional, sat down, and fought claustrophobia. It's always been my opinion that padded seats in the confessional would provide comfort, which, in turn, would encourage honesty. The one exception to my theory would be the Irish, who need to suffer and therefore would rather have the hard, narrow wooden seat, preferably with bits of broken glass on top.

My mind has always had a tendency to wander under stressful conditions. Church, and the prospect of facing Michael, rated a ten on my stress meter. I loved him, and at times needed him like hell; I just didn't know how to approach him.

The small door opened at mouth level.

"Forgive me, Father, for I have . . . I have a knock-knock joke for you, Father," I said in a whisper.

"Pardon me?" The voice on the other side of the screen was indignant.

"I have a knock-knock joke for you," I whispered louder. "You start."

After a long moment of silence, a chuckle, and then, "Knock-knock," the voice whispered back. "Damn it, Phoebe," he muttered. "Get serious. Are you trying to get me fired?"

"I thought God was an equal-opportunity employer." I giggled. "And had a sense of humor."

"Yes, on both counts. He'd have to have a sense of humor with you. Do you feel like coffee?"

"Sure," I said, still speaking in a whisper.

"Meet me in the rectory in ten minutes."

"Father, won't people talk?"

"Come on, Phoebe, there are people with real problems out there. Give me a break. I was going to get in touch with you, anyway. I had a disturbing call from Kehly."

"That figures," I said under my breath as I left the confessional, smiled piously at the obese woman still trying to free herself from the pew, and walked over to the rectory.

Michael was there within minutes. Each time I saw him in his robes, I wondered how my remarkably handsome brother could ever have committed to celibacy.

Michael was one of those charismatic touchers who had hugging down to a science. His arms felt good around me.

"Michael—"

"Fee, before we go into anything else, you and I are going to have a talk. A talk we should have had three years ago."

"Where's this coming from?" I asked. A feeling of dread clutched at my chest. "I was only kidding about the knock-knock joke."

"Like I told you, Kehly called me," he said, frowning as he set a cup of coffee down in front of me. "She was upset, Fee. She wasn't making a lot of sense. For one terrorizing minute I thought maybe she was—"

"She's clean, Michael. I had dinner with her, and she's great. Trust me."

"Phoebe—"

"Phoebe is it? This must be serious."

"It is," he said as he looked me straight in the eyes. "We're going to talk about Ben."

"Look, Michael," I said as I stood, "this is apparently a bad time for—"

"Sit down, damn it. We've both avoided this for far too long."

"Avoided what?" I asked, trying my damnedest to come back at him from strength.

"Kehly is scared to death that something is going to happen to you. Just like it did Ben," Michael said. "Ben killed himself, Phoebe. He shot himself in the head because at that moment he felt that was his only choice."

My throat constricted, my pulse raced, and tears, as though summoned by truth, rushed to my eyes.

"Don't, Michael," I pleaded, "don't do this to me, to us."

"Phoebe." He slumped in his chair. "We've been through so much as a family, but we're on the other side of it now. Kehly is just a kid, and something you—"

"She's a woman, Michael. Not a kid. A woman. But you wouldn't know about those, would you?"

"As I was trying to say, something brought this whole thing with Ben up again in her mind. You can get as nasty as you want, but . . . it scares me, Fee, really scares me." A veil of sadness draped itself over his face. "I should have done this a long time ago."

"Done what?" I felt weak.

"You were away, Fee. You were at the academy when things started." His voice was soft, regretful, and troubled. "A couple of months before . . . before it happened, Ben started coming down here. He was agitated, eaten up by something. I tried to find out what was going on but couldn't get him to open up. You knew he was working with some kids, off time, right?"

I nodded my head and stared at his face.

"He was struggling with something. He talked like he was paranoid or scared. Maybe both." Michael shook his head. "It was rambling, but I knew it was, I don't know, crucial to him. He said he was having a hard time figuring out what was right and what was wrong. I found him out in the church praying a couple of times. He was visibly upset."

"Come on, Michael. That doesn't even sound like Ben. Religion was never a big thing in his life. At least not like it was for you."

"He was in trouble, Fee. Emotionally in trouble. He rambled on and on like a madman about how he had pushed too hard and that now it was too late to turn back. Maybe it was the stress of the job, maybe he and Charlene were having problems, though I doubt it, and maybe—"

"Ben was more stable than all of us put together," I said and slapped the table. "Are you trying to tell me that he had some weird breakdown? The guys at work, or at least Charlene, would have caught that."

"All I can tell you is what I heard with my own ears. Two days before they found him on the Rims, he called me in the middle of the night. He said he had something he wanted me to keep for him, *just in case,* and that he'd mail it to me." Michael looked up at me, tears filling his eyes.

"He was crying, Fee. Sobbing like a man who was tortured beyond our imagination. I begged him to tell me where he was. He wouldn't—" Michael's voice broke off. He cleared his throat and continued. "Then he calmed down. He told me that he loved me, loved us all, and asked me to pray for him. I got him to promise me that he'd come down in a couple of days and talk to me. The day he was supposed to come, I had a death call and had to leave. I called the rectory. He was there, waiting. He sounded fine."

I stood and glared down at Michael. "You thought our brother was in trouble and you left? You left him here?"

"Phoebe, he sounded fine. I had a death call, for God's sake . . ."

"For God's sake." I sneered. "Everything has always been for God's sake with you, you pious bastard. Now you want to tell me, after three years, that he was nuts. You could have saved your own brother and you made the choice."

My hand flew out so fast it seemed like someone else's hand. His face turned sharply as I slapped him with everything I had.

"Take that to your God, Michael. Ask him to forgive you. I never will."

He just sat there, numb, staring back at me, and never said a word. I walked out of the rectory, got in the truck, and tried to start it. It didn't cooperate. Each time I tromped on the gas, I could hear the battery wearing down.

Finally, the engine kicked in. I leaned forward, and in one overpowering contraction my own soul screamed out in pain. My stomach cramped as nausea stroked it toward heaving. God, I wanted to cry. It didn't happen.

I was barely aware of the uniformed man standing beside the truck, reaching in, and turning off the key in the ignition.

5

GEORGE SHANKLIN WAS A consummate bully as a kid. I'd spent a lot of time around him in those days when he and Ben were inseparable. And later, when Ben fell in love with Charlene, they became a threesome.

Charlene was gentle, totally devoted to my brother, and motherly toward George. Charlene was a born caregiver. As I slipped the key into the lock of my apartment door, I wondered if she still was. Then I turned and faced him. We hadn't talked for two and half years.

"I'll be fine," I said as I looked up into his face. "Thanks for the ride home. I'll pick up the truck later."

I turned away, opened the door, and started to walk into the apartment.

"It's good seeing you again, Phoebe. It's been a long time. I see Kehly now and then . . . ," he said with the first hint of humility I had ever heard in his voice.

I felt drained. The confrontation with Michael was screaming over and over again in my head, and I wasn't in the mood for nostalgic reunions, but something drew me to George, comforted me that he was there at that precise moment.

I sighed, braced myself, and pulled what resembled gratitude from my gut as I turned to face him again.

"Why don't you come in for a minute?" I asked and forced a smile. "Can you take a break?"

"That'd be great," he answered and followed me into the apartment.

Once inside, I walked into the kitchen, got myself a bottle of Coke out of the fridge, and watched him as he called the dispatcher on his hand-held radio.

"What's the number here, Phoebe?"

I hesitated. My number had been unlisted since I'd had my phone installed. I knew who had it and felt good that when it rang I knew who it would be. But I figured what the hell and gave it to him. When he was through, he walked to a chair, took off his hat, and sat down.

I'd forgotten how tall he was, well over six feet and built like a defensive end. He was drop-dead good looking and had a wry way of smiling that was both seductive and boyish. I took a swallow of Coke and just stared at him, hoping the carbonated fluid would wash the resentment I had toward him down my throat.

For a minute neither of us said anything. He just sat there looking down at the floor, rolling his hat over and over through his fingers. When he finally looked up, I knew he could see contempt in my eyes.

"We gotta break through this, Fee. Shit, it's been over two years, and I haven't seen or talked to you once. If it's about Charlene and me, I understand," he said and looked back down at the floor. "Damn it, Fee. She was family to you, and I was damn close to you my whole life. What can I do?"

I took another drink of Coke and continued to stare at him. He just sat there looking pitiful. It didn't sit well on George. He knew it and I knew it.

"I want to know about Ben."

"What about Ben?" There was a defensiveness in his voice that disturbed me, a look that flashed through his eyes.

"I want to know why the department didn't investigate his death."

"Christ, Fee. They did." He reached into his shirt pocket, took out a cigarette, and lit it. "You know that."

"How was Ben those weeks before it happened?"

He was good. Nothing flickered through his eyes, not a muscle twitched, but I knew it unnerved him. He waited, watching my face for a long time, before he answered.

Finally. "Uptight. Troubled," he said quietly.

"Troubled about what? Charlene? The job?"

George stood and started to leave. "You don't want to get into this, Phoebe. Neither do I."

"What about Jennifer Kuntz?"

"What the . . . who? What did you just say?"

"Jennifer Kuntz. What was the deal on her?" I looked at him and smiled. "I already know for a fact that you knew about the whole damn thing, George."

"Where's this coming from? Hell, Phoebe, you're not the only one March is tough on."

I seized on that last remark so quickly I felt like I had been clubbed. Could it be that George and I did have something in common? Doubtful, but the mere mention of March and the look on his face softened me a little and relaxed my posture.

"Sit down, George. I've had a bad day, and I shouldn't be taking it out on you."

"You had me there for a minute, Fee. You came on like the Grand Inquisitor," he said and laughed uncomfortably.

"Would you like something to drink?"

"No thanks, I don't have that much time. I've got to head home for dinner pretty soon. So . . . how have you been, Fee?"

"I've been great," I lied. "Thanks for stopping when you did. I must have an ulcer or something. I get those attacks once in a while."

"How's your mom, and Michael? I bet he's saving souls left and right down there."

"Mama's fine, and you know Michael. I really do need to know about Ben. Was he okay, George?"

"Leave it alone," he said. His face changed. "We're all under pressure all the time. Hell, you know that, Phoebe. All the political bullshit we put up with, and crap in the streets. This isn't a place you want to dig in . . ."

"Right. Like today, I bet today was tough with that kid hanging himself. It must have been as tough as the letter that Jennifer Kuntz wrote."

Now something changed in him. Barely perceptible, but a change anyway. His jaw twitched. He didn't answer.

"What about it, George? Was it as tough as the letter?"

"Shit," he mumbled and looked away from me and then back again. "How the hell did you hear about that? It was nothing. Another hysterical, doped-out kid. It didn't go anywhere."

"Did Ben think it was nothing? He was dead two days after John got the letter. How much *nothing* was it, George?"

He stood there. Fear, anger, pain, and rage alternated in his dark brown eyes and ignited a searing sense of guilt deep within me.

"Look, I'm sorry. I . . . I found out about the letter and I . . ."

"Forget it," he said softly. "Fee, Charlene doesn't know about any of that. Please, don't say anything. Only John and I and maybe a couple of others even knew that the letter existed. You'll hurt a lot of people if you push it. And Mom? What the hell would it do to her?"

I bristled. "You believed it, didn't you? You thought that Ben actually—"

"Hell no, I didn't believe it. Not for a minute, but you know how those things go. One damn seed of doubt, and it can ruin a career. Shit, you know I would never have believed anything like that." George shifted uncomfortably and looked around the room.

I raised my hand in mock surrender. "George, it's just been a strange couple of days. Weird information. . . ."

"It's over. Forget it," he said, shuffled his feet, and tried to laugh. It came out like a raspy cough. "It's been a tough day all around."

"The Padilla kid?"

"There's going to be a stink over this one. The kid was in Oz. Lucky he didn't take out his family. Just another punk, in my book." He sneered, stood, and put his cap back on. "I gotta go." George reached out and touched my shoulder. "Let's not make it such a long time between visits, Fee. Charlene would love to see you. We've done a lot to the house—"

At that precise moment, George spun around and let out a yell so loud it shocked me. I jumped up off the couch not knowing what to expect. As he turned, there was Stud, all twenty-five pounds of him, clinging to George's back, claws sunk deep through his jacket and into his skin beneath it.

"Shit," he screamed. In a mad dance, he twirled and reached for Stud, grabbed him, and threw him across the room. "What the hell was that?"

Stud landed on his feet, swished his tail a couple of times, and strutted off into the kitchen.

"That was my cat," I said, trying not to smile. "I'm sorry; he's unpredictable at times."

"Christ, he's dangerous."

George tried to slough it off, walked over to the door, and opened it.

"It was good to see you again." He forced a smile. "Keep in touch."

"Right," I said solemnly. "I will. You take care, George."

I closed the door after him and leaned against it, laughing harder than I had in a long time. I walked into the kitchen and bent down to where Stud was lying flat on his back, legs spread wide open. I scratched his stomach and cooed to the little killer.

"You did good, you little devil," I said. "Tonight, I'm going to let you out and you can pee on that old poodle as long as you want."

* * *

49

I spent the next two hours waiting for Roger to show up with Chinese takeout and decided to pass the time by watching Mary's slides. I had a projector of my own, but using it would have meant digging through my less-than-organized closet, so I opted to use hers.

I had to take a couple of pictures down to use the white, textured walls as a screen. The texture gave everyone a bumpy look and took away some of the resolution, but it did nothing to alleviate the boredom that soon settled over me.

I yawned my way through Jennifer Kuntz and another little girl who seemed to be her constant companion from the time Jennifer was a nude one-year-old in an inflatable pool to Jennifer with her arms around a white-faced calf with a blue ribbon in her hand. She was a cute kid with white-blond Germanic hair and blushing, chubby cheeks.

The older Jennifer grew on the wall, the more bored I became. I finished five boxes of slides and put in the last one.

Come on, Jennifer, honey. Do something shocking.

The first few pictures of the last set were not out of the ordinary. She was older, pretty in a plain way, and had an angular face that would have been attractive if it'd had some makeup on it. Her companion had disappeared from the pictures; now it was Jennifer on her own.

As I clicked through the slides, slower this time, there were some subtle changes. She started looking sullen and unkempt. But still, nothing shocking. Then I came upon something blatantly visible: Jennifer definitely stoned. She was leaning up against the house, flipping off whoever was taking the picture. The almost shy-looking teenager now looked street tough and sleazy. Very sleazy.

The next shot showed her bent over, pointing her denim-covered rear end in the direction of the camera. I backed the slides up and flashed them on the wall again.

"Hey, why didn't you tell me you had home movies?" Roger said as he walked in the door. One of the great loves of Roger's life was home movies.

I had been concentrating so hard on what was in front of me, I jumped when I heard him.

"Who is that?"

"A client's kid," I answered halfheartedly.

I only had five or six slides left. Roger sat down on the couch beside me and watched the wall. The next picture flashed on.

"Wow!" Roger commented. "That's some kid."

He was right. Spread out over my living room wall was one of the most beautiful young women I had ever seen. Her elbow propped on a fence post, her chin resting on her hand, Jennifer Kuntz looked close to angelic. The bright sun highlighted her hair with an iridescent glow and glinted off the shiny bracelet encircling her wrist. Her face was exquisite. She was strikingly beautiful in a haunting sort of way. I flipped back a slide and then forward again.

"This can't be the same kid," I said under my breath.

"Looks like the same kid to me. She just grew up," Roger said, his eyes fixed on the wall. "How old is she?"

"Eighteen."

"No way. God, look at those eyes. They look spooky, out of control or something. Makes you wonder whether you want to hug her or hide from her. Ya know, she looks familiar as hell. Who did you say she was?"

"I didn't. It's too long to go into, Roger."

I was stunned at what I was seeing. Something was definitely different about Jennifer Kuntz, but I wasn't sure it was just the blossoming of a troubled Plain Jane into this gorgeous creature.

I went back to the girl with the calf and worked my way forward through the defiant teenager and finally to the beauty who looked back at me. Beyond the beauty, something was missing. A quality. Something I wasn't sure I wanted to know. I turned off the projector, leaned back, and rubbed my eyes.

"Ready for dinner?" Roger asked.

"Sure," I answered as I stared at the blank white wall.

The strong odor of stir fry, sweet and sour, and fried rice bombarded my senses and set off my salivary glands, as Roger swung a little white box under my nose.

"Let's eat," he said as he kissed me lightly on the lips. "We'll do dessert in there." He motioned with his head toward the bedroom.

Roger was timid about sex, and his approach was, more often than not, a little juvenile and corny, but he threw himself into it heart and soul. It was just that, on that particular night, something else had seduced me first: the enigma of Jennifer Kuntz.

I had tossed and turned for a couple of hours, unable to sleep. Stud had wanted out, in, and then out again. Roger, sleepily, had moved close to me, pulled me into his arms, and snuggled up.

"What's the matter, baby?" he asked, half awake.

"It was just a bad day. Go to sleep. I've got to wait for Stud to come in."

"We need to talk about that cat." Roger's words were muffled as he started kissing me lightly on my neck.

"What about him?"

"He's psycho, Phoebe."

I tried not to giggle. When it came down to a choice between Stud and mice, Stud won hands down.

"I think he's mellowing," I murmured as I moved in closer to Roger. His body felt warm and responsive. I almost laughed out loud remembering how Stud had attacked George.

"Roger?"

"Hmmm?"

"Could we talk?"

"Sure."

"I had a bad scene with Michael today," I said. "He tried to tell me that Ben was having emotional problems."

"Maybe he was." Roger moved away, propped himself up on one elbow, and looked at me.

Roger was the only person in my life that I allowed to tread into dangerous waters where my family was concerned. I always told myself I could take or leave the relationship, but, looking back, I could see that he was my touchstone. I needed him, in all of his klutziness, for a reality check once in a while.

"There's some stuff going on, some people bouncing back into my life. I can't figure it out."

"Like who?"

"Like Lanny Wilson, and George Shanklin."

Roger and I never talked about my marriage, and therefore never talked about Lanny. So it made sense when he ignored the name and went straight to George.

"Isn't he the guy that married—"

"Yes," I said and touched his lips with my finger. "I'm feeling pretty raw right now."

"How'd you run into this George?"

I explained to him what had transpired with Michael and how George had seen the truck and stopped, given me a ride home, and come in for a minute.

"Maybe you both needed to touch base and deal with some past stuff. From what Kehly has told me, Ben and this guy were close."

I hated it when he made sense.

"He hasn't changed much," I said, reflecting on the feelings I'd had when he was sitting in that chair. "He's still damn sure of himself."

"That's not a character defect, Phoebe. Maybe the guy just knows who he is." He moved closer to me again. "You know we have some unfinished business from last night."

Like I said, sometimes he was just downright corny.

"We do?" I giggled.

Roger slid his arm under my neck, pulled me as close as possible, and gave me one of those long, wet kisses that there's no return from. Just as I started getting those fuzzy feelings, Roger shifted and moved his arm. Pain shot up the back of my head and paralyzed me. I yelled. It startled him and made him move again. This time the pain was more than I could take.

"Your damn watch is stuck in my hair, Roger," I squealed.

With my free arm I reached for the lamp on the ledge above the bed and pushed the button. The high-intensity light focused on his face.

His arm flew up and covered his eyes. "Turn that thing in another direction," he yelled.

"Wait a minute!" I untangled my hair and jumped out of bed.

"Where the hell are you going?"

"That's it, Roger. Her wrist!"

"Oh God, don't do this to me again. I'm begging you, Phoebe."

I bolted into the living room and turned on the projector. I fumbled with the slides, spilled one box on the floor, and finally came up with the ones I wanted. I flashed them on the wall, and then flashed them again.

It was so obvious; how had I missed it? Mary had told me to watch carefully. The last handful of slides all revealed the same thing: the bracelet encircling her wrist. I went back to the slide where her chin rested on her hand and zoomed in on the bracelet, walked to the wall, and touched it.

There must be hundreds of thousands of Medic Alert bracelets *similar* to the one she was wearing. But the chance of there being even one *exactly* like it was so remote you'd have better odds winning the lottery.

Charlene had had it custom made while she and Ben were still in high school. Ben had taken penicillin for a strep throat and had gone into anaphylactic shock almost immediately. The doctors had told him that the next dose, given inadvertently, could well be fatal.

His sense of macho fought against wearing an alert bracelet until Charlene presented him with a sterling silver one. The only changes were his initials and hers on either side of the caduceus and the Celtic braid chain that replaced the links.

My eyes were drawn to Jennifer's face. Her pupils, like two foreboding, dark caves, were completely dilated in the bright sunshine. She was smiling, almost posing for the camera. But that look; Roger was right. It was like nothing I had ever seen before, and it filled me with a cold, sinister fear.

I backed up a few slides and went through them again. The bracelet was there. A sinking feeling moved from the pit of my stomach and crawled over my skin. Nothing in those hollow, haunted eyes could answer the question screaming, hammering my mind: why the hell was she wearing the bracelet that should have been buried with Ben three years ago? The only thing those eyes did confirm was that there was definitely something wrong with Mary's Jennifer.

$\triangledown$

6

I DIDN'T FEEL LIKE fighting the truck, so I talked Roger out of his BMW and had started out to Mary's farm by seven thirty the next morning. I had tried to phone first, but the line had been busy up to my seventh try. It made sense to me that any self-respecting farm wife would be up and at 'em and up to her arms in bread dough or chicken feed.

By the time I pulled onto the gravel road that led to the farm, the sun was losing its battle with a darkening cloud cover that threatened snow or rain. Or both. A chill hung in the air, but it was mild compared with the one I was generating on my own, wondering if looking into Jennifer Kuntz's eyes would reveal any answers. I was definitely determined to look into those eyes and more determined to find out why Mary had chosen to let me find the bracelet, instead of telling me about it.

When I reached the gate, I stopped and just sat there. The mountains in the distance still wore a white-bearded mantle of snow that would last until midsummer. It was a sharp contrast against the deep-blue illusion of the pine-covered Beartooth Mountains some sixty miles away. Nothing was what it seemed to be.

I had second thoughts. Christ. The thoughts running through my mind multiplied by tens every split second. None of it made sense. Mary was right. Maybe not in the sense she thought she was, but she was onto something.

I got out of the car and pulled the iron gate open, got back in, and pulled through. Then I repeated the whole process again. No wonder they were in better shape than us city slickers.

Farms give me the creeps. I sneeze around hay, cows terrify me, and I'm probably the only person who doesn't think it's very funny to call those flat brown liquid piles that cows leave, after they are sun dried, Montana Frisbees.

Chickens, with their little pointed beaks, can do great harm to your ankles, and God only knows what would happen if they got you on the ground. Many dangerous things live on a farm. If you've ever been chased by a psycho goose, you know exactly what I mean.

The place was quiet. A new Ford Escort was parked near the back door, so I got out of the BMW and walked up to the house, knocked, and waited for someone to answer. No one did. I looked around and didn't see anything or anyone move. I tried the knob. The door was unlocked.

I pushed it open and yelled through the doorway. Still, no answer. Inside I could hear a radio playing. Feeling like an intruder, I stepped in and yelled again. Nothing. The quiet that hung in the air was making me more and more uncomfortable, so I walked back outside and around the house. I'm convinced that no one in a rural area uses a front door. They may all have them, but no one uses them.

Before I reached the front of the house, I thought I heard a noise up ahead. The ground was still wet from the spring thaw, and my Nikes were gaining layers of gumbo with each step I took. I'd picked up a couple of pounds of weight on each foot when I heard the noise again. Metal, buckets or something, was clanging.

I walked around the corner of the house and saw a barn at the bottom of the hill. It was one of the old, massive, red kind that always look like the first strong wind would carry them away. The noise seemed to be coming from there. A corral stretched around one end of the barn and disappeared. It looked empty. There were no more noises. I headed for the open door at the opposite end of the barn, figuring I'd find Mary.

The barn was dim inside. Spectral, shapeless shadows crouched in every corner. The air inside smelled heavy, sweet.

"Mary!" I yelled. Within the cavernous space of the barn, I thought I heard an echo. "Mary! It's Phoebe!" I yelled again.

"M-a-a-a-r-y," the sound, zephyrlike, haunting, floated through the air toward me. I shivered. This was no echo.

I didn't like the place. It was dark, dank, and farmy.

"Where are you? I . . . I tried to call but the line was busy."

"Over he-e-e-r-e . . . ," the singsong voice answered from the darkness.

I inched my way along. My eyes started itching; my nose twitched and tickled from the dust and faint smell of mold. I tightened my upper lip and unsuccessfully tried to block a sneeze. The braying sound filled the barn.

"Bless you," the disembodied voice said.

A low, tortured groan sounded from the far end of the barn. I strained my eyes as the unmistakable sound of weary and worn hinges groaned ahead of me. A square of light appeared. I picked up my pace and headed for it.

As I neared, I could see it was a small door leading outside. By my calculations, it would bring me into the corral I had seen from the yard.

"Mary . . ." I was growing impatient with the bizarre game of hide-and-seek. Granted, the woman was under a lot of stress, but this was getting ridiculous. "Maybe we could go up to the house and talk."

I ducked down and stepped out into the light. After the stifling atmosphere of the barn, the cool air felt like pure oxygen. "Mary?"

Something moved behind me. I turned just as the door slammed shut. I pushed on it with my hands. It gave a little for a split second. Then I heard a bolt slide on the other side and a shrill, nerve-shattering burst of laughter.

"Open this damn door!" I screamed and beat on the rough wood. Bits of dried and peeling brick-red paint fell to the ground by my feet. "Open it up!"

"You don't want to get too noisy out there," a voice said from inside the barn. It wasn't Mary.

I quit banging and stepped back from the door, shocked. "Jennifer?"

"Have we met?" she asked.

"No, we haven't. This seems like a good time. Why don't you open the door and join me out here?" I didn't want to meet this kid in the dark barn.

"Uh, I don't think so. I'm late for an appointment as it is. Gotta go." She sounded smug, triumphant. Little did I know.

"I don't have time for this shit," I said and started beating on the door.

"I tried to tell you not to do that. Blacky doesn't like noises. The vet thinks he might be crazy and will have to be put down." There was a feigned dramatic quality in her speech now. "Even the slightest little noise puts him on edge. Mother dropped a bucket up at the house the other day, and he broke two of the corral rails."

"Look, Jennifer, your little joke is cute. Real cute. I'm going over to the fence now and crawl under. Your mother isn't going to like this one bit. Do you hear me?"

I started backing up. For a couple of minutes it was quiet. Suddenly, she spoke from behind me. I spun around. Jennifer stood on the other side of the fence holding a metal bucket and a wrench.

"What makes you think Mother will know?" She hit the side of the bucket with the wrench.

"I see you're in a band. How nice for you." I took a step toward the fence, wondering if I would have to disarm her, when the ground vibrated under my feet. A high-pitched whinny filled the air. I froze in my tracks and turned around.

A great obsidian stallion rose high above me and pawed the air. His ears were flat against his head. His eyes rolled in a wild frenzy. He flared his nostrils, curled his upper lip, and screamed again toward the darkening sky. He dropped to all fours and dug at the ground between us ten feet away.

I looked over my shoulder and knew damn well I wouldn't be able to vault that fence before he compressed my spine with one blow of his hoof.

Jennifer laughed behind me. "I tried to tell you. He doesn't like noises. He's crazy."

She didn't have to convince me. I didn't utter a word. In fact, I didn't draw a breath. I felt barrel-chested from the acre of air I had drawn in when I saw him.

He settled down, if you could call it that, and paced back and forth in the corral. We did a peculiar dance, he and I. He moved one way, I inched another. He was cleverly positioning himself between me and the fence.

Then it started, the laughter and the drumming on the bucket. Every muscle on that horse tensed and then started twitching. In pulsating time, Jennifer was slowly, steadily increasing her death tempo with the wrench.

He came at me like a black freight train, reared up, and brought his hooves down so close to my head I felt the air move past my face like a contrail. I stumbled backward and crawled, crab style, out of his way. Now the sound was deafening, and he was on a homicidal roll.

He reared again. Missed me again. I had visions of his hoof breaking into my skull and the further damage it would do when he tried to dislodge me. I knew I'd had it.

"Jennifer, stop! My God, what are you doing?" I heard Mary scream from a distance. "For God's sake, stop!"

I was too busy to be impressed with her intervention. Besides, unless she decided to get in the corral with me and deflect the blows, there wasn't much she could do. A bucket flew past me and bounced off the horse's head. He backed up. His flanks quivered and glistened under a blanket of white, frothy sweat. Everything went quiet at once. Mary appeared at my side, grabbed me under the shoulders, and tried to pull me toward the fence.

"I can walk," I said. I was shaking so bad my teeth were chattering.

"Just do it slow, nice and slow. He's calming down."

I don't even remember climbing the fence. Maybe I crawled under. It didn't matter. All I cared was that those six-inch poles were between me and that black beast.

"Come up to the house. Are you hurt?" Mary's voice was shaking as bad as mine. "I don't know how this could have happened."

I tried to brush my jeans off, but my hands wouldn't work. A spasm grabbed my diaphragm and tore at my throat. Nothing came up with it. I started up the hill toward the house.

"You definitely have a problem there, Mary." I knew I sounded hoarse, breathless. "Where the hell were you?" I asked.

"I . . . there was a cow out. I had to get him back inside the fence. Why didn't you call first?"

"I did!" I yelled, took a deep breath, and lowered my voice an octave. "I did call. The line was busy. Christ, look at me."

My clothes were covered with mud, and something more disgusting. Trying to brush it off only smeared it.

"I'm so sorry. My God, you could have been killed." Mary's hands flew over me as she tried to rid my clothes of the horseshit.

By the time we crested the hill, I saw the back end of the Escort pulling down the driveway. Mary looked distraught and near tears. I reached out and touched her shoulder and considered why the hell I was trying to make her feel good.

"I gotta get out of here, Mary. I'll call you when I get back to town. I saw the damn bracelet by the way. Cute. We are going to talk, Mary."

"I'm so sorry." I could feel her hands brushing down my back. "I . . . maybe I should have told you about . . ."

It had started raining. I stepped toward the car, through the puddles that had formed on the dirt driveway, without even acknowledging her feeble attempt at an explanation. When I reached the BMW, I looked down and saw that one of my Nikes was missing.

"The hell with it," I said, got into the car, and got the hell out of there.

I looked once in the rearview mirror. Mary just stood, in the rain, watching me drive away.

* * *

After a shower, I dressed and took my filthy clothes to a Laundromat. I couldn't see running horseshit and gumbo through Mama's washing machine. Roger's car was another story. I took it to a detailing shop, left it, walked back to the apartment, and called Mary. She was still shook up when she answered the phone.

"Are you okay?" she asked.

"Fine. Never better. I'm going to try and come back out—"

"No . . . no, don't do that." She sounded hysterical. "That wouldn't work."

"We need to talk, Mary. As soon as possible."

"I know that, but it can't be here. You should understand that now."

"Hey, that's fine with me, but—"

"I'm looking for Jennifer's diary. She's kept one from the time she could write. It may have something that will help you."

"Great," I said without much enthusiasm. "Where do you want to meet?"

She was adamant about the place and the time; a truck stop halfway between Laurel and Billings, between nine and nine thirty, Wednesday night. The line went dead.

It had been three days since I had seen the projected image of Jennifer Kuntz on my living room wall and two days since I had seen my life flash before me at the Kuntz farm. I still hadn't gotten over my encounter with Jennifer and her black avenger.

Roger had been right, her eyes were spooky. Spooky enough that I couldn't get them out of my mind. I was convinced that the kid was still using, or at least was on some type of heavy medication that obviously wasn't working.

After much begging and pleading, he had given in, as Roger always did, and agreed to run Stroud's name through MIB. Today he was supposed to give me any information he found.

I had picked myself up a new pair of shoes and was admiring them as I sat in the reception area of the MIB, waiting for Roger to emerge from behind the closed door leading to his office.

If power had an odor, it would smell like Old English wood polish. If it had a feel, it would feel like three inches of padding under the most luxuriant carpet money could buy. Of course, word had it that the MIB got a helluva deal on the building, hence the built-in luxury.

I thumbed through the latest issue of *Glamour* magazine the receptionist had loaned me and pretended I knew what it was about. Every once in a while I smiled up at her. It was all I could do to keep from laughing each time someone walked through the door to her desk. Her red, high-gloss lips slid back and flashed a toothy white smile.

If a woman walked in, she slipped into a solicitous monotone of forced congeniality. If it was a man, her voice dropped seductively. She would lean forward, upper arms held tightly against her body to accentuate her cleavage, and, I swear to God, she cooed any tough act that walked through the door into submission as she gave him a teasing glimpse of her breasts. So much for class.

When Roger came into the reception area and saw me, panic glazed his eyes. He glanced at me briefly as he shook hands with a big, good-looking guy flanked by a ferret-faced smaller man who was looking me up and down. He was good at it. I could feel my skin crawl as his pale-blue eyes met mine.

With a not-too-subtle motion of his head, he pointed out my presence to the man who was shaking Roger's hand. All three of them turned toward me in unison. The bigger man's frame obliterated Roger as he stepped in front of him.

"Roger, you're always two steps ahead of the game. I like that," he said as he moved toward me. Without looking at her, he spoke to the gaudy blond receptionist. "Hold all my calls, Linda," he said as he walked toward me with his hand extended.

Roger stepped from behind the guy and started making a series of cryptic faces I couldn't decipher. Watching Roger and his facial tics and the other two move toward me made me feel like I was walking on coals.

"How fortuitous for both of us," he said as we shook hands.

Roger moved swiftly toward me. "Phoebe, I didn't know you were going to be here. Isn't this going to make you late for your—"

"Uh . . ." I tried like hell to get the drift of what he was saying with his eye rolling and acrobatic eyebrows. "I thought maybe you could break for lunch if you—"

"Bad timing," he answered. I was starting to pick up on his desperation. "Bad timing."

"Roger"—the big one put his arm around my shoulder and started guiding me toward Roger's office—"has been telling me about you. From what I hear, we should have met a long time ago."

There wasn't much to do after I glanced at Roger and saw him shrug in helplessness, so I followed the big guy's lead. He waved me through the door of Roger's office, guided me to a chair, and proceeded to sit down in Roger's chair and put his feet up on the desk.

"Close the doors, Roger old buddy," he said and smiled solicitously. "On your way out, that is. It'll give us a little more privacy to get to know this woman of yours. How about you and Earl go over that matter we were discussing?"

Without a word, Roger and Earl left the office. The big man watched me, folded his hands up under his chin, and settled back in the chair.

"I'm Cutter Gage," he said simply.

It was effective. Anyone with ears knew the name. Malcolm "Cutter" Gage was old money. He had run, successfully, for four terms as state senator, was now the head of the MIB, and purportedly had his eyes on a U.S. Senate seat in a couple of years.

There were a few other things rumored about Cutter Gage. He was ruthless in whatever he pursued, was known for his redneck racist views, and thought fences should be built around the Indian reservations. He had a lot of supporters. Word was that he was a shoo-in for the U.S. Senate if and when he decided to run. Women were said to swoon in his presence. Sitting there looking at him, I understood why. Men cringed. That I understood, too.

There were no neutral views when it came to the infamous Cutter Gage. He was either revered or hated, depending on who you talked to. The guy exuded a presence, a power that reached out and made you pay attention. I didn't know what to say.

"I understand you were at Quantico."

"Right. I—"

"Big change. How long have you been doing this?"

"For about three years. Listen, I really have things to—"

"I guess I should get down to brass tacks. I don't approach things any other way."

"I . . ." I was dumbfounded. What do you say in the face of the Grand Inquisitor? "Uh . . ." I was quickly expending my verbal defense.

"Roger's one of my main men around here, Miss Siegel. Hell, how 'bout I call you Phoebe?"

"Fine. Cutter." My chest felt tight. I wanted to get up, slowly, and just walk out of the room.

He laughed, leaned back in the chair, and put his hands behind his head. "I like that. A woman after my own heart. I bet you keep him on his toes. Am I right?"

"What's this all about?"

"You're marking up some points here." He laughed again and continued to look me dead in the eyes. "Fish or cut bait, well, I'm for that."

He got up, walked around the desk, and stood behind where I was sitting. I could feel the tips of his fingers against my back as he gripped the top of the chair.

"This is difficult for me." His voice dropped. He paused, took a deep breath. I could hear the leather on the chair compress as he tightened his hands. "You've recently been retained, on a professional level, by my daughter. There are a few things you should be aware of."

"Your daughter?" I asked incredulously. "I don't think so."

I started to stand. His hand reached out, held my shoulder, and exerted just enough pressure to keep me in the chair. He walked back around me and sat down at the desk.

"God, I wish she would have come to me."

"Who?"

"I'm not surprised she didn't tell you. She's always had a thing about that. Mary is, how shall I say it—"

"Mary is your—"

"She exaggerates, blows things out of proportion." He shook his head sadly. "She's always been a bit high strung. Compulsive."

My mouth was hanging open wide enough for a dentist to walk in and sit down on a molar.

"Mary's mother and I were divorced when she was quite young. Her mother moved back to Missoula and, unfortunately, did everything in her power to discourage a relationship between Mary and me. I didn't see Mary until she had graduated from high school and moved back to Billings."

"Wait a minute here." I held my hand up before I was even aware of what I was doing. "Back up. Mary Kuntz is your daughter?"

"That's right. I know this puts you in an awkward position. And I appreciate that. But the fact of the matter is—"

"The fact of the matter is, it doesn't put me in an awkward position at all. It doesn't *put* me in *any* position. I can't discuss anything with you, *Cutter*." I stood and stared him down.

Totally controlled, his lips parted slowly as he smiled. His eyes flashed, just for an instant, and then narrowed. I could see the movement of his tongue against the inside of his cheek. He reached up and ran his hand through his thick, dark hair. Then his whole body relaxed and he burst into laughter.

"God damn! No wonder that boy is—"

"I have an appointment. It's good to have met you, Mr. Gage."
I started to stand.

"Now hold on there. I told you I'd help and I will," he said as
he buzzed his secretary.

I stood there in silence. Inside I was shaking like a leaf and mad
as hell. He kept on smiling that self-assured smile as he waited for
her to pick up on the other end. When she did, he kept his eyes
riveted on me.

"Have Earl come on in here, will you, please?"

Within seconds Earl entered the room from behind me. In seconds I had both of them, Earl sitting on the edge of the desk, Gage
behind it, grinning at me.

"I'm going to make Earl available to you should the need arise.
This man has been my confidant and my aide for many years. He's
aware of my family and of Mary's *problems*." He leaned forward
on the desk and clasped his hands in front of him. "I'd like you to
humor my daughter. Do what it is she asks within reason."

"I'm afraid—"

He waved me silent and continued. "I'm not a man who takes
no kindly. Particularly when it comes to my family. A man who
holds a position of responsibility like I do, Phoebe, has to be careful. Has to live his life above reproach, as does his family."

"What Mr. Gage is trying to tell you is that—" Earl started to
say, but I cut him off.

"I'm uncomfortable with this whole conversation. Mary has
retained me and—"

"I would consider it a personal favor if you'd let me open a few
doors for you if you should find them closed. I have some favors I
can call in that might be of benefit."

I wondered just how many and what kind of personal favors he
had to call in. He walked around the desk toward me; Gage's arm
felt heavy as he placed it across my shoulders and led me toward
the door.

The intercom buzzed on the desk. He picked up the phone,
listened for a moment, hung it back up, and turned toward Earl.

"The governor is on the phone and ready for that conference
call. Would you see to it that everything is taken care of?" Gage's
voice echoed authority.

Earl nodded, shot me a dirty look, and left the room.

"Now all you need to do is get hold of Earl, should the need
arise. We'll talk again, Phoebe. My family is important to me.
There's nothing, absolutely nothing, I wouldn't do to protect—"

He stopped and looked down at me. His face was void of expression. His eyes were iced, cold. "Why am I telling *you* about family? Yes, we'll talk again."

He opened the door, led me into the reception area, and walked away without saying another word. As he disappeared down a long corridor, I saw Roger out of the corner of my eye, coming from another one.

"Phoebe, shit."

"That's the understatement of all time. What the hell did you do, give him my life history?"

"I swear to God, I didn't say a thing. I ran that name through the computer, and five minutes later he was in my office. He approached me, Phoebe," he whispered. "You didn't know she was his daughter?"

"Do I look like I knew? I've got to get out of here, Roger." I started for the door. "Boy, do we have to talk soon."

"I don't know. I'll call you."

"Roger," the receptionist called out, "Earl needs you in his office ASAP."

"Right," he answered. "Later, Phoebe. Jeez, I tried to warn you."

"I thought you were exercising your scalp. Thanks. Thanks a lot." I walked out, the muscles in my neck starting to knot up from what felt like an invisible noose from a not-so-invisible hangman.

7

ALPHA FOOD WAS THE biggest wholesale outfit in the area, so it only made sense that if Whispering Pines bought locally, it would be from Alpha. Cutter Gage might be able to open the front door of Whispering Pines for me, but I couldn't afford not to cover all the angles, one of which was finding access to the back door if I needed it.

With the luck of the Irish, I learned that the dock foreman was a guy I had known in high school, Jerry Bean. You hear things in a town the size of Billings, and I knew he was married and had three or four kids, which meant he was probably living from paycheck to paycheck.

I stopped by the bank, got two hundred bucks in fifty-dollar bills, and, instead of calling, I drove down to the warehouse in the '49, pulling in by the loading docks. The old truck always brought a lot of attention, and as soon as I got out three or four guys had walked up and started looking it over.

Jerry was standing at one end of the dock holding a clipboard, cussing out some skinny kid who was loading a small van. When he finally looked my way, he smiled and jumped down off the dock.

"Hey, Phoebe."

"Hey, Jerry." I'd known Jerry long enough to know I wouldn't have to snow him. "I need a favor."

"Shoot."

I started by making an assumption; most people figured you already knew. "You guys deliver up at that treatment center on top of the Rims, don't you?"

"Whispering Pines? Sure do. Why? Are you investigating a complaint on us or something?" He stiffened, puffed up a couple of inches taller, and frowned.

"No, nothing like that. I'm just trying to do a little research."

"What's up?"

"You know I can't talk about it, Jerry. I can make it worth your time, though."

I pulled the four fifty-dollar bills out of my shirt pocket and tucked them in his.

"How's the wife and kids?" God, if you had to buy someone off, it was a helluva lot more pleasant to know the money went to a worthy cause.

Jerry reached into his pocket, took out the money, and counted it. He looked around, rather obviously, and grinned.

"I guess my boy can finally get that Nintendo game he's been wanting. Life must be good, Phoebe. What can I do?"

So much for worthy causes. "I might need to get in the back door up there. Is that possible?"

"For that much money I'd get you in *my* back door. That place used to be on my route. They're real flakes."

"How so?"

"They only take deliveries on Saturday nights. And they pay in cash. Big cash. They had a couple of real killer dogs up there that tried to deball one of my drivers. Before we could even complain, they had picked up the hospital tab, settled a couple of thou on us, and guaranteed the dogs would be locked up when we delivered."

"Quick thinkers."

"Big money," he countered. "Let me check when our next delivery is. I've got a new guy named Crank on that route now. He's been with us about eight months."

"Crank?"

"Don't ask," he answered and laughed. "Crank's the one the dogs nailed. They went right for his crotch. If you get lucky, he might show you his scars. There's some ugly rumor going around that he's had a hard time getting it up since then. I'll be right back."

He reached out, patted me on the shoulder, and walked toward my truck. I watched as he started talking to one guy and motioned the rest of the group back to work. In a couple of minutes he waved me over.

It wasn't hard to figure out why they called the guy Crank. Everything about him was wired. He had a cocky grin that turned me off immediately. As soon as I approached, he looked me up and down with one of those looks that made me wish I was wearing a shroud. His eyes settled on my chest.

"I hear you're a dick," he said.

"I hear you're not."

His mouth dropped open, and his face turned a deep crimson. He looked toward Jerry.

"Damn it, Jerry. You didn't tell her . . ." His entire posture changed to that of an offended boy.

"You better watch her, Crank. She'll eat you up and spit you out. What do ya say? It's an easy fifty bucks."

Crank eyed me suspiciously for a minute.

"Sure. What the hell? I go tomorrow night."

"What time?"

"Between nine and nine thirty. It's real tight up there. They let those damn rottweilers out at ten sharp."

"This is still tentative," I said. "I'll be here before nine if I need a ride." I turned toward Jerry. "Won't they wonder about two people in the van?"

"No problem. We always send two drivers. If you're here, someone will get a couple of hours off."

"Thanks, Jerry. Crank? If it's a go, okay?"

"Great," he answered. It didn't ring with a lot of enthusiasm.

I turned and left. At fifty bucks, Crank was just another sign of a bad economy.

I had called the center and gotten the VIP treatment from a honey-voiced woman on the other end of the line. Stroud could see me at *my* convenience. The next day, disguised as someone who knew how to dress (I was amazed at how much I resembled Zelda), I climbed into Roger's BMW and drove out to the city.

In less than fifteen minutes I was driving down a narrow lane leading to Whispering Pines. I stopped at the massive iron gates, got out of the car, and read the sign bolted to one of them.

WHISPERING PINES
INSTITUTE OF
HOLISTIC HEALING
Press buzzer for admittance

Through the trees I could see the three-story stone building that had once been the Odd Fellows' Nursing Home. It seemed appropriate. There wasn't a soul in sight. No sooner had my hands touched the gate than a steely feminine voice broadcast out of nowhere.

"What is your business, please?"

I let go of the bars, stepped back, and looked around. Set into one of the columns was a speaker, a buzzer, and what I assumed to be a microphone.

"I have an appointment with Dr. Stroud," I said.

"Your name?"

"Helen Jenkins."

In a moment the gates started opening slowly. I got back in the BMW and drove through, watching the gates close almost immediately behind me. A television camera rotated high atop one of the columns and tracked my entrance.

A stone wall at least ten feet high stretched from either front corner as far as I could see. The place was a fortress. I pulled up at the base of the wide stone stairs leading to the front door, turned off the car engine, and got out.

I glanced up the stairs and saw a woman standing in a window to the left of the doors, a pair of binoculars hung around her neck. The climb up those stairs was risky at best. My ankles ached and threatened to buckle at any moment. I had barely touched one of the doorknobs when a buzzer sounded from within the building. The doors swung open. Tricky. Fake doorknobs, I thought to myself.

Before the doors closed behind me, the woman I had seen in the window walked up to me, extended her hand, and said nothing. Our clothes were so similar in a benign sort of way, I wondered who she was imitating.

"I'm Ms. Jenkins. I phoned for an appointment. Dr. Stroud is expecting me . . ."

Her expression changed. It didn't soften, it just changed. What was supposed to pass for a smile opened above her pointed chin. Her handshake nearly crushed my knuckles.

"Dr. Stroud will be with you in a moment. He likes to have dinner with our residents and should be finishing now. He has an extremely structured schedule, Ms. Jenkins."

I was intrigued with her lipless mouth as it formed words. There was an edge to her features that was sharp, angular. No softness, just flesh stretched over bone. I didn't answer right away.

"It is Ms. Jenkins, isn't it?"

She caught me off guard. For a second I didn't know who the hell she was talking to.

"Sorry. I was, uh . . . I was thinking how nice it is up here. This is rather spread out, isn't it? My late husband would have appreciated it," I said, trying to make conversation. It wasn't hard to tell she wasn't interested in my life story.

The place was as quiet as a tomb except for the click of our heels echoing around us in a strange lopsided rhythm. I tightened the muscles in my calves and tried to block out the sharp pains that were shooting up from my feet. I hadn't had a pair of pumps on for three years. They were starting to feel like Vise-Grips on my feet. Beads of sweat were forming under the wig and felt like hundreds of little beasties scurrying back and forth across my scalp.

She finally stopped in front of a door, opened it, and ushered me through. The room was expansive, plush, and definitely male. There was no doubt that the man who occupied this space was top dog. Whoever he was, he was a collector. Masks, primitive and garish, long, tapered swords, and ornate daggers filled every nook and cranny on the paneled walls. Some were even propped on marble-topped tables or held protectively within glass showcases.

"Dr. Stroud will be with you in a moment," she said as she led me to a large overstuffed leather armchair.

I sat down, grateful for the opportunity to take the weight off my feet. She leaned down close and looked me straight in the eyes.

"I'm Dr. Stroud's assistant. My name is Claire," she said. "Now don't you budge."

Again, that smile opened up above her witchy chin. Then she disappeared. There I was, watched by hundreds of black, empty eye sockets, a faint scent of sickeningly sweet incense wafting through the air, and surrounded by enough sharp instruments to make me extremely nervous. Odd decor for a treatment center. So this was Whispering Pines.

Minutes slipped by. I was tempted to slip my shoes off but knew if I did I would end up barefooting it when my feet puffed up like pumpkins. Leaning back in the chair, I looked around the office. It was half as big as most tract homes and furnished with more antiquity than most museums.

I couldn't resist the urge to explore and touch. Grimacing, I stood and cruised the perimeter of the room. Shelves of books covered one whole wall. I browsed through the titles. Many, stuffed between psychiatric journals and psychiatric texts, were penned by Rama-this or Rama-that. Had the bhagwan resurfaced in Montana?

There were two chaise lounges, several leather chairs, and a colossal wooden desk that would have made a queen-sized bed look diminutive. Behind the desk, two French doors stood open and led onto a stone porch. A chilling March breeze wound in from outdoors and shuffled the papers around on top of the desk.

I checked my watch. I'd been waiting nearly fifteen minutes. I threw the clutch bag I was carrying down on the chair and walked over to a low counter that seemed to hold the largest trove of treasures. My hand reached out and touched a long, slender, mahogany-colored stick that resembled varnished rawhide. I picked it up and ran my hand up and down the smooth, twisted surface.

I was born curious and loved a puzzle, but this one had me stumped. I tapped one end on the floor, leaned my weight on it, and breathed a sigh of relief when it took some of the tension out of my ankles. I stood there, using it for support, and tried to stare down the empty eyes that followed my every move.

"That's quite astute. Most people wouldn't recognize that as a walking stick."

The voice, deep and commanding, bearing a subtle but strong accent, came through the air from behind me like a javelin. I turned and faced him.

Victor Stroud walked across the room and stood a couple of feet from me. Every old horror movie I had ever seen flashed across my mind. I knew if I tried to flee, his taloned hand would reach out, grab my throat, and lift me six feet off the floor. I'd hang there, struggling helplessly. My shoes would slip from my feet and fall to the carpet right before he effortlessly pitched me twenty feet across the room. Sometimes a good imagination can be a real downer.

I cleared my mind and reached out to shake his hand. His skin was soft; his grip gave a new definition to the word *flaccid*. My eyes were riveted on his thin red lips as his tongue moved rapidly over them, giving them a spittle sheen.

"I'm Dr. Stroud, and you are Helen Jenkins," he said as he lowered his forehead slightly and looked down into my face.

A crooked etch formed in the space between his eyebrows as he wrinkled his forehead. He was tall, lean, and wore his silver-flecked black hair brushed starkly back from his face. The guy was handsome in a malefic sort of way, but when he smiled it didn't involve his eyes.

"I appreciate your seeing me on such short notice." It took everything I had to maintain some sense of authority.

He reached out, took the cane from my hand, and, holding it in the air, turned it slowly in the space between us.

"This is a bull's penis, Helen," he stated matter-of-factly without looking at me. "They shove a steel rod down them and dry them in the sun. After surgical removal, of course."

He shifted his gaze to my face.

"Of course." I twittered like a fucking fool. If shock was his game, it succeeded. He was unnerving me. Intentionally.

Without a word, he touched the side of my cheek with the stick, which now had taken on a life of its own. I could feel the smooth, cold surface as it moved across my skin.

"They always feel cool to the touch. Curious, isn't it?"

"Oh definitely, definitely curious."

A picture flashed through my mind of this guy prodding my wig off with a bull's penis, which in turn would allow my own hair to spring forth in all of its tangled, auburn glory. It would be tough to explain. Something told me that this was child's play and that this guy was capable of anything.

"Have a seat, Helen," he said as he walked to his desk and sat down behind it.

It felt good having the five feet or so of wood between us as I settled back into the overstuffed leather chair and tried to look the part I was playing.

"When my assistant informed me that you had called and made an appointment, I wish she would have told you that accepting a local referral would be against the norm for us. There are always exceptions, but they would be few and far between."

My mind immediately wondered how much more *local* you could get than Jennifer Kuntz.

"I . . . uh, have never considered myself one of the locals," I tried to say with as much indignation as I could muster.

"Because of our policy, it will more than likely necessitate your finding accommodations for your daughter elsewhere. We have found that geographic distance takes some of the wind out of our clients' sails. The percentage of clients running away from the institute is probably one of the lowest in the country."

He articulated each word with cunning precision. He folded his hands in front of him and looked at me directly. I've always been good at holding it together under the toughest circumstances. It wasn't working. There was an energy about him that crawled under my skin and stroked something raw on my nerves.

I reached into the clutch bag and withdrew Kehly's picture. I hesitated, feeling that the minute his hands touched the photo, she would be soiled.

"I don't foresee that as a problem. We're not from here. My husband was. We maintain a seasonal home above Red Lodge that we frequent during the summer, but I prefer West Palm Beach, which is my home. My daughter," I said as I handed the picture of Kehly across the desk, "has spent most of her time abroad in foreign schools. It was when I allowed her to spend the summer in Florida last year that she was, shall we say, led astray. I have no skill in handling the behavior she has been displaying. I am at my wit's end."

I sat back in the chair to read his reaction to her picture.

"Very attractive young woman," he said without a trace of interest.

"For reasons I won't go into, I need to handle this matter with the utmost discretion. I was impressed with the security you have."

"We've found it necessary." He put the photo down and rested his open hand on top of it. He looked toward me, licked his lips quickly, and said nothing for a moment.

"Dr. Stroud, I'm a woman alone. Virtually without family. Motherhood hasn't been easy for me, to be quite frank." I even surprised myself with the charade. "Rachael is my stepdaughter, and we've never, what's the word? Bonded? Of course, I'm rising to the occasion. She's troubled and needs help."

"Hmmm," he muttered and continued to look at Kehly's picture.

"How long have you operated this facility?"

"I maintained a private practice outside of Washington, D.C., for several years before moving out here. I took over a practice, and shortly thereafter an opportunity arose that I took." He motioned around the room with his hand. "Hence, Whispering Pines."

"Montana must have been a radical change."

"Not really." He shifted in his chair.

"You must miss the nightlife in D.C.?"

"My work and involvement with my clients have always limited me socially. Although I now have a larger volume of clients, I still pride myself on being involved with each one on an individual basis."

I sat back in the chair to read his reaction to my questions about him personally. He was giving me more than I had expected. Victor Stroud was a man who didn't like discussing himself. Or his past.

"Back to the security I noticed. I'd like to reiterate how closely supervised everything seems."

He pulled himself together, looked toward me, licked his lips quickly, and said nothing for a moment. "Most of our clients are from well-to-do families. Their problems run the gamut. We treat psychiatric problems, drug and alcohol dependency, and good old-fashioned rebellious adolescent behavior. Because of this, we protect the privacy of the parents as well as minister to their children.

"Let me show you our facilities. I can't take you everywhere. It's a further precaution to protect our clients, but I'm sure we can impress you with what Whispering Pines has to offer. And it will give us a chance to chat a little." A beeper lying on the desk chirped. "Excuse me, please." He turned toward a phone and picked up the receiver.

It was impossible to hear the conversation, but when he turned around, I saw a chink in his self-assured armor. Fear? Rage? Whatever it was, it was intense.

"We have a minor difficulty," he said quickly. "I must ask you not to leave this area, Helen. Please stay right here. This won't take long."

He walked from the room through a door that was camouflaged in the paneling. I walked to the French doors and looked out over the manicured grounds. I could hear muffled voices coming from somewhere but couldn't see anyone.

I walked toward one of the showcases and bent down to get a closer look at a jeweled dagger that had to be worth thousands. My breath was creating little patches of humidity on the glass.

Something stirred behind me. The hair stood up on the back of my neck. I knew someone was there, not speaking, not moving, just breathing.

A hand reached out and grabbed my shoulder from behind. I tried to keep from wetting myself as I turned slowly around. She wasn't much taller than I was. Her hair was blond, frosted, and hung in thin, wispy tangles around her face. Her blue eyes were glassy and stretched so wide that I wondered what was holding her eyeballs in. Her teeth were working at one corner of her bottom lip. I doubt that she was even aware of the small drop of blood forming under their persistent gnawing.

"God, help me," she whispered. "You . . . you have to help me get out of here. Oh God, please."

"Who are you?" I whispered back.

Her eyes were wild, darting back and forth, searching my face for a place she could hide, an opening she could crawl into. She kept looking behind her and out the French doors. I reached up and held her by her shoulders.

"It's all right. Calm down," I whispered again. "Who are you?"

"They've been holding me in the infirmary." She jerked her head toward the wall. "You've got to help me, now, before . . ."

Something in her voice reached into my chest and held my breath bursting in my lungs. "What can I do?"

"Call my father. Oh God, call anyone. He's in Denver. Tell him to forget what I told him. Not to say anything. Oh God."

She moved quickly around the desk and grabbed a pencil, tore a piece of paper off a notepad, and hurriedly started writing something down. Her body shuddered; she was on the verge of collapse. I moved toward her. The lead broke on the pencil. A sob burst from her throat.

I reached out, touched her face, tried to turn it toward me. Her right hand stiffened and dropped the pencil. She doubled up, grimaced in pain, and clutched her stomach. It lasted only seconds before a new expression, almost cunning and sharply alert, crept over her face. She straightened up and faced me.

"Don't touch me." Her voice was low and sharply insistent. A smile formed on her lips for an instant, until the madness in her eyes yielded to tears, which rolled down her cheeks. "Please, before it's too late. Please call my father. Oh God, oh God," she sobbed as she tried once more to scribble something on the paper.

She folded it quickly and shoved it into my hand. My palms were wringing wet. Her knees buckled, and she sank to the floor. I kneeled down beside her and tried to figure out what she was saying.

"Do you know . . ." She half-sobbed, half-whispered. Then she started to giggle. "Do you have any idea what they—"

"Shawna, you shouldn't scare us like this." The voice paralyzed me. I felt the hand reach out and touch my shoulder. "Ms. Jenkins was just about ready to take a tour of the institute. Now what is she going to think about us with you carrying on like this?"

I turned and looked at Stroud. A muscle twitched high on the side of his temple. With a wave of his hand, two orderlies entered and roughly pulled the young girl from the floor. She looked at me only once before she hung her head in defeat as they led her off.

"My apologies. Shawna is new to the program and going through a rather rough period of adjustment. It's uncommon, but it does happen."

His hold on my elbow was tight enough to let me know he wasn't about to let me out of his sight. The iron maiden, Claire, stood back and watched me. I clenched my hand around the note. Before I knew it, Stroud had led me to the front of the building.

"As I'm sure you'll understand, I need to deal with this situation. We'll be in touch, Ms. Jenkins. Better yet, call and we'll set up another appointment." He turned and walked off down the hall.

His assistant had disappeared, and in her place was a big, muscle-bound blond who sized me up one side and down the other. He raised one paw of a hand and pushed the button beside the front doors. They opened and I left.

A helpless knot of guilt formed in my stomach as I got into the car and drove toward the main gates. Glancing into the rearview mirror, I could see someone standing at the same window watching my departure through binoculars. As the massive gates swung open to allow me passage through, the sun slipped down behind the mountains to the west.

I slammed on the brakes. Kehly's picture was still lying on top of Stroud's desk. I had to get it back, and there was only one way to do that. "Hell," I muttered under my breath. "I guess it's going to be me and you, Crank. I hope you're up to it."

I checked my watch. I had forty-five minutes to get Roger's car back to him and catch Crank at the warehouse.

$\triangledown$

8

CRANK HAD A COUPLE of things against him from the start. He had an excess of energy, which I assume was chemically induced. Something was always moving. Also, Crank was a punk, but, as reality would have it, there wasn't an accountant, realtor, or any other white-collar type who could have gotten me back through those gates at that hour. He was the type my little sister had been involved with on the street. It made my skin crawl.

We made two stops on Crank's route before we started up North Twenty-seventh Street, a main artery that cut Billings in half from east to west. I had avoided it on my first trip to Whispering Pines because it passed the spot on top of the Rims where they had found Ben's body.

When I knew we were approaching the area, I looked out the window and watched a United Airlines 737 rise from the ground, lights blinking on its wings. I wanted to be on it, going somewhere else. Anywhere March couldn't find me. But I knew it already had.

It was dark outside by then. Conversation was at a minimum. I couldn't get Shawna's face out of my mind. I had seen that look once before. Believe it or not, on a rabbit. One of the darker sides of the great white hunters in Montana is an old trick to call in coyotes for the slaughter.

I'd been approached a couple of years ago by a man saying that something odd was going on in the garage next door to his. To make a long story short, a couple of college kids were torturing rabbits in their garage, recording the pitiful responses, and selling the tapes to coyote bounty hunters.

On the day the cops busted them, I was there. I had reached into a cage to pet a sable-colored loop-eared bunny that cowered in the farthest corner of its mesh enclosure. I'll never forget those eyes. The same helpless terror lurked in them that lurked in

Shawna's eyes. Shit. I had cried for two days. I had that same feeling now.

Shawna's note was tucked in my pocket. I pulled it out and read it again.

DANIEL UNGER
THE GRAY GOOSE
FIVE POINT DENVER

I had so many things colliding in my mind, so many voices, that I couldn't make anything out of it except that she was desperate and she was scared. There was a distinct possibility that she was going through a tough withdrawal. Kehly had created quite a commotion the first couple of weeks she had been in treatment, so I couldn't rule out the same thing for the wild-eyed Shawna. Or could I?

I glanced over at Crank. Christ, what was I doing here? At that point I still could have pulled out, called Mary Kuntz, told her we were digging in sand, adding also that she had a psycho for a kid, and gotten on a 737 the next morning and split. The words were rolling around in my mouth waiting for me to give them life. As fate would have it, Crank broke the silence, scattered those unspoken words, and sealed my fate.

"I've never been involved in undercover work before," he said as he tapped-out a mindless rhythm on the steering wheel.

Everything about him was like a rubber band ready to snap. The music of some tripped-out heavy-metal band was blaring from the dashboard speakers and driving spikes through my already throbbing head. I'm purely a fifties and sixties listener with a dose of the blues thrown in for good measure. This was crap.

"Like, is this your everyday gig?" he asked.

"What?" I yelled.

"Do you do this a lot?" he screamed back.

I heard him but didn't answer. He reached over and turned the volume down.

"No, Crank. I don't do it a lot."

"Breakin' someone out?"

"No, Crank." This time I emphasized his name and shot him a disdainful smile. "I'm not."

"Checking in?" He burst into gales of slobbering laughter and slapped his thigh. Chew leaked out of the corner of his mouth. He reached up and wiped it off with his sleeve.

The van veered over the center yellow line.

"Watch what the hell you're doing! Christ!" I reached out and grabbed the dash. "I've got a lot on my mind, Crank. Let's just find a place where you can pick me up when you're through."

His expression changed. He looked more serious than I thought he was capable of looking.

"Nope, that won't work. You've got to come back out with me."

"Why?"

"You won't get out any other way. I know this place. Gaines Burgers city."

I looked at him and tried to figure if the guy was lucid enough to call the situation accurately. He glanced at me sideways, grinned, grabbed his crotch, and gave it a little macho shake.

"Jerry told ya about the Hounds of the Baskervilles," he said and kept grinning. "Damn near cost me the family jewels."

I don't know what threw me the most, the fact that he even knew the name of a book, or the assault on his crotch.

"And?"

"It takes me about thirty minutes to unload. Fifteen more to sign it off. That's all I can give ya."

"Where do you unload?"

"In the back. Right into the kitchen. It's a drive-through underneath some big porch. There's usually one dude hanging around for the first five minutes. Then he wanders off down the hill for a hit or two."

"How do you know what he's doing down the hill?"

Crank reached up and turned on the dome light, pulled two neatly rolled joints out of his pocket, and held them up in the air.

"He smokes, and I get a couple of boxes of shrimp, game hens, whatever catches the old eye."

My success hinged on this obnoxious Dr. Feelgood? Great. Voices were whispering warnings in my ear. I should have listened.

His mention of a porch, hopefully *the* porch, caught my attention. Maybe the gods would be with me. We turned off the highway and followed the road I had taken only a couple of hours before. I felt sick. I didn't know what the hell was going on at that place, but the desperate, trapped look in that girl's eyes haunted me.

When we reached the gates, Crank got out, pushed the buzzer, and identified himself. Within minutes we were pulling around behind the institution. The van headlights created shadows that moved in and out of the darkness as he slowed down and stopped.

"This would be a good spot for you to get out," he said and looked toward me.

"Here?"

"Right here. They've always got some broad watching me with a pair of binoculars when I come in. She wasn't there."

I looked around and saw stone stairs leading up and around the corner of the building.

"Is that the porch you were talking about?"

"Yup. You've got forty-five minutes. Max. I'll catch you right here on my way out. I don't wait," he said as he gave his crotch another quick squeeze and raised his eyebrows for emphasis.

"Right."

I closed the door quietly, trailing my hand along the side of the van as he drove slowly down the hill toward the door. Then I took a deep breath and ducked around behind the van and up the stairs.

Doing the kind of work that I do, up to that point, had not required much 007 stunt shit. But there I was, creeping up those stairs, sideways, with my back pressed against the wall. I needed those French doors to be there. I needed them open, and I definitely needed them to lead into that office.

They gave me all of that, and more. The office was empty. It was no more than five steps inside those open doors to the desk. Only one lamp was on it, and it washed the room in a sepia tone. I walked to the desk. Kehly's picture wasn't there. The door to the right of the desk that Stroud had disappeared through was open, revealing a hallway that stretched twenty-five feet before it turned left.

I shuffled a few papers around as a huge surge of panic gripped my chest. Then I heard it. Those same clicking echoes that Claire and I had created earlier that evening when she steered me into the room. The steps moved closer to the turn in the hallway.

My first instinct was to bolt back out the door. I took my next-best shot, which was to duck under the desk and squeeze myself as far back in the kneehole as possible. It was at least four feet deep and dark as hell. My heart was beating so hard I could hear it. The footsteps came closer. As they neared, I could hear Claire's spirit-less voice. The sound of those clicking heels disappeared into the carpet. She was in the room.

"Sit down over there," she said. Someone was with her. "Doctor will be right in. And don't turn on any other lights. Doctor likes them turned low in the evening."

I strained to listen for her footsteps as they walked back over the carpet and clicked down the hallway. I was trapped. I had no idea who was sitting in that room. For all I knew, Crank could have gotten busted unloading his shrimp.

I pushed the button on the side of my watch and read the time. I had exactly thirty-nine minutes before I had to meet him. I knew he wouldn't hesitate to leave me behind as fodder for the hounds. The thought crossed my mind that I could attempt crawling toward the French doors and take my chances. Then I heard them. Heavier footsteps coming down the hall.

To get under the desk, I'd had to move a high-backed leather swivel chair away from the kneehole. Some unseen hand was now moving it toward my lair. Almost instantly I found myself looking straight at Victor Stroud's knees as he rolled up to the desk in the chair.

If I had thought it was dark when I crawled in there, it didn't compare with the blackness that descended on me when he moved closer. I felt caught in a tomb with no possible escape. The sound of a pencil tapping on the desktop kept me spellbound.

"Gina," he said. The deep timbre of his voice filtered down to me. "Claire told me you've been having some second thoughts. Would you care to tell me about them?"

His voice was seductively compassionate. Whoever was sitting on the other side of the desk didn't feel like talking.

"You were doing so well. I thought that we had reached some accord, some conclusions that would be beneficial, not only to you, my dear, but to your family as well. What happened?"

For a moment I thought that maybe Gina whoever-she-was was answering and I just couldn't hear her. Stroud's legs stiffened. The desk exploded. Cool, controlled Stroud apparently lost it and slammed his fist down on top of the desk. The sound reverberated through the kneehole. I damn near blew it and had to bite down on my lip to stay still.

"I don't have time for this, Gina. You're not some little princess that everyone has to walk on eggshells around," he said with contempt. "Maybe, just maybe, you're missing those vomit-coated old men that you let—"

Stroud relaxed at the same time that I heard a soft mewing sound coming from somewhere. It didn't take much to figure out she was crying.

"I don't enjoy talking to you like that. You know that, don't you?"

"Yes." It was hard to hear her.

"Yes what, Gina?" His voice was lower now, commanding and sinister.

"Yes, Dr. Stroud. I know you don't like talking to me that way."

"Then why do you put me in that position? Why do you push me?"

"I don't know," she said and started crying harder. "I just feel so—"

"How do you feel, Gina? What's brought this on?"

"I . . . I feel like I can't trust anyone here."

"How could that be? Unless you have secrets."

"Secrets." Her voice broke, choked in a sob. "How can you have secrets when everything you say to anyone is written down in those . . ."

"The Book of Shadows is what frees us, Gina. This is not done for the sake of cruelty. It is done to shatter the secrets, the lies that we all hide behind."

"It's snitching, Dr. Stroud. Plain snitching." Her voice dropped to a pathetic whisper. "Claire . . . Claire told me about my family." She spoke after a moment.

"What did Claire tell you?"

"She . . . she told me they didn't want anything more to do with me. They," she said and muffled a sob. "Claire said that my father says that I hurt him with my lies and that was why they wouldn't accept my calls."

"Can you blame them? You've brought quite a bit of shame down upon them, Gina. Your father became ill over it and almost died. You can't expect them to sacrifice his life, now can you?"

I still didn't know what his game was. All I knew was that I wanted to reach out and grab *his* family jewels and dry them in the sun. He was baiting this kid. Mercilessly. Purposefully. And the Book of Shadows bullshit spoke for itself. He had them controlling and spying on each other.

"I thought they'd, uh . . . I mean he would forgive me. I thought that . . . I just want to die, Dr. Stroud. I mean it. I want to die. I won't lie anymore. Please."

I could hear the desperation and grief in her voice as she let loose. Stroud shifted and must have knocked a file off the desk. Papers floated down to the side of his feet. I was ready to do anything necessary the moment he leaned over to pick them up. But he didn't.

"I understand your wanting to die, Gina. I don't blame you one bit. I have always considered myself a strong man, very strong, and I'm not sure I could bear up under what you've created in your life. Maybe," he said and then stopped.

The girl continued to sob openly for another minute or two. I moved slowly and pushed the button on my watch again. I had fifteen minutes or I had nothing. Then Stroud rolled the chair back and leaned down to pick up the papers. I could smell his sickeningly sweet after-shave as he scooped the papers together and sat back up.

"What am I going to do, Dr. Stroud? I know you don't believe me, but I want to die. God, I just want it to be over."

"Like I said, I understand. Here I sit with your file in front of me. It's . . . it's shocking. You can't blame your parents. I certainly don't. They're decent people, Gina. They didn't ask for this. When you ran away you made your own choices."

"What's left? Where can I go?"

"Maybe we need to talk about your options, Gina. It may take me some time. There is a way that—"

"A way?"

"Yes. A long-term treatment. I've suggested this already to your parents, and they are in agreement. You and I need time to come to know one another. We'll talk about it in more detail. Of course, a lot depends on how you respond to the program."

"I'll try hard. I promise," she said between sobs. "Anything, Dr. Stroud, anything . . . but I've been here six months, Dr. Stroud."

I calculated six months at six hundred dollars a day and tried not to choke audibly.

"What about your father? What did you and I decide about your father?"

"I . . . I don't remember." Her voice was pitiful. Small.

"You can remember if you try. Drugs distort our perception, Gina. There's a period of time when those drugs are working their way out of our systems that we experience the same sense of distortion as when we were using. As I recall, I helped you straighten out some of those *distorted perceptions* about your treatment here. Didn't I, Gina?"

"Yes. I guess so."

"Then are you ready to write the letter to your father telling him you will work harder and wish to lengthen your stay here with us?"

"I don't know if I can take any more," she said and started crying again. "He loves me. He was concerned about how unhappy I was here."

"Only after you wrote him all those lies. Now, since he and I have talked he has a better perception of what's been happening here."

"I . . . I can't, Dr. Stroud. . . . I want to be home."

"They don't want you home, Gina. Not until you're better. I want that letter by tomorrow morning." His voice boomed. "Do you understand? Tomorrow morning."

"Yes, sir," she whimpered.

"Let's get a good night's sleep."

Without warning, I heard Claire's voice. I had been so wrapped up in the conversation I was hearing, I must have missed the sound of her coming down the hall.

"Claire," Stroud said, "I was just about to buzz you. I think Gina needs to get some rest tonight. Would you help her on that, please?"

"Certainly, Doctor."

"Gina, go on back to your room. Claire will get you something to take the edge off this anxiety of yours, and bring it there."

"Yes, Dr. Stroud."

"And, Gina? I'm looking forward to the letter. We'll talk about it tomorrow."

This time I heard the steps of the girl retreating from the office.

"How'd it go?" Claire asked.

"She's close. Real close. Call her parents and tell them not to accept any of her calls. Tell them that it's in her best interest at this time in her treatment. Leave word for her imbecilic father to call me on my private line. He's desperate enough to buy anything. It's time to tighten the screws a little bit."

He stood, closed the French doors, and turned out the light.

"What were those lights I saw coming through the gates?"

"Our food delivery," she answered. "He's almost done."

Both of their voices were fading away from the room.

"Go down and make sure they're through. And keep an eye on Shawna. I've got a feeling she's going to be a problem."

I waited until I couldn't hear anything, came out from the knee-hole, and looked around the desk again for Kehly's picture. Only the faint illumination from the moon coming up outside the French doors cast any light into the dark office. Then I found it, tucked in between two letters.

I hurriedly shoved it into my pocket and held the letter the picture had been under up to the faint light. It looked interesting enough for a closer look-see, so I crammed it into my pocket also. As quietly as possible I opened the French doors and stepped onto the porch. I fully expected alarms to go off.

It was pitch black as I felt my way along the wall toward the stairs. One by one I edged down them. I stopped and let my eyes adjust to the darkness, trying to figure out how the hell I was going to get off the grounds. I checked my watch again. It was 10:00 P.M. Time for the dogs. Then I felt a hand touch my head.

"Where the hell have you been?" Crank whispered.

"Waiting for you. Let's get out of here."

Just as we both opened our doors and got in, two dark, bulky figures appeared in the headlights about ten feet in front of us. The dogs just stood there and stared. Crank pulled forward slowly and then leaned on the car horn. Not overly impressed, they moved calmly aside. Crank bounced up and down in his seat.

"Big suckers, aren't they? That horn should wake the dead and split a few eardrums."

"Let's draw as much attention to ourselves as possible, okay?"

"Sounds good to me." He leaned on the horn again as we passed through the gates.

Within minutes we were winding down the Rims. The city looked ethereal. Nighttime covers all kinds of defects, hides all kinds of secrets. I couldn't get Shawna's face, or Gina's voice, out of my mind.

"Did you get what you were after?" Crank asked.

"Yeah, I did," I answered as I grabbed the sides of my seat. I couldn't stop shaking.

$\triangledown$

9

BY THE TIME I parted company with Crank and started driving home, the asphalt streets glistened with rain and absorbed my headlight beams even on high. I stopped a couple of times to make sure they were working.

I swung by Uncle John's house and breathed a sigh of relief when his lights were off. I didn't know how I was going to tell him about Shawna and Gina; either scene I had witnessed could easily be chalked up to kids fighting rehabilitation.

John would not approve of my methods. He played everything by the book where his job was concerned, and my escapade with Crank wasn't in his book. Cops on the whole don't have a lot of use for PI's. Blood tie or not, Uncle John was no different.

I pulled up in front of my apartment, parked, and got out of the truck. The streets were empty. Victor Stroud was lurking in every darkened corner, Shawna's haunting desperation looked back at me from my own reflection in each darkened window I passed, and Gina's pitiful cries echoed through my mind.

Footsteps sounded behind me just as I was putting my key in the lock. Claire reached from my mind and unleashed the little restraint I had on a bad case of jitters. The keys fell from my hand and to the ground. I turned.

"I'm Mrs. Wickersham from next door. We have to talk about your cat's assaults on my Susie, Miss Siegel. I saw you pull up and said to myself, there's no time like the present."

Her voice was high pitched and worse than nails on a chalkboard. My adrenaline rush waned the moment I looked into her shriveled, greasy face. The rain formed little beads on her cheeks. She stood clutching her raincoat around her. I looked her up and down and had to fight a sudden urge to laugh.

"Excuse me?"

"Susie is asthmatic, Miss Siegel. Every time your cat assaults her, she wheezes for days."

"Look, I've had a real bitch of a day myself."

"I've tried all the legal avenues, and upon advice from the animal control officer, I have borrowed a cat trap and just wanted you to know that Susie and I will not tolerate it anymore."

"You won't, huh?" Something about her was pissing me off.

A cold, steady drip from the eaves was hitting me square on the top of my head, splitting, and running down behind each of my ears.

"Susie doesn't want a problem with your cat."

"You're sure of that."

"Oh yes, I'm sure," she answered and managed an artificial smile. I could tell she thought reconciliation was imminent.

"Well, I'll tell you what. The next time you talk to Susie"—I leaned closer to her—"tell her that Stud says, get fucked, Susie."

Disbelief covered her face. She didn't move; she held her pose and looked at me. Our faces were no more than six inches apart.

"And while we're at it, Stud thinks you should follow his advice for Susie, too. It could do wonders for your attitude. I know it does mine."

She bolted, her slippered feet clicking into the darkness down the sidewalk, toward her house. "The trap, Miss Siegel. I have the trap. Susie just can't take it anymore," she shrieked over her shoulder.

"He didn't assault her, he pissed on her, Mrs. . . . Mrs. Wicker-shit!" I yelled back. "He pissed on her!"

I heard her door slam, picked up my keys, and let myself into my apartment. I pulled the letter I had taken from Stroud's desk out of my pocket, flipped on a light, laid the crumpled piece of paper on the table, and smoothed it out.

It was brief and to the point.

Find enclosed my personal check in the amount of $18,400.00. As per our conversation, this takes care of any outstanding balance in regards to my daughter's treatment at your facility. Dinah is doing well and is back in school.

I reiterate that I see no need for any further correspondence between us.

Jeffrey Lord

I read it again. There was nothing outstanding in the content. Red flags didn't pop up in my mind. If anything, I found it curious. That was a hunk of money, and apparently a last payment. The grand total must have been something else. But why did Jeffrey Lord, whoever he was, so bluntly cut any ties to Stroud?

I checked out the letterhead.

LORD MANUFACTURING, INC.
Jeffrey Lord—President
Tymer, Wisconsin

Neatly, at the bottom, done in small italics, was one simply, if not obtuse, statement.

A Lord makes you think you've died and gone to heaven.
Fine mattresses since 1900

It was one of those statements that left you not knowing whether to laugh or take it seriously. I folded the letter and tucked it in a drawer in the phone stand. I figured the name might come in handy.

The message reminder on my answering machine showed four calls. I pushed play and sat down on the couch to listen. Stud jumped up on my lap and declared with his low, guttural purring that he was in need of some affection. Weren't we all?

"We're in deep shit, my friend. You better stick close to home for a while."

The deep, resonant vibration from his chest felt good against my own as he snuggled and pushed his nose up under my chin. I was so damn drained that even lifting my hand to stroke it down over Stud's back took strength I didn't have. I pushed back into the softness of the sofa and listened to my messages.

The first and second calls were from my mother. I hadn't checked in with her for over a week. I made a mental note to make my obligatory coffee stop the next day. The third call was from Roger saying he had a backlog of depositions he had to take care of and would stop by later, if it didn't get too late.

The fourth call threw me. I ran the tape back and listened to it again. There was a pause in the beginning.

"Fee, it's Charlene. If you're there, pick up the phone." Again, another pause. "I guess you're not. I, uh . . . George told me he ran into you. I," she said and paused again. "*We* want you to come for dinner on Friday. Please, Fee. Friday at six, okay?"

I ran the tape back once more and listened for a third time. There was uncertainty in her voice. The call must have been hard for her to make, but even so, she sounded the same, all warm and caring.

Dinner. The thought of sitting down to dinner with George in my brother's house, with my brother's widow, was ridiculous. Completely out of the question. But I knew I'd go. I needed to. I needed to talk to Charlene about Ben's last few weeks. Maybe, just maybe, there was something she would remember after three years, something she had forgotten at the time. And what had happened to his Medic Alert bracelet?

Some nagging little voice tucked back in the darkest recesses of my mind replayed my conversation with Kehly over and over again. Ben had asked the same questions about Whispering Pines. Why? I dialed Kehly's number.

"Are you still up?" I asked when she answered.

"Yes. I just got home from an AA meeting. What do you need?"

"I'd like you to elaborate on the conversation we had the other night. What questions did Ben ask you?"

"Fee, I was way out of line calling you like that. Sometimes . . . uh, I guess it freaked me out. Forget it, okay?"

"I can't. It could be important."

"To further your neurosis? No way. I said I was out of line, Fee."

"Kehly, I'm working on something that involves a kid that's hooked in up there. Maybe Ben knew something about the place, maybe he—"

"I didn't know that much, so I couldn't give him a lot of information. I told you what I told him, they were weird kids. Snobs. It was the one and only time our AA group got in there. They never showed up at any of our meetings."

"Did any of the kids you saw seem like they were, I don't know, unwilling to be there?"

"No, not really. There were class acts. You know the types. Real mainliners. They were more interested in each other than in us," she said. "They all clutched some kind of book that they wrote in every so often. It was weird."

"Books?"

"Notebooks, something like that."

"That's it?"

"That's it. I think Ben thought it was a cult or something. He never said that, but I got the feeling he thought it was a weird place. It definitely gave me the creeps. Listen," she said. "Rudy's home. I gotta go."

"Thanks, Kehly. Talk to you soon."

"Right . . . thanks."

It was midnight before I turned out the lights and crawled into bed. The rain hammered against the bedroom window and pulled me willingly into a hypnotic dream state. Blacky raced out of the darkness and reared up in front of me. His hooves flashed razor sharp, slicing through the darkness.

I shot up in bed; cool air in the bedroom crawled across my sweat-covered body, leaving me shivering. Something moved beside me. I grabbed the top of the covers, jumped from the bed, and shook them with everything I had. I reached for the light and turned it on. The blankets, in a heap at the foot of the bed, took on a life of their own as something struggled beneath them.

A second later, Stud crawled out and looked up at me, as confused and pissed as I had ever seen him. He arched his back, stretched one leg out in front of him, and walked out of the room.

"Shit," I mumbled and started remaking the bed. When Stud didn't come back into the bedroom, I had to chuckle, knowing I'd pay.

If Roger hadn't shown up by then, I knew he wouldn't. It was probably for the best. I needed to sort out my thoughts. But there was a part of me that needed to be held, loved, stroked a little. Feeling vulnerable, in need, or feeling anything for that matter definitely took me out of my comfort zone. So I turned on my police scanner. It picked up both Billings Police and ambulance signals, and on a night when the natives were restless—like I was—it made for some interesting listening. Concentrating on those flashing red numbers, melting in and out of each other, had become my own form of meditation.

With the scanner on, I got back into bed and turned out the light. I could hear Stud in the kitchen trying to turn the trash over. His vengeance was always creative and usually knew no bounds. One of his favorites was shredding the toilet paper into such minuscule shreds that an ant couldn't use it to wipe.

I started drifting into an uneasy sleep. I listened to a couple of dog-barking calls and a domestic in-progress and was just about to slip into other realms when another call came through on a police band.

"Prepare to copy a runaway from the Whispering Pines Institute. A female, Shawna Unger, five foot four, one hundred fifteen pounds, blond and blue. Last seen wearing a light-green institutional gown and blue jeans. Reported missing at approximately 1400 hours. Complainant would like to be contacted at this time. If located, hold for complainant."

"Forty-six to Dispatch." By this time I was sitting up in bed.

"Go ahead, Forty-six."

"Who's the complainant?" The voice was vaguely familiar.

"Dr. Victor Stroud."

"Ten four."

"Eleven to Forty-six." A new voice cut in.

"Go ahead."

"Crummy night to be running around in a nightgown."

"You got that right."

"I'm in that area, let me take it for ya."

"Are you sure?"

"Yup. I'm already on my way up the hill."

"Thanks. I was about to hit Perkins for some coffee."

The red numbers on the scanner started tumbling over each other, melting into an unrecognizable mess of red. My stomach contracted and threatened to erupt. I turned over and looked out the window. Shawna was out there somewhere, cold, alone, and definitely afraid. Or maybe she wasn't missing at all.

It was barely daylight when I made the call to a cop I knew, Henry Wayne Williams, in Denver. I'd met him at Quantico. He hadn't been there that long, just long enough for us to have a short-lived but intense relationship. Henry was an odd but nice guy who always identified himself by all three names and insisted that he also be introduced that way. It ended up with me sounding a lot like Elmer Fudd. I just couldn't get the *R* right in *Henry*.

We had written each other on and off until he had gotten married. In three years he had gone from a beat cop to a detective on Vice, right where I needed him to be. I gave him the only information I had on Daniel Unger, which was three little words: *Five Point* and *Denver*. He promised to get on it right away, for old times' sake, and get back to me as soon as he knew anything. The name sounded familiar to him, but he couldn't put a face with it.

There's an odd process that I've found among investigators. They all tell you that they go by the facts and the facts alone. Not true. At least not for me. They like to think of themselves as Sherlockian. Me? I've always taken old Sherlock to the furthest possible conclusion.

In one of Doyle's best, *The Sign of the Four*, there's a clear formula that can be applied nine and a half times out of ten. It goes something like this: when you have eliminated the impossible, whatever remains, no matter how improbable, must be the truth.

It always made sense to me and left the sky the limit. Within bounds, of course.

An hour slid by before Henry called back.

"What did you come up with?"

"What do you have going on this guy, Phoebe?"

"Come on, Henry. I told you he's got a kid up here on the run from a drug rehab program."

"That's all?"

"That's all."

"Have they picked up the kid?"

"I don't think so. She may have taken the first ride headed for Denver."

"There's nothing down here for her anymore. Her old man blew his brains out in the back of a bar, the Gray Goose, down in the Five Point area. I knew I had heard that name."

"When?"

"A couple of days ago. The old gal that owns the place found him when she opened up the next morning."

"You're sure that's who it is?"

"I'm sure. I just pulled the report. Let's see what her name is," he said and paused. I could hear him shuffling through papers. "Here it is, Dorothy Morgan. According to this, they had a fight. They've been living together for about ten years. The night they had the falling-out, he opted to sleep at the bar. She owns it, by the way. When she came down the next morning to open the place, she found him. He blew his head off with a twelve gauge. Messy."

"Thanks, Henry. Would you give me her phone number?"

"No problem."

I took the number and listened to Henry chatter on for a minute before I was able to thank him and hang up, only to start dialing.

Dorothy answered on the first ring. I told her who I was and that Shawna had taken off.

"That poor kid," she said softly, "that poor damn kid."

"Is there any chance she'll get in touch with you?"

"I'm sure she will. What will I tell her? Should I tell her about Dan?"

I thought about it for a moment and decided to take a big chance. "No, don't tell her. Dorothy, this is a strange situation up here. I can't go into it, but—"

"It's that son of a bitch from that center, isn't it?" She startled me when she said it.

"Why do you say that?"

"I knew the SOB was slime. I knew the kid had problems when she came out here, but she didn't need that creep in her life."

"What do you mean 'came out here'?"

"Her ma died back east, and the kid decided to look up her old man. What a shock that must have been." She chuckled. "Dan had his good points, but he'd sell his own mother if he had a chance."

"So Shawna hadn't lived with him long?"

"Shawna lived with me, honey," she said and laughed smugly. "And with Dan when he decided to show up. He's, or I guess *was* would be more appropriate, a big money mover. He had a place up in the hills, but he liked the nightlife down here. Slumming appealed to him."

"Then what about Shawna? He just dumped her off on you?"

"No way. Me and the kid hit it off. I think she missed her mama. She's a good girl, that one. But she's seen too much. Smart as hell, too."

"Who put her in treatment?"

"Her old man. She came out here with an ax to grind, started running with a rough crowd. He got all paranoid about her ending up with some Crip or Blood," she said. "We got them all over, ya know?"

"So I heard. And?"

"He figured she was using the same shit they were, or so he said. Myself? I never bought it. I think the old man was worried about his little girl getting into trouble and bringing some bad publicity down on his head. Then that slick-talking SOB met up with Dan somewhere and told him he had a program that he could get Shawna into."

"Did you ever see him?"

"No. But he called here a couple of times. Real slick gentleman type."

"Was she on drugs?"

"Hell no. I doubt if the kid had even been laid," she said, laughing. "The next thing I knew, Shawna was gone. Dan had money. Big money. But not enough to buy off his own conscience. Things went downhill from there. He had a high time treating all his friends and spending big on his floozies. I'd had it and told him to take a hike."

"Did he?"

"With that twelve gauge he did." I could hear her voice break. "Damn his ass anyway. The fool never even bothered to pay me back the money he owed me. The last couple of days he just talked out of his head."

"Like how?"

"Crazy shit. About how Shawna was just like her old lady and wanted to ruin his life. They had a helluva fight right before she left for that place. Poor kid."

"What were they fighting about?"

"Stuff. She was at a tough age. He didn't know how the hell to be a father to her. Christ, that's all they did was fight. About drove me crazy. He hadn't seen her since she was five or six. She wanted to know why."

"And?"

"Nothing. I don't interfere with family stuff. I just kept my nose out of it. The kid should have guessed the first time she saw him that he wasn't going to be any help to her."

"What happened after she came up here?"

"He figured in the beginning that he was doing what was best for Shawna, until he talked with that SOB from the center and found out she'd be up there for a long time. Then he just cried all the time. Said he'd failed her, that he should have listened to what she told him."

"What did she tell him?"

"I don't know. Honestly don't. Wait a minute, I do too know a little about that. It had something to do with some girl she met and some book she had read. Didn't make much sense. I thought he'd burned his mind out on all that gin. Shawna said they had to keep 'snitch books' on each other. I talked to her once, and she told me she had found photocopies of a lot of these books. I figured it was some pretty juicy information."

"Listen, Dorothy. If Shawna calls you, tell her it's urgent she get in touch with me. Urgent," I reiterated. "Don't tell her about her father. And don't tell anyone else who calls that you've talked to me, or that Dan is dead. Okay?"

"Well . . ." She hesitated. "Sure, you sound concerned about the kid. By the way, you keep my secret and I'll keep yours."

"What's that?"

"I found Dan. Did they tell you that?"

"Yes."

"I also found what he had left of his money roll. I wasn't keeping it for myself, you understand. I thought maybe . . ." Her voice broke again. "I thought maybe the kid could use it when she got out. I didn't tell the cops. I figured the county could bury the bastard."

"Sounds fair to me."

"The old boy really went out in style and left a slug trail of bills and bad deals ten miles long. I guess me and the kid will have to make it on our own."

"Thanks for the information, Dorothy. I appreciate it."

"Life don't make much sense, does it?"

Her voice slurred, and I started wondering how I was going to get off the phone when the line went dead. It was time to start eliminating the impossible.

$\bigtriangledown$

10

I T CAME DOWN TO A CHOICE: either stop by Mama's first or hit the cemetery. I had avoided both for over a week, but the mood I was in, I knew damn well I couldn't handle Mama without a good heart-to-heart talk with Zelda.

Times like this were when I missed Zelda the most; she always managed to come up with some clear, simple solution to each and every one of life's problems.

Life was never a dress rehearsal to Zelda; this was it. One chance to get it right. Laughter was the ultimate healer, and tears only ran your mascara. If she didn't have an immediate solution, she laughed it off, and the problem mystically, magically disappeared.

Mama, on the other hand, relied on a source that had long ago lost credibility with me. She burned up more votive candles than the church could supply, so she started buying the little scented jobs at K mart. The house smelled of vanilla, bayberry, God, and burning wax. It made sense to Mama.

In the center of the cemetery hundreds of symmetrical white headstones formed a concentric pattern separating veterans from the plain, undecorated folk who were scattered throughout the rolling hills and along the twisting, narrow road. It always struck me as odd that the separation existed. They'd all died from acts of aggression: man to man, God to man.

Up the hill from the fallen soldiers, the Siegels had the best view. I pulled under the towering spruce tree that formed a canopy over the family plot and got out. Off in the distance I heard a siren as it raced to some unknown crisis. I sat down on the stone bench at the foot of the plots and did what I always did first. I read their headstones.

BENJAMIN AARON SIEGEL
1925–1979
Loving husband & father

SAMUEL AARON SIEGEL
1949–1969
Sgt. U.S. Army – Vietnam
We love you, Sam

BENJAMIN AARON SIEGEL, JR.
1952–1986
Our star in heaven
Shine brightly for us
Beloved son, beloved husband and brother

**ZELDA DEBORAH SIEGEL, FINK,
ABRAMS, MORGAN, FEINSTEIN**
1925–1986
Oi vey, Oi vey

Even dead, Zelda was good for a laugh.

"I saw you pull in here." Roger walked up behind me and put his arms around me. I hadn't even heard his car. His breath felt good on my neck as he snuggled his face in my collar. "I thought maybe you'd gotten a job as caretaker."

He walked around and sat down beside me. "Hi, Pop," he said and waved in that direction. "It's one of two places I can get her to sit still. What does a guy do?" he said and shrugged.

"Don't make fun of me, Roger. Besides, I'm damn angry at you."

"I'm not making fun of you." He reached out and softly held my chin with his hand and turned my face toward him. A hint of melancholy edged his voice.

"Feeling bad that you threw me to the wolves?"

"You know better than that. Christ. I was as surprised as you were. Why the hell didn't Mary what's-her-name . . ."

"Mary Kuntz, Roger."

"Why didn't she mention the fact that her father was Cutter Gage?"

He had me on that one.

"Phoebe, the man could have gotten any answers, any time, from anyone out there. Why didn't she go to him? It doesn't make sense."

"There's a lot of things that aren't making sense. Let's drop it for now. How are things going for you?" His questions were valid. The same ones had been boring a hole in my gut since my meeting with Gage.

"Tense. Everything is tense. Cutter has been uptight. Earl's been riding my ass and watching my every move." He ran his hand through his hair. He looked beat. "Look, Phoebe, since you talked with him—"

"Wasn't it more like him talking to me?"

"Whatever. I think he's monitoring my calls."

"Get serious. It wouldn't be a paranoia virus, would it?"

"You're right. I am being paranoid. We've got a lot of heavy cases all going on at the same time."

"I called the office, and they told me you were in court."

"I was. The judge granted a continuance. I ended up with some out-of-the-office time on my hands, so I decided to play hooky, and when I couldn't find you, I found myself in your mother's kitchen with a cup of coffee in my hand."

I stood up and looked down at him.

"And?"

"And nothing. It was good to see her." Roger stood and grabbed my hand. "Let's walk."

He led me down a narrow path that wound through the cemetery. We must have made a strange sight. Roger, dressed as neat and classy as a mortician, me in my Reeboks, jeans, and pullover hooded sweatshirt. But the relationship worked. On some weird level, it really did work.

"Phoebe, what I'm about to say . . ."

"I knew this was coming as soon as you said you'd seen Mama," I said, pulled my hand away, and turned to face him. "I'm not in any mood for one of Mama's secondhand Epistle of the Apostle lectures."

He just stood there, half-smiling, his brow furrowed. Without warning he pulled me into his arms and kissed me. It was different from other times. Roger wasn't exactly known for his spontaneous shows of affection. He just held me, tight and close to his chest. I could feel the abrasiveness of his wool topcoat against my cheek. After a moment he held me at arm's length and looked into my face. "Maybe this isn't the time or the place," he said softly.

"Go for it."

"This isn't working out for either of us."

"What isn't?" I knew damn well what he meant.

"Us. Me." He tapped his chest with his index finger. "And you." He gently poked me.

"Roger, let's not get into—"

"I don't want to lose you, Phoebe. I don't want to lose the best friend I've ever had."

"Are we having a personal funeral here?" It didn't come off as funny as I meant it to.

"I guess you could say that."

We just looked at each other for a minute, neither one of us saying a damn thing. I had the sudden urge to burst into tears. I saw Roger's chest heave a couple of times and prepared myself to deal with some heavy emotion.

And it came. Roger finally lost control. He leaned back and started laughing so hard I thought he'd make himself puke.

"Sorry it tears you up so much," I said, scowling.

"It's not that, Phoebe. Here we are in the middle of the cemetery, where it all started, sort of, knowing damn well that this relationship will never be any more than it is, and a few things just strike me as funny."

"Like what, for God's sake?"

"Like how you looked when I got serious. You were afraid I was going to pin you down to marriage."

I smiled. It had crossed my mind.

"And this damned cemetery. God, for two years we've been hanging out here. It's creepy. Funny . . . but still creepy."

"Friends? Forever?"

"You got that right. Now loosen up and tell me what all this crap with Cutter is about." Roger placed his arm around my shoulder.

We started walking again, and before I knew it I had spilled my guts about Mary Kuntz, repeated my near swan song in the old corral, the late-night call from Kehly, and what I had encountered both times at Whispering Pines. I expected him to get angry, but he didn't. I braced myself for a tirade of legal jargon covering everything from trespassing to anything else he could think of. It didn't come.

He listened to the whole story without so much as a comment. He didn't bat an eye when I told him about Shawna, or hiding under Stroud's desk. I did elicit a sideways glance and one raised eyebrow relaying the Daniel Unger–Dorothy Morgan story. In the end, Roger's advice was what I would expect from him.

"If you're convinced something is wrong up there, call your uncle. I don't see any other choice. But you're going in with pretty weak evidence, Phoebe."

"There are always options, Roger."

"And, where there aren't any, you'll make some."

"There's more to this."

"How much more can there be?" he asked.

"At this point, the sky is the limit," I answered.

"Think you can cut me some time later?"

"I've got to meet Mary Kuntz tonight. Why don't we do some *friendly* Chinese takeout after that? It won't be late." I snuggled back against him.

"Sounds good."

"Guess I should run home and get my trench coat and fedora and do a little skulking."

"Be careful, Phoebe," he said as he tilted my chin up and kissed me lightly on the lips.

"Why did you say that?"

"What?"

"Be careful. You've never said that before."

For a moment he was quiet, his face reflecting some obscure concern. "I don't know. Just one of those days, I guess. But I mean it. Be careful."

I hummed my best "Twilight Zone" for him, kissed him quickly on the cheek, and walked to the truck.

"You're six days into March and functioning. I'm proud of you," he said and smiled.

"The month isn't over yet," I answered and left.

The stiff frosted grass beneath my feet crunched like a thousand shards of glass. Teasings of green showed through the white, promising a spring in which some things dead could live again.

As I followed the dirt road toward the exit that would get me onto Central Avenue, I saw a cop car parked at the far end of the cemetery. I damn near turned the truck around and drove by to see if it was anyone I knew but decided against it. I should have looked.

Most people are unaware of the volumes of information that are available about them. They fill in one form here, an application for credit there, and before you know it, any credit bureau rep worth the wage can find out your shoe size, where your kids go to school, and the nastier details of your divorce petition.

I'd built up quite a few contacts after three years in the business. All I needed to do was call in a few favors. It just happened that Donna Jo Johnson owed me a favor and, conveniently, had worked her way up as assistant shark in one of the more bloodthirsty credit services in Billings.

A young shark trainee met me at the counter with a look that would have cowed Mother Teresa into genuflecting before a Dun & Bradstreet sign. I could see past her toward the back of the room, where Donna was talking with a young man who looked to be on the verge of hysteria. She looked up when she heard me talking to the young woman at the counter, waved, motioned me to wait, and went back to what she was doing.

It wasn't long before I was in the same chair the flustered young man had occupied minutes before.

"What can I do for you, Phoebe?" she asked, grinning.

"I need you to get me everything you can on this name," I answered, reached for a pencil lying in front of her, and wrote it down on a scratch pad she had shoved in front of me.

She looked at the name and shrugged.

"I don't recall it. Need anything specific?"

"Everything and as specific as you can get."

"No difference," she said and shrugged. "Let me see what I can do. How's life?"

"Great. Yours?"

"Not so great. I don't know if I have the stomach for this crap. The pay is more than I could have made waiting tables, and I even get a commission for making people feel like pieces of shit, but it stinks. I'm thinking of quitting."

"Don't do that before you run this for me. It's real important, Donna. I need it—"

"Yesterday. Right?"

"Right. I'll get back to you."

I found Mama crying over a sink of dishes that she was meticulously washing, rinsing, and placing in a drainer. She jumped when I walked in the back door.

"Phoebe, honey. I wish you wouldn't startle me like that," she said as she dried her hands on a white cotton towel that was draped over her shoulder.

It usually took me about one minute to determine Mama's mood. I broke my own records as soon as I took a look at her face. She was definitely on a pity trip. She called it the weeps.

I kissed her on her cheek, grabbed a cup from the drainer, and poured myself some coffee.

"Sorry, Mama. Next time I'll do a little Irish jig up the walk and burst into the kitchen in full song."

She started to smile, caught herself, and wiped a tear from her eye instead.

"What's going on? Roger told me he came by for coffee. That should have made your day."

"That poor, dear boy." She sighed, effectively dramatic. "I'm disappointed in you. He's what we called, in my day, a good catch."

"What are you talking about?"

"About you and him."

"There is no me and him. I mean . . . God! You weren't pushing that marriage thing with him, were you?"

"I may have mentioned it," she said innocently. "In passing, that is."

"Jesus, Mama. Sometimes I wonder who was Jewish, you or Daddy. Have you ever heard of the words *adult* or *privacy*?"

"Those things don't apply to your mother, Phoebe."

"Well, they are going to start to apply to you, Mama." It was hard to be tough with Mama, but a little emotional strong-arm usually backed her off. "So don't start on me."

"I'm not starting on anything. You're going to be moving into that big house, if it doesn't fall in on itself first. You should really think about resale value, dear," she said as she jumped from one thing to the next. "If you were married, I wouldn't worry about you so much."

"Mama. . . . Don't start . . ."

"I'm not starting anything, dear. We'll just drop it."

I had to give her credit. She could dropkick you with her not-so-subtle lead-ins and change plays in midstream.

We spent the next hour talking about the safe things: my problems with Stud, which she immediately suggested would be cured by having Stud neutered, and her problems with the old bachelor across the alley who backed over her garbage can each time he pulled his car out of the garage. I suggested the same surgical cure for him as she did for Stud. Mama didn't laugh.

When we'd exhausted all the mundane things and had verbally tarred and feathered most of the neighbors, we lapsed into a familiar quiet that left both of us smiling smugly down into our coffee cups. No matter how grown I thought I was, how estranged I thought I was from my family, it was easy, even comfortable to slip back into the fold.

"Mama? What happened to all of Ben's personal effects?"

"That's an odd thing to ask about, Phoebe honey. What in particular were you looking for?"

"Oh, I don't know. Things . . . notebooks, anything he kept track of his day-to-day stuff in. And that bracelet Charlene got him when he had a reaction to that shot."

"Now what would make you think about that old bracelet after all these years?"

"I was in the drugstore and saw some bracelets like it hanging there, and I just thought of the one that she had made for him. Does she have it?"

"I don't know about that bracelet, but I think Charlene has the rest of everything. Michael helped her pack most of it away about a year or so after he . . . Phoebe, you're not having a hard time, since it's March and all, are you, honey?"

"No," I answered and avoided her stare. She reached up and touched my cheek with her hand. "Well, maybe a little. You know how it is."

"Did you want to talk about it, dear?"

"No, Mama. I'll get through. Are you sure Charlene kept his things?"

"I don't see why she wouldn't. But I would have thought they'd have left that bracelet with Ben. After all, he wore it all the time."

"Thanks, Mama. I'll check into it."

"Michael is dropping by in a few minutes," she said as she looked up at the clock. "He'll be glad to see you."

"Why didn't you tell me he was coming by?" My voice sounded accusatory, angry, even to my own ears. "That's the last person I need to deal with right now."

"What?"

Mama said the word *what* like no one else on earth. Her whole facial expression changed. The *w* was drawn out, riding on a burst of air that reached you right before she snapped the *t* off her tongue. Anyone who's ever seen Maureen O'Hara in *The Quiet Man* knows you shouldn't piss off these flame-haired Irish women.

"I . . . I just didn't know that . . ."

"How could you? He called this morning. You and Michael haven't had a falling-out or something, have you, Phoebe?"

"No, Mama. I just have to run. I'm working on something." I stood and started for the door. "I'll call you in the next couple of days, and maybe Roger and I can bring Frieda over for—"

My hand had just pushed the back screen open, which gave me an unobstructed view of the backyard. From my vantage point I was high enough to see the light bar of a cop car parked in the alley. The weathered, six-foot wooden fence that separated the house from the alley blocked everything else. Slowly the car started moving down the alley and within seconds was out of sight.

"Were you suggesting dinner, honey? I'd like that very much, and it would probably be good for Roger's mother to get out a little more."

"Sure, Mama . . ."

"What is it?" she asked and walked over to where I stood, frozen.

"Nothing, it's . . . nothing," I answered. "I thought there was a police car in the alley." Thought hell. I knew there was.

"Not around here, dear. We never see a policeman, unless your uncle John drops by for coffee. Are you sure?"

"No, I'm not sure. Forget it, I'll see you later."

I kissed her on the cheek and left. I knew damn well what I had seen. It wouldn't have been such a big deal except for the cruiser at the cemetery. It unnerved me. Big time.

$\triangledown$

11

THERE ARE TIMES I ask myself why I stay in Montana. I toyed with the thought of moving to the West Coast and opening up a security business that would cater to the rich and famous. The fact of the matter is, I couldn't leave if I wanted to.

Something keeps people here. Sixty miles east of Billings, General Custer decided to stay beside the Little Bighorn River. Of course, it was at Chief Sitting Bull's insistence. Signs are rumored to exist at the Dakota border which warn motorists entering Montana that CUSTER WAS HEALTHY WHEN HE LEFT HERE.

You can stay near the Little Bighorn cheaper today. It cost Custer over two hundred fifty lives, plus his own. Now, for $10.50, which includes electricity and water, you can park an RV and be able to leave alive the next morning. People still get scalped at the numerous trading posts in the area, but that's another story.

The bottom line for me is the seasons. I need the cyclical changes, so I stay. Each season is well defined, each month different from the one before. March is the most unpredictable. It hides up north across the Canadian border, waiting, ever changing. Striking without warning, it can spring across the Forty-ninth Parallel with the ferocity of a lion, drop the temperature forty degrees in five hours, and dump a foot of snow over the High Plains.

When that happens I throw a couple of inner tubes filled with sand in the back of the '49 for added traction. I had debated doing just that a couple of hours after I left Mama's. The rain was heavier, colder than it had been earlier in the day.

I finally ran down Jackie, the polyester realtor, and tried to find out when we could close the deal on my dream house. She went into a lengthy explanation about the holder of the deed, who was a ninety-five-year-old woman, a longtime resident of a local private nursing home who slipped in and out of reality. Jackie hadn't been able to catch her in one of her lucid moments but promised it would be any day now. Sure, Jackie.

The colder it got, the more I thought about Shawna Unger. On the off chance she might have called, I swung by the apartment and checked the answering machine. There were three hang-ups and no messages. I wrestled the inner tubes out of the garage and into the back of the truck and headed for the county courthouse.

Up to this point, I had nothing on Victor Stroud except my own conviction that he was a slimeball, and that somehow, three years ago, Ben had had an interest in his place. That, and a mother's instinct, and a close encounter with Jennifer Kuntz.

There are a few rules I follow, contrary to the purists, concerning investigations of any kind. Never assume, never wear blinders, and never *not* follow your instincts. The conversation I had overheard between Stroud and the girl in his office was, at the very least, disquieting. I was aware of tough love as a therapeutic tool. You couldn't turn on a talk show without someone expounding the virtues of pain and heavy confrontation. But something in Stroud's voice had stepped through the bounds of therapy and into the shadows.

By the time the county clerk and recorder was ready to close, I had gotten what I needed. Whispering Pines and the ten or so acres it sat on had been sold for back taxes, its halls vacated of the elderly waiting to die. Eventually it was sold to an outfit by the name of United Investments Corporation.

I was making a few last-minute notes when Krisa Poole walked up to where I was sitting. Krisa and I had gone through school together. She was a short, fluffy blond who had never quite lost her perky cheerleader personality. I liked Krisa. But through some delusion, she thought we were friends. I used that to my advantage every time I needed to browse the records department, and I felt bad about it. Not so bad, though, that I didn't keep the delusion going.

"Did you find what you needed, Phoebe?"

"I could have used a little more time," I answered, glancing at my watch. "This place doesn't ring any bells with you, does it?"

She leaned down and looked at the name I had written on a piece of paper.

"UIC? I don't think so. Business is booming. There are so many deals coming through that it's hard to keep track. What's the property?"

"The old Odd Fellows' Nursing Home."

She was pensive for a moment. "I do know that place. Didn't they put some kind of hospital up there?"

"Hospital?"

"Oh, you know what I mean. One of those drug places where they treat people. Windy Pines, Whispering Pines, something like that."

"Whispering Pines."

"As I recall, that was part of a bigger deal," she said and thought for a moment. "I can't pull it up," she said and tapped her temples with her index finger. "I'll check it out tomorrow. Okay?"

"That would be great, Krisa. What time?"

"Come in around noon. I take a late lunch, and it will give us some time to catch up on each other."

I flashed her my best smile. "Good, I'll see you then."

I walked out of the courthouse and around the corner of the building to the parking lot. The wind was driving sleet against my forehead, giving me an instant headache. I was walking, chin down, when a car horn blasted. It lifted me a foot off the pavement.

"Watch where the hell you're backing—" I started to yell and looked up. Leaning out of the driver's side of a white Chevy Blazer was Lanny, grinning.

I walked over to him. "It doesn't look good for cops to run over pedestrians," I said.

"Need a ride?"

"Nope. I'm parked right over there. Are you just getting off?"

"I covered someone on days. I've got to come back out at midnight."

"Rough shift."

"I saw you at the counter in the Clerk and Recorder's Office."

"I'm buying a place on the edge of town. Just getting a little history on it," I lied, uncomfortable that I did.

"Which place?"

"That abandoned mausoleum on Two Moon Road."

"The mansion?" He pursed his lips and whistled. "Shit, it's been condemned for years. You're throwing your money away. I've been running kids out of there; it's one of their favorite kegger hangouts."

"Have they found the girl who took off from that treatment center yet?" I asked, ignoring his gales of laughter.

He didn't say anything for a minute. "What kid?"

"I heard on the scanner that—"

"Still listening in, huh? There's a slot opening up, you know. Baker is leaving, you'd be a shoo-in."

"No, thanks. Have they found her?"

"No, they haven't. Why the interest?"

"The weather's turning. I hate to see a kid on the streets in this shit."

"Listen, I've got to get home and catch a couple of hours. If these streets freeze over, we're in for a busy night."

"Catch you later," I yelled over my shoulder, walked to the truck, and got in.

My hair was soaking wet and my forehead was throbbing from the cold. I pulled out of the lot and headed down Twenty-seventh Street toward the South Side. There were a lot of places a kid on the run could find down there to get in out of the cold. I had some time to kill so I thought I could cruise a few blocks before I had to head out the interstate for my meeting with Mary Kuntz.

Who knows what lurks in the subconscious of the guilty? I'd kicked myself for not hanging around Mama's long enough to make amends with Michael. I'd reached for the phone several times but just couldn't make the call.

I figured that since I was in the area, maybe I could just drop in and act like nothing had happened. I swung down by the church and parked across the street. A couple of Hispanic kids were in front, under the eaves, sharing a cigarette. Their shoulders were pulled up practically under their ears as they braced themselves against the cold.

I sat in the truck and watched them. The taller of the two looked up, saw me, and nudged his partner. It didn't take much to know that there was something going on inside. It was too early for a wake and too late for a funeral.

Just as I was about to pull away, Michael walked out of the church, his arm around a short Mexican woman. They stopped; the woman turned toward Michael and leaned against him. The two boys dropped their cigarettes and walked over to them.

Michael shook their hands. As he was talking he looked toward where I was parked and did a double take. My first instinct was to get the hell out of there, but I fought it, knowing damn well I'd gone too far by even being there.

The two boys helped the woman into a car parked in front of the church and roared off. Michael waved me over. I made a dash for the door he was holding open and ran inside. I was trapped and tongue-tied. Without a word, he pulled me close and hugged me.

"Let's sit down," he said as he led me toward a back pew. "I'm glad you're here, Phoebe. I was going to call you later anyway."

God, he was handsome. What a waste. Neither of us said anything for a minute. Then we both spoke at the same time and started laughing.

I knew Michael, and I knew me. We didn't approach what had happened between us. Laughter shared, we just shoved it behind us.

"You look tired, Michael."

He leaned forward and pinched the bridge of his nose with his thumb and index finger.

"It's been rough. That was Jimmy Padilla's mother and a couple of his cousins. Sometimes . . . ," he said reflectively. "Sometimes I just don't know what to say."

I found that hard to believe. Michael's faith was notoriously unshakable.

"How're they doing?"

"Not that hot. Did you read about it in the paper?"

"Who hasn't?"

"It really piss—" He stopped, grinned uncomfortably, and started over. "It's hard to accept that a kid could hang himself in jail without someone getting to him in time."

"Well, Michael . . ." I groped for words. I owed him something. I wish it could have been something I had. "If he was loaded . . ."

"He was so close to making it." He turned to me and scowled.

"Close only counts in horseshoes, Michael. The papers said that he was on something and—"

Michael shook his head and looked away from me. I could see the color rising in his cheeks.

"Ya know, if this had been some kid from up under the Rims, or out around the country club, they would have watched him like a hawk . . ."

"Or he wouldn't have been locked up at all."

"Right," he responded and hung his head. "I talked to his cousin. He'd been clean a long time. For some reason, he started doing cocaine again and anything else he could get his hands on." His voice was muted. I could barely hear him. "Something to do with some girl."

"What?"

"A girl. He threw it away for some girl." Michael looked up at me. "Angela Padilla just gave me the news on the drug thing. The toxicology report came back. It was all there. She also told me that Jimmy had talked with this girl a couple of hours before he freaked out."

"Do you know her name?"

"No. I asked Angela because I thought it might be someone from the parish. It scares the hell out of me. One kid kills himself and then another picks up on it, and before you know it . . . But the girl wasn't from around here. Angela didn't know her name."

It wasn't hard to figure out who it was. "Sometimes they just slip over the edge, Michael."

"These kids down here don't just slip over the edge. They're too busy surviving. They make bad choices, and when those choices involve drugs, they become the throwaways. They're up for grabs to the first creep, the first Dr. Feelgood that comes down the pike."

"I'm sorry." I stood up and placed my hand on his shoulder.

"Yeah, me too. I've got a couple of kids coming in for a consultation. She's fourteen and pregnant. He's fifteen and . . . well, they think they can make it. Makes you wonder, doesn't it? Call me sometime?"

"You bet."

I left him sitting in the silence, God's silence. It made sense.

Mary Kuntz walked into the Pelican Truck Stop fifteen minutes after I did. I had already secured us a booth up front, beneath the heavy plate-glass windows. Each time the door opened, a gush of air carried the heavy scent of diesel inside the coffee shop.

Everything she wore was identical to what she had on the day I'd met her. Even her expression had the same determined look she had stared me down with at our first meeting. There was something about her I liked. Nothing in Mary's appearance and nothing in how she handled herself would ever lead anyone to suspect she was the daughter of one of the most powerful and controversial men in Montana.

I still wasn't completely convinced she wasn't whacked out, but as the days wore on, the cards kept stacking auspiciously in her favor.

"Am I late?" she asked as she removed her windbreaker and slid into the booth. "I should have worn something heavier. It's nippy out there."

She placed the jacket on the seat beside her, vigorously rubbed her hands together, and looked around for the waitress.

"I ordered us both coffee when I got here."

"You remembered. How nice," she replied. "I—"

"Mary, I'm not going to beat around the bush. Why the hell didn't you tell me your father was Cutter Gage?"

The color left her face. She lowered her eyes and then raised them and looked directly into mine. "I didn't lie to you, Phoebe. I just didn't see the necessity of bringing it up. Besides, I knew you'd eventually find out on your own." She smiled wryly.

"Why didn't you go to him? Why didn't you use his . . . uh, connections to check out Stroud?"

"Oh, I tried all right," she said and laughed cynically. "Don't underestimate him." She raised her index finger and shook it toward me. "Nothing matters to him but his public standing, his famous, or should I say infamous, career, and his control over people. Anything, anything at all that smacks of bad publicity, he squashes like a bug under his foot. You won't hear dirt about Cutter Gage. He won't tolerate it."

"Look, Mary—"

"No, you look," she said. "Do you see this jacket?" She grabbed one of the sleeves of her windbreaker and held it in the air. "It comes from Cutter Gage's money. Just like every other thing I have on. The dishes I eat off, the bed I sleep in, the grass I mow; it all belongs, one way or the other, to Cutter Gage. The only things I have in this world are my . . ." She paused. "Uh . . . Jennifer. Jennifer is mine."

I was sitting there looking into a face I barely recognized. Her eyes darkened, hardened, and never left my face.

"What about Frank? Doesn't he . . ."

"Frank?" She laughed. "Frank sold out the day he married me. Little did he know how much it would cost him. The difference between my husband and myself is that I'm not afraid of Cutter," she said and laughed. "The fact of the matter is, I never knew him at all until I was eighteen years old. My mother and he separated when I was very young. He was nothing more than a name in the paper, or a face on television."

"How did you end up here?"

"Curiosity. I wanted to know my father. My mother had effectively cut him out of our lives, so when I finished school I left Missoula, came here, and walked into his open arms and all that Gage charm."

She and Shawna Unger had a couple of things in common. She looked down at the table and shook her head. When she looked back up again, she was smiling.

"Frank was working on the farm for Cutter. Six months later Frank and I snuck off to Wyoming and got married."

"And?" It was hard to picture a younger, giggling Mary eloping with the hired help.

"We came back the next day and all hell broke loose. Cutter

whipped Frank, beat him up, right in front of me. It was the first time I really knew what he was capable of." Mary seemed drawn back to a painful moment in time, reliving it. "It was never mentioned again. Cutter moved into town, put Frank in charge of the farm, and from then on it was business as usual. Most of Cutter's relationships are business as usual."

"Why didn't you and Frank leave, get the hell out of there?"

"Frank comes from poor people. They were good, hardworking folks, but Frank hated the poverty. To Frank, poverty is some ugly birth defect, something dirty that he's been trying to clean up and change his whole life."

Instinctively, I reached out and touched her hand. "I'm sorry, Mary."

"No reason to feel sorry for me. You get what you ask for in this life. We've worked hard, had a good life, and can hold our heads up. For the most part, Cutter lets us be."

I didn't know what to say. At that moment I wasn't sure that it even mattered who the hell her father was, but it did pique my curiosity about why the guy had pulled me into Roger's office.

"Is there anything, anything at all, that you haven't told me, Mary? I don't like these little surprises. Like the bracelet?"

She studied me but said nothing for a minute. "Mary?"

"Then it was his? Do you know that for certain?"

"There's no way to tell, unless I see it. Does Jennifer still have it?"

"I don't think so. I've gone through her room, but I can't find it. She left it in the bathroom on the sink one day and I came across it. I tried to figure out why she would have one. She's never had any allergies or—"

"If it belonged to my brother, it was for penicillin. And there would have been initials on the front—"

"B.S. and C.D. And yes, it was for penicillin. I knew immediately it wasn't hers when I saw the initials. It didn't take much to figure out who it belonged to."

"How did she get it, Mary? Where the hell did it come from?"

"I don't have the slightest idea. We had company over one Sunday after church and we were taking some pictures. Jenny was leaning on a fence post and I got the most beautiful picture of her. You saw it, the one that shows the bracelet real plain."

I nodded and let her continue.

"I hadn't even realized she was wearing the bracelet until I looked at the slides myself. When I questioned her about it, she flew into this rage and accused me of spying on her. I haven't seen it since then."

"Is there anything else?"

"No, there's nothing more."

"You're sure?"

"I'm sure."

There wasn't any place to go but forward, so I dropped it. "I guess you've read the papers . . ."

"About that Padilla boy? Yes. Yes I have. My heart goes out to his family. I haven't been able to get him off my mind."

"Does Jennifer know?"

"Yes. I showed her the obituary," she answered and lowered her eyes. "I'm afraid she didn't show much interest."

"None?"

"No. Nothing."

The waitress placed a cup of coffee in front of each of us. Mary picked hers up and held it in both hands.

"Take care of your hands, Phoebe. I'm afraid these old things are wearing out. This heat feels so good."

I hadn't noticed her hands before. She had kept them on her lap in the office most of the time, and to be honest I'm just not a hand person. Now I noticed that a couple of her knuckles were enlarged and the skin on the back of her hands was read and mottled. They looked painful. It made me wonder how she produced the beautiful afghans she had shown me.

"Mary, I've put some feelers out. I don't have much for you yet."

She reached out and patted my hand. "I'm so sorry about the other day, Phoebe. I don't even know what to say to you. She's changed. Do you at least believe that?"

"I think she's sick, Mary. I don't have a lot to compare it to. I didn't know her before, and for that matter, I don't really know her now." *She needs to go to Blacky's vet and be put down with him*, I thought to myself and then felt immediately guilty.

"What happened down at the barn was something that *my* Jennifer would never have done. You could have been killed. When Jennifer came home that night, she laughed it off and refused to talk about it."

"Where had she been all day?"

"Who knows? Phoebe, something else is going on. I'm not sure what it is, but something's building." Her eyes filled with tears. "I thought I heard Jennifer up in the middle of the night. When I started down the stairs—" Her voice broke.

She looked out the window to hide her face. I watched her try to pull it together. ". . . I started down the stairs and met her coming up. She was smiling and never said a word. I went on downstairs and found Frank, sitting in the dark, crying."

"Frank?" The man just didn't strike me as the crying kind.

"Yes," she answered. "He wasn't openly crying, he just had tears running down his face, but it was the pain he was in. A deep kinda pain that I've never seen in him before."

"Did you talk to him?"

"I tried," she said and shook her head. "He wouldn't have any of it. He just sat there with that . . . that . . ."

Again, Mary looked away from me and out the window.

"Did you approach Jennifer?"

"I went back upstairs. She was in bed." Mary stopped, bit her bottom lip, and continued. "It's just so hard to talk about. Jennifer asked me to come into her room and tuck her in. I was shocked. She barely talks to me, much less . . ." She broke down and cried.

I reached over and held her hand. My palms were clammy. I didn't like feeling this much for this woman. "Try to go on, please."

"She wanted me to sing a lullaby to her. One I sang when she was little. I just held her in my arms and sang to her until she fell asleep. I stayed there, all night like that . . . God . . ." She took a deep breath and stared out into the rainy night. "The next morning, she was ice cold. I want my little girl back. Please. I can't lose—" She stopped.

"Go on," I urged.

"I can't lose Jennifer. Have you talked with Stroud?"

"Yes."

"What did you think?"

"I didn't like the guy." My thoughts went back to the conversation I had overheard. "That doesn't mean a damn thing. Has Jennifer ever mentioned any other names to you? Any other kids that were up there with her?"

"No . . . maybe, I don't know. What name?"

"Lord?"

"Pardon me?" she asked and grinned.

"Dinah Lord. Does that strike a bell?"

She thought a minute. "No. It doesn't. Phoebe, what about Stroud?"

"He's a creep. But, like I said, it takes time to compile information. Even the basic stuff."

I picked up my coffee cup and took a drink. The steaming liquid seared my tongue. It took everything I had not to spit it across the table. I grabbed the water in front of me and drank all my mouth would hold. I didn't swallow, I just let it bathe my buds. Mary handed me a napkin when I started leaking.

When the crisis was over, I decided to dive right in.

"Look, Mary, I want to talk to Jennifer."

"That's impossible."

"I'd like to get a feel of her. Something."

"In the beginning, I told you she had changed. I thought you understood that. Particularly after the other—"

"I did, I mean I do, but—"

"She can't be involved. She's crippled, hurt. If you approach her . . . You can't, Phoebe. She's sick."

This time, she had no control. With a muffled, agonizing sob, she reached out and grabbed my hand.

"I've prayed. God, how I've prayed. Something is going to happen. I feel it. Know it. Please . . ."

Now it was time for me to look away. The red neon sign attached to the plate glass a few inches above our heads buzzed. The tubular cursive letters ran together and spelled CAFE—OPEN. I could see the reflection of the letters blink on and off against her pale skin.

"Mary, if there is anything that you know that will help me, I need the information."

She turned back toward me.

"I've told you all I can."

"All?" They never tell you everything. With Mary that had been borne out early on. "Are you sure?"

"Mary . . . ," someone said from beside us.

Mary turned and smiled. A petite woman, with rosebud lips and flushed cheeks, stood by the table. She wore a rain slicker that glistened with water and a plastic fluted scarf on her head.

"What on earth are you doing out on a night like this? Where's Frank? Isn't he with you?"

Mary's face turned red. She glanced at me quickly and then looked back to the woman standing beside our booth. She didn't address the remark about Frank, but I could tell it made her uncomfortable.

"I guess I could ask you the same thing. You look soaked to the gills."

"We just had a horrid experience. We had to take a load of hay out toward Blue Creek and wanted to get it there and get home before this weather turned any worse. They had the whole bridge blocked off."

"Was there a wreck?" Mary asked politely.

"We thought so."

"Come on, Karen," someone yelled from a few booths down.

The woman waved her hand toward that direction and continued.

"There were cop cars all over the place. Some girl jumped off South Bridge. They have those boats out there, in this weather if you can imagine it, dragging those huge grappling hooks up and down the river."

Something snaked up my neck.

"How horrible," Mary replied. "Did they find her?"

"We left. Jerry knew the deputy that was directing traffic, more like holding traffic up really."

By this time, I felt like I wanted to throw up.

"What did the deputy say?" I asked, butting in. Both women turned and looked at me curiously.

"He told Jerry that some passing motorist had seen a blond girl jump out of a car as it was crossing the bridge. They almost hit her. She jumped up on the rail and went over the side."

"Mary, I have to go. I'll call you." I got up, dug some money out of my purse, and put it on the table.

"What—"

"I'll call you, Mary," I said again and took off.

I got in my truck and had to wait for a sixteen-wheeler to pull through before I could get out of the lot. I looked toward the cafe. I could see Mary sitting in the booth. Water ran from the eaves and down over the plate glass, carrying crimson streams of neon down into the dark.

▽

12

MY HANDS WERE SHAKING so bad that I had a hard time getting the key in my apartment door. I had expected Roger to be there, but the apartment was dark. I flipped on a light, walked straight to the answering machine, and pushed the play button on the machine. After three or four hang-ups, Shawna's pitiful, desperate voice broke the silence on the machine.

"Dorothy Morgan . . . in . . . ," she said and paused. I could tell she had covered the mouthpiece of the phone. When she came back on seconds later, she was crying. "A friend of my father's gave me your number. She's wiring me some money tomorrow and said—" Her voice broke again. "She said you'd help me," she blurted. "I'm at a mall . . ." I could hear her ask someone where she was.

"Damn it, Shawna. Give me the name," I said more to myself than the unresponsive machine.

"I'm at West Park Plaza . . . on Grand Avenue. I'll call back."

The dial tone kicked in, and my machine hummed for what seemed like an eternity.

"Cheap piece of shit!" I yelled and slapped the desk with my hand. I'd paid top money for a voice-activated machine that recorded dial tones better than voices.

She came on again.

"There's a security guard watching me. I can't stay here much longer," she said as she struggled for words. "I . . . I couldn't find your address in the phone book. I'll wait by the phone. Please . . ."

By this time, I had a knot in my throat the size of a fist.

"Please come and get me. I'll be by the phone. It's back by the rest rooms."

I fast-forwarded it past the dial tone and listened to her last message.

"I've got to leave here. A couple of guys said they'd give me a ride if I needed one . . ."

There was silence for a moment. I knew she was debating the ride.

"Don't take it . . . don't take it," I said. "Just wait outside." I checked my watch. It was already nearly 10:00 P.M. "Shit!"

"I'm going with these guys. I'll call you in half an hour."

The line went dead. There were no other messages. I sat down on the couch and willed that phone to ring. It didn't. I knew it wouldn't, and deep inside I knew why.

As I maneuvered the ice-clad streets across town and onto South Billings Boulevard, Shawna's haunting voice clawed at my mind. Those feral eyes stared deep into mine, accusing me, begging me, reaching out to me.

From the description that Mary's friend had relayed, things had quieted down some on the bridge. Traffic was not blocked when I got there. Three or four squad cars from the Sheriff's Department had pulled off the road and parked near the edge of the river.

There was a lot of activity around a search and rescue van. My first instinct was that they had found whoever they had been looking for. I sat in the truck and watched. My legs were rubber. I couldn't have gotten out if I had had to.

The way I was parked, my headlights illuminated the rescue van and several deputies who were standing around it. I could hear someone yelling and saw an agitated arm waving toward where I sat in the truck. I rolled down the window and leaned out.

"Turn off your damned lights," one of the deputies yelled.

I pushed in the switch and sat there in the dark. One of the figures started walking up the hill toward me. The gait, the long, lanky legs, and the tip of his cowboy hat were unmistakable.

Kyle Old Wolf was the only Indian either on the police force or in the Sheriff's Department. That, and the fact that he was the best they had, didn't make his professional life easy. We had taken a few classes together at Eastern Montana College. He was the definition of "hunk," with chiseled features and raven-black hair. His quiet, brooding personality and intense brown eyes made him all the more appealing. He was traditional, at least as traditional as any Indian can be in the '90s.

"I thought that was your truck. Going for a late-night swim?" he said as he leaned on the door and grinned in at me.

"Right, Kyle," I answered cynically. "I hear someone did."

"We don't know for sure. We've only got a statement from a couple that was driving across the bridge when she jumped."

"And . . ."

"And what?"

"Well? Are you going to tell me about it?"

Kyle leaned his head down and laughed. "You're digging for something. What is it?"

I knew I could trust him, but I still didn't tell him all the details, only that I knew a girl was on the run from Whispering Pines and that she had been given my number through a connection in Denver. I also told him what she looked like.

He scowled, pulled his hat down on his forehead, and shook his head. His breath was white vapor on the cold night air as he spoke.

"Could be, Phoebe. It matches what the kids that picked her up said."

"You've got them?"

"They're down at the office giving a statement. One of the kids stayed down by the bank and the other called it in."

"What went down?"

"They picked her up at the mall on Grand Avenue. One of the guys working security had been watching her. These two kids saw she was in some tight spot and told the guy she was their sister."

"He bought it?"

"We haven't talked to him yet. Anyway, these kids are pretty shook up. They were heading out to Blue Creek for a booze bash. According to them, she was acting real paranoid."

"Like how?"

"Like looking out the back window and crouching down in the seat every time a car passed them. She got real excited about a cop car she thought was following them."

"Was there?"

"Not that we can track down. One guy swears he saw it too, following a block or so back. The other kid didn't see a thing. She got hysterical and said it had trailed them from the mall and started screaming and tried to get out of the car."

Kyle shook his head again. "They probably had a couple of cans of beer, and she thought she was going to get popped for possession. There wasn't a damn thing in the car when I checked it out."

"So how the hell did she end up on the bridge?"

"Like I said, they got into a real wrestling match. The guy driving was trying to pull off to the side and stop while the other guy had a hold of the girl."

"Two guys couldn't keep her in the car?"

"She was out before they knew it. The kid driving threw it into park, got out, and chased her. She made it to the center and dived off."

"Fuck," I said and hit the steering wheel with my hands. "What about the car following them?"

"A cop? I doubt it. I suppose someone from the city could have been on their tail, but it could have been anybody. One of the kids swears a car was stopped way back behind them with its lights out. When they started yelling for help, it turned around and took off."

"Is it possible, Kyle?"

"Anything is possible. I checked it out with Dispatch. The kids were driving a 'sixty-nine black Camaro with personalized plates that said BATMAN. Someone would have remembered it, had anyone called it in and run it through. Think she's your girl?"

I shook my head. All I felt was a warm, sick knowledge crawl through me. I didn't even feel the cold.

"I saw them loading the back of the van. I thought maybe they found her."

"They're calling it quits for the night. Shit. Look at it out there, and it's going to get worse before it gets better. They'll be back down first thing in the morning."

"Kyle, let me use your pen." I scribbled my phone number down on an old envelope out of my glove box and handed it to him. "Give me a call if something comes up on this, could you?"

"Sure," he answered and put the number in his pocket. "What are you onto here?"

"Could she have made it? Have you checked the bank?"

"They're still checking. I'd say the odds aren't in her favor. Even if she got out, she couldn't last long in this shit, being wet to the bone." He reached in and placed his hand on my arm. "What's up?"

"If I could tell you I would. Maybe later. Okay?"

He looked at me for a minute, turned, and left. I pulled back up on the road and headed home. The temperature had dropped enough that snow was sticking to the ground. A stiff wind was coming out of the north, freezing everything solid in its path.

Somewhere on the edge of reality I must have heard the phone ringing and picked up the receiver. All I heard was my own voice asking someone to leave a message and three good reasons why I should return their call. It was an odd sensation.

"Pick up the damned phone, Phoebe," a voice screamed.

I held the phone to my ear.

"This is the stupidest thing I've ever heard on one of these machines," the voice continued. "But . . . I'll give you a damned good reason why you should return my call. If you don't I'll send a car to your place to bring you in. You've got one hour."

The line went dead. Uncle John, pissed off, was enough to bring anyone out of a stupor. I could only guess what it was about. Guess hell, I knew, or thought I did. The clock by the bed said it was almost noon.

It's never taken me an hour to get ready for anything, but this one I played down to the wire. Why not? Who the hell did he think he was, anyway? I've never played beat me, whip me, call me trash that well, and I sure wasn't starting now.

When I walked out of the apartment, the phone was ringing. I ignored it and walked into City Hall with only two minutes to spare.

"I think you blew it this time, honey," Tillie said as she looked up from her desk.

"What's he on, high-grade testosterone?" I managed a nervous smile and tried to look confident.

"Aspartame. Don't push him. Ever hear of the Twinkie killer?" She giggled. "Want a cup of coffee before . . ."

"That sounds ominous. Got any 'real' food?"

She nodded her head toward a small cabinet that held a coffee maker and a tray of doughnuts.

"Help yourself. I only wait on people for money anymore. Too damned old and mean for anything else."

I had just poured myself a cup of coffee and taken a big bite out of a maple bar when John walked out of his office. He shot me one of the dirtiest looks I had ever gotten. He didn't say a word to me, he just leaned down, said something to Tillie I couldn't hear, stomped off, and proceeded to assault a four-drawer file cabinet.

I stood with my mouth full of carbohydrates and watched him as he pulled open the top drawer and tore through some files. This was a new mad-on he was exhibiting, and it scared me.

"Phoebe?"

"Hmmm?" I answered as I took a drink of coffee and tried to break down the stale hardness of the maple bar.

"He wants you to wait inside his office. He'll be in, in a second."

"Thanks, Tillie," I mumbled around my mouthful. "Can I choose lethal injection?" I grinned.

"You're drinking it." She smiled back at me.

I took another bite of maple bar and walked into John's office. A tall man, with his back toward me, was standing behind John's desk, looking down at the jumble of pictures John had on the ledge above the radiator. A faint, sweet odor assailed my nostrils and opened one of my mental this-is-familiar files.

Before I could nail it down he turned. He had a perplexed look on his face. I took another drink of coffee, washing everything down my throat, and hoped like hell I could control the look of disbelief in my eyes. John walked into the room and put his hand on my shoulder. His voice was formal, threatening.

"Take a chair," he said as he tightened his grip on my shoulder. "This is Dr. Victor Stroud. He's the director up at the treatment facility on the Rims."

John was enunciating his words carefully. There was a message in his tone, one meant for me, its meaning unclear. Victor Stroud walked to me and extended his hand.

John sunk his fingers into my shoulders and snapped me out of my paralysis. "This is my niece, Miss Siegel."

"How do you do," Stroud responded and stretched out his hand. His eyes searched my face. He looked puzzled. "Have we met before by any . . ."

At John's prodding and the pain in my shoulder, I set my coffee down on the edge of the desk and reached out to grasp Stroud's hand. It was cold and unresponsive to my grip. When he pulled his away, I wanted to shake mine off. I swallowed and mumbled something. He lowered his eyes and continued to look at me. He was struggling with something, processing information.

"Phoebe, a young girl who was a patient at this center—"

"Was?" I asked before I could stop the word from popping out.

"They found her this morning."

I couldn't say a thing. Couldn't look anywhere except straight at Uncle John. His eyes hardened and commanded any reaction I had to stay hidden. I got the message real quick, picked my cup of coffee back up, and tried to swallow some over the lump in my throat.

John picked up a piece of paper and looked at it briefly before he let it fall back down on his cluttered desk. I watched it flutter, mesmerized, until it came to rest in front of him.

I glanced at Stroud. He was watching me, not Uncle John.

"We've pretty much figured out what happened. The night she ran, she walked across county a mile or two and connected up with

Airport Road at the top of Twenty-seventh Street. She either hitched or, my guess is, she walked down to an all-night Laundromat that's about a block from the college. We had a report of some clothes taken from there around midnight. We'll probably be able to match it up with what she was wearing when they snagged her."

Snagged her. Shit. The callousness, even from John, even knowing it was for self-protection, bothered the hell out of me.

"We don't now how she spent the day, but she did end up at West Park Plaza that night. We've got a statement from a security guard who remembers seeing her. We've also got a statement from the kids who picked her up."

"Unfortunate matter," Stroud said, again without any emotion.

"We've also talked with a friend of her father's," John said as he picked up another piece of paper from the desk, took his glasses off his head, and put them on. "A woman in Denver who apparently was close to the girl. She said that Shawna called her three or four times yesterday and that she gave Shawna your phone number."

Without warning, Stroud's voice, strong now, addressed me.

"Did you know this young woman, Miss Siegel?"

"No, I—"

"Did you know her father or her friend in Denver?"

"Uh—"

"My niece is a private investigator," John interjected and then turned toward me. "I'm assuming that this woman contacted you when she heard from the young lady. Am I right?"

The anger hadn't left John's eyes, but for some reason he was trying to cover my ass. I went for it.

"Yes . . . uh . . . that's it. I was going to give it a couple of days before I decided to take the job."

"Then that would account for your phone number being found in the pocket of the jacket Miss Unger was wearing." John's voice deepened.

"Then you didn't know the deceased or her father?" Stroud pushed.

"No, I didn't know either of them." I spoke from conviction, hoping my voice carried the message to Stroud.

"Dr. Stroud has been concerned for the safety of the girl since she took off. It crossed his mind that someone may have been hiding the girl, and that perhaps you could shed some light on the fact that she had your number."

I braced myself. "If she had my number, it came from the woman I talked with in Denver. I did not know Miss Unger."

John turned his attention to Stroud. "We're not in the habit of withholding information from any party concerned in something like this, Doctor. I hope this alleviates your concerns. I can vouch for my niece," he said without once looking at me. "She's always conducted herself within the limits that govern her *chosen* profession."

God, he could bullshit with the best of them.

"Now," John said and stood. "If there's anything else we can do for you, let me know."

John reached out and met Stroud's hand halfway across the desk. "We'll have the autopsy reports back—"

"Autopsy?" Stroud asked. For one second, I could see that he had lost a little piece of the calm, cool reserve. "I don't think the family—"

"It's state law in cases like this. We don't need anyone's permission."

"I wasn't . . ." Stroud's temple was twitching. "It's such a degrading assault upon the dead."

"Sorry," John replied and shrugged.

"Thank you again, Captain. Please come up to the center and have a look around. We're proud of our facility. Perhaps it would improve our link with the community."

"I just might do that one of these days." Uncle John smiled and followed Stroud to the door. As soon as she closed the door, I could feel him watching me.

"What the hell do you think you're doing? My phone has been ringing off the hook. And, mysteriously, a few of those calls have been about you. What the hell have you done to get Cutter Gage on your ass?"

Before I could say anything, he had walked back around to his desk and sat down. He leaned back in his swivel chair and looked at me hard. Without taking his eyes from mine, he reached out and pushed the buzzer on his intercom.

"Tillie, hold all my calls. I don't give a damn who it is. Hold 'em."

$\triangledown$

13

T HE ONLY THING THAT had been missing in my encounter with Uncle John was the chair in the basement, and the light shining in my eyes. He used words as effectively as a rubber hose. I had managed to come out of it with only a bad case of acid indigestion from Tillie's coffee, and a warning from John that the "State giveth, and the state taketh away" in reference to my license.

Then the real harassment started. We spent the rest of the time pleasantly, if not comfortably, chatting about the family.

Late though I was, I decided to stop at the Clerk and Recorder's Office and glean what I could from Krisa. She was helping someone at the counter when I walked in. I waved and mouthed "I'll be back" only to have her scowl, so I hung around for another fifteen minutes.

"Sorry about that," she said when the elderly gentleman she had been waiting on turned and walked out the door. "I think I may have something for you."

I was running a little low on enthusiasm but forced an ah gee, Krisa, I-couldn't-do-life-without-you smile. She walked to her desk, picked up a spiral notebook, and came back to where I was standing. In a low, secretive voice that made me want to laugh, she leaned close and started whispering.

"Remember when I told you that something rang a bell somewhere about the transaction for the old nursing home?"

"Right. I take it you found something."

"I don't know. You'll have to be the judge of that."

"Shoot."

"We get a lot of traffic in and out of here. Real estate people, attorneys, surveyors, just to name a few. Every once in a while the same name keeps coming up. Someone can't find something, or it's been ripped off."

"They rip you off in here?" I asked.

"You'd be surprised," she said and frowned. "They usually like the old-time documents, the ones with the old fancy writing on them. Some are very collectible," she said with conviction.

"I didn't know that." Nor did I give a shit.

"Anyway, you usually know what documents are up for grabs. They can copy anything, but that usually isn't good enough. They end up tearing out the pages."

"Does this lead anywhere?" I asked, getting irritated.

"The transaction on the nursing home, now doing business as Whispering Pines, was done in two deals. The first was purchased by UIC. Cash. Two hundred thousand dollars."

"Whew!" I exclaimed.

"Then there were another forty acres adjacent to that land that had a small airstrip . . ."

"Airstrip?"

"On the second purchase, UIC shows up with a partner and buys up the forty acres, which includes the airstrip. It was part of an estate handled by a local law firm, and a conflict of interest came up. Some other people were interested in the land. The law firm claimed there were no heirs—"

"How the hell did you find out about all of this?"

"The job, for the most part, is pretty boring, so we end up listening in on conversations a lot, little bits and pieces from all over the building, and start putting two and two together. Plus the fact that when any one particular area gets busy, it also gets juicy."

"If you're ever looking for another job, look me up."

Krisa laughed, effectively stroked.

"There's also the paranoia about outside investors buying up the state," she added confidentially, like this was little-known information.

"I still don't know how this relates to what I'm looking for."

"Doesn't the guy you're dating work for MIB?"

"Yes, he does. How'd you know that?"

"A good-looking guy like that? Single? It doesn't take long before the bevy of beauties around here know everything but the color of his toothbrush."

"Go on."

"Malcolm Gage held the title on not only the forty acres but also Whispering Pines. The state cried foul, so he had to sell. And guess who he sold it to."

"Who?"

"His son-in-law. A, let's see"—she shuffled through her notes—"Franklin Kuntz. Odd thing is, he turned around and sold it ten days later to one Victor Stroud. And Victor Stroud is—"

"UIC," I interjected. "How long ago?"

"Around three years ago."

I just stood there, dumbfounded. "Can you copy any of it?"

"Sure, what do you need?"

"All of it."

"Give me an hour or so?"

"You've got it. Krisa, you're a genius." I leaned over the counter and hugged her.

I'd avoided my own office since the end of February. I found myself parking in front of the Hart Albin Building, looking up at the arched window that I contemplated life from eleven months out of the year.

The sun, still moving in a southerly arch, had pushed the temperature into the forties, a far cry from the bitter ice storm of the night before. What had started as ice and snow had been rendered to a sloppy slush. Steam rose from the sidewalks and streets.

I opened the front door to the building, got into the coffin-sized elevator, and rode it up to the second floor. Very few of the offices were rented out. The building was vintage 1890, and it must have been grand in its day. Now it stood like an old woman in dire need of a face-lift.

Pigeons cooed seductively from under the eaves and shared their droppings with passersby far below. Roger hated the place. I loved the antiquity, the embossed tin ceilings, the oak trim, and the rail on the staircase that shone with the oil of the many hands of people who had climbed five flights to the top floor. My floor. I called it atmosphere. Roger called it decay.

Next to me, a CPA kept a low profile balancing debits and credits and reading *Penthouse*. On the other side, Sharon, a massage therapist, plied her trade on willing flesh five days a week.

The CPA gave me the creeps. But I frequented the gal with the nimble fingers. She had a mystical way of working all the knots out of my body and the kinks out of my mind. I walked into her office and found her sitting behind her desk reading a murder mystery.

"Phoebe, you just missed that guy of yours," she said, laid the book down, and smiled. "He said to tell you he'd be by later."

"Roger?"

"Looked like him." She grinned. "Is there more than one?"

I walked over to her Mr. Coffee and filled up a Styrofoam cup.

"Why do you read that stuff?" I asked and sat down in a chair opposite her.

"You live it, I read it. And besides, with a real live private eye—"

"Investigator," I said. "Private investigator."

"Private eye sounds much more romantic," she replied. "By the way, you must have heard on your house."

"I haven't. Why?"

"What were you doing, then? Spring housecleaning?"

"I don't know what you're getting at, Sharon."

"All the racket—"

"What the hell are you talking about?"

"I had a late appointment last night and didn't get out of here until almost eleven. At about ten thirty," she said and pointed toward the wall that divided her office from mine, "God, Phoebe, it sounded like you called the movers—"

Before she could finish her sentence I was up, out of my chair, and out of her office. My hand was shaking so bad I could hardly get the key in the lock. I turned the knob, heard the bolt slide from the catch and the grating of the hinges as I pushed the door slowly open. It was the only sound in the hallway. There weren't any surprises.

Every file cabinet drawer and desk drawer was open and empty. A few drawers were lying on the floor hidden beneath the blizzard of paper that had hit the room. Nothing was left untouched. My one attempt at a green thumb, a tall, neurotic rubber tree I called Bud, was lodged between my chair and the radiator, its rich black sustenance spread from one end of the window ledge to the other.

"Whoa," Sharon said over my shoulder. "The bastards mugged Bud. Time to call a private eye."

"I'll stick to nine one one."

A couple of detectives, no one I knew, spent an hour taking a short statement from me, a longer, more dramatic one from Sharon. To her, this was something out of one of her mystery books, and she was a key witness.

She had gotten to the office around 9:00 P.M.; her appointment showed up a little after that. Around ten thirty, just as she was finishing up, she heard someone, presumably me, in the office next door.

Knowing I kept some pretty odd hours, she'd thought nothing

of it and had planned to look in on me before she left for the night. She heard commotion right up to the last couple of minutes before she finished up, but when she locked up her office and walked next door to mine, the place was dark and quiet.

She had not heard anyone come up the stairs, which were notorious for their creaking, nor had she heard the elevator, which vibrated each time it came from downstairs. Sound carried throughout the building under any circumstances. Last night, the only sound she'd heard had filtered through the walls between our offices.

Sharon stayed and offered to help me clean up. She grabbed a couple of boxes out of a storage closet in the hall, and between the two of us we gathered everything off the floor and stacked it inside. We stuffed Bud back in his pot, packed in what soil we could gather from the ledge, and hoped for the best. I told Sharon I could handle the rest on my own.

"I've got to go back next door," she said when she looked at her watch. "God, I'm sorry, Phoebe. It could just as easily have been my place."

"Right," I said, even though I knew full well that whoever did this had no interest in massage oils and nimble fingers. "Thanks for the help."

"I feel a little guilty. All of this going on with me next door and—"

"Forget it," I said, trying to let her off her own hook. "Things could have been worse."

I spent the rest of the day sorting files and trying to maintain some semblance of normalcy. Several times I caught myself flinching when I heard footsteps in the hall. The phone was on answer and clicked in several times. Whoever it was would have to wait.

It wasn't only the files I was trying to put back together. My nerves were shot. My mind kept creating, with graphic detail, visions of Shawna's bloated body being snagged by a grappling hook.

If I had been home . . . if I had checked my messages. If . . . if only. Hundreds of scenarios plagued me. Kehly called them the woulda-shoulda-coulda's and said they were worse than the delirium tremens. I was beginning to believe her.

The sun was slipping down over the edge of the western horizon and had cast the entire valley in a golden glow. I'd pulled up in front of the apartment and turned off the ignition when two things caught my eye. The first was the tail end of a cruiser as it pulled slowly around the corner at the end of the block. The second was

Roger's car parked across the street. I wondered briefly why a cruiser was in the area and then let it slide. I had too many other things on my mind, like some answers to questions I wasn't even sure existed.

I walked around to the rear of the apartment and let myself in through the sliding glass doors. I turned on the tape deck, kicked my shoes off, and dropped into my favorite chair, an overstuffed, vintage 1930 mohair number, and let it envelop me. My head fell back into the softness.

The low, crooning sounds of B. B. King filled the room and drowned out the sound of the shower and Roger's rendition of "The Sloop John B." My mind focused only on the emotional exhaustion that held it captive, and I slid, willingly, into a restless sleep.

I was twelve again. The air around me was filled with Zelda's laughter. I walked cautiously on the tips of white patent-leather shoes toward the exaggerated heart-shaped bathtub that stretched before me. An icy vapor mist hung a few feet above the tub. I felt no fear as I crept closer and knelt on the bottom stair leading to the platform.

The giant hook fell from far above my head and sliced deep into the water. For a split second I shuddered and then leaned closer to peer down into the crystal clearness. The hook started to rise, stopped momentarily, then rose again. My heart beat wildly and my mind screamed.

As the hook rose higher, a face appeared, disembodied only for a second. Impaled fast on the gleaming steel, Shawna smiled at me. Water cascaded from her hair, her mouth, her hands as she hung suspended over the tub.

Her mouth formed garbled words as dead eyes stared toward me.

"I needed you," she spewed. "I needed you, and you weren't there."

I stumbled backward as heads crowded in the watery tomb. Zelda, Ben, Daddy, and Sam rose, dripping, and smiled at me. My breath caught in my throat; water splashed around my feet, beading on my sparkling white shoes. I stumbled and fell, eyes riveted on Shawna, her accusations lost in the haunting laughter. Someone reached down and picked me up.

"Shit!" Roger yelled and moved back from the chair. I stopped the scream coming from my mouth. Stud flew from my lap and landed a few feet away. "All I said was dinner is ready. Christ! Where were you?"

"Sleeping," I yelled back. "I was fucking sleeping, Roger. Have you ever heard of sleep?"

"God, I'm sorry. You looked beat, so I cooked a little something—"

"What the hell were you doing in my shower? How did you get in here?" I lashed out. "I thought this damn relationship was over." As soon as the garbage flew out of my mouth, I had an urge to bite down hard enough to make my tongue bleed.

"My intention was to pick up the rest of my stuff, and a shower seemed pretty appealing. Excuse the hell out of me. And this should cover your second question." He reached into his pocket, pulled out a key, and tossed it onto my lap.

I reached out and held his arm. "I'm sorry. Everything is so . . ." My nose was assaulted with the smell of hickory-smoked bacon and eggs, and my salivary glands kicked in. "I smell breakfast."

"I thought your favorite thing for dinner was breakfast." His voice was still tense, untrusting.

"It is, Roger. Look . . . I've had a helluva day . . . and night. Plus the fact I just had this really bizarre dream."

"Let's eat. We'll talk later."

It dawned on me how he always came through. I reached out and touched his cheek.

"Roger?"

"What?"

"Forgive me?"

"Maybe in ten years or so."

"Thank God. I was worried you'd hold a grudge."

Roger's bark bacon and plasticized eggs rattled in the hollowness in my stomach. Krisa Poole had tied Gage and Frank Kuntz to Whispering Pines and therefore to Victor Stroud, and therefore to Jennifer Kuntz, Shawna Unger, and Ben. There couldn't have been a more unlikely group.

I snuggled back in the chair, listening to Roger clean up in the kitchen and struggling to make sense out of the cast of characters. Shawna, Daniel Unger, and the Padilla kid weren't talking. Mary Kuntz was, but she wasn't making much sense. It was the strength of her conviction that had halfway hooked me in the first place, and the mention of my brother Ben that had reeled me in. And there was the ruthless and powerful Cutter Gage.

I got up from the chair, walked out the back door, and stood looking out into the night. I turned my face up to the rain that was falling in a fine mist. A door slammed and startled me.

"Susie," the voice cooed. "Susie honey, come in out of the rain or you'll catch your death. Come on, baby. Come to Mama."

Right, have enough sense to come in out of the rain, I thought to myself as I stood in the dark. I looked toward the street and stiffened. On the opposite side, halfway down the block, a car pulled up to the curb, parked, and turned out its lights. Exhaust from the tail pipe hovered close to the pavement. Someone inside struck a match. The end of a cigarette glowed bright for just a minute and then disappeared.

It didn't take much to spot the light bar on top of the cruiser.

"'Phoebe, come on in," Roger said as he leaned out the door. "Shit. It's raining out here. I'm about to leave."

"I'm coming," I whispered. "Just give me a minute."

I paused up against the wall as Mrs. Wickersham yelled out her back door again.

"Susie, I mean it. You'll catch your death. Now you get on in here."

I heard the tiny nails of the dog's paws click up the sidewalk as she came around the corner of the apartment building. She stopped at my feet, sat back, and looked up at me.

"Get out of here." I spoke as quietly and, at the same time, as menacingly as I could. "Go on."

Susie wasn't budging. She growled and started barking up at me. Each time the nerve-racking sound erupted from her mouth, her entire body bounced, lifting her front feet off the ground. The porch light went on behind Mrs. Wickersham's. I kept my eye on the cruiser. It wasn't budging either. Without warning, Susie's "mama" materialized around the corner, flashlight in hand. The beam of the light scanned the yard in front of her as she moved toward the front of her property.

She didn't see me at first. Susie stopped barking and ran toward her. Before I knew it, she had turned the beam up into my face. I brought an arm up to cover my eyes and looked away toward the cruiser. Whoever was inside flipped the cigarette out the window and pulled slowly away from the curb.

"Well!" Mrs. Wickersham huffed. "Come on, Susie. You have to stay away from that woman and that . . . that marauding cat. Let's go in, sweetie."

The prissy poodle ran to her. Without a word to me, she redirected the beam of light, picked up her dog, and walked around to the back of her house. I watched the cruiser as it disappeared around the corner into the night.

14

A STIFF WIND BATTERED the apartment and chilled the room. At some point Stud had crawled up on the bed and settled at my feet. He just added to the weight that already rested on me.

I didn't get to sleep right away. The wind quieted down and then died. At some point I got up, let Stud out the back door, and waited for him to do his thing. When he didn't return I closed the door, opened one of the windows just enough to give him space to crawl through, and went back to bed. I don't know how long I had been sleeping when I heard Stud growling.

It was one of those moments when you're torn between doing the right thing, like getting up and seeing if Stud was all right, and slipping back into that comfortable sleep realm that verges on comatose. I chose the latter.

I've always slept with one leg sticking out from under the covers, bedclothes pulled tight up under my chin, on my side, balanced precariously on the edge of the bed. Tonight was no different. I'm also a deep breather. There's nothing like pulling in all that frigid air when you're snuggled under a mountain of covers. On some level of my awareness, the air suddenly changed.

The warm, panting breath hit my face in soft synchronized bursts. It was moist, heavy, and nauseating. I moved just a little and immediately heard a low, even growl inches from the side of the bed. I froze and slowly opened my eyes. Nothing came into focus right away in the darkness of the room, but every one of my other senses screamed for attention.

As things cleared in front of my eyes, I blinked and willed myself out of the dream I knew was not a dream at all. Not more than two feet from my face was the broadest black, growling face that any nightmare could conjure up. It was inlaid with two dark, beady eyes that were staring straight into mine. This was no nightmare. This was real.

Again I tried shifting my weight. The effort immediately prompted a menacing growl from the massive dog standing beside the bed. For a moment I stayed as still as possible. My mind knotted up and threw nothing but garbled thoughts at me. Again I tried moving. Again the dog's forehead wrinkled, its jaw dropped to reveal a set of long, saliva-coated canines that seemed to go on forever and the ever-present rumbling.

My mind was fuzzy. Roger was there. Next to me. Or was he? I moved my foot as slowly as possible toward where his leg should be. It hit me like a glass of ice water in the face: he'd gone home. It was just me and the dog. The dog didn't seem to notice the hidden movement beneath the layers of blankets. I kept my eyes on its face.

Someone was moving around in the living room. Shadows slid over the walls. Drawers opened and closed. My eyes had adjusted to the darkness, but my heart, on an adrenaline surge, refused to slow down. Cujo and I were in an eye lock. A cramp started knotting on the bottom of my foot. I moved slightly. The dog placed both of its front paws on the side of the bed and leaned down over me. Droplets of saliva slid from its jowls and landed on the side of my face. I was too scared to be repulsed. The doorway darkened. Out of the corner of my eye I could see a tall, dark, featureless figure.

"Watch," the specter whispered. "Good boy."

And that's just what "Good Boy" did. His eyes never left my face. My hand was inching under the pillow toward the brass lamp on the stand next to the bed. Good Boy had caught on to the subversive movements and gave me his menacing best. This time he pulled it up from inside and growled so deeply that the air around me vibrated.

I considered throwing the blankets over his head, until I decided it would take him under sixty seconds to shred them as he went for my throat. I also considered screaming but hated the thought of being cut off midscream. So I just stayed still. The dog's syrupy drool was building into a rivulet of slime that started to slide down my neck.

Then it began. That teasing, hair-grazing sensation that courses softly over the inside of your nose just before you sneeze. I tried holding my breath and stretching my nostrils, to no avail. It was building, gathering force. Nothing I could do, short of moving my hand up in front of my face, would slow the increasing tension.

The constant blasts of hot air from the dog's mouth only fueled what I knew would be my last act on earth. I judged him to be around 150 pounds of killing power. With a little luck it would be quick.

"Come," the voice said huskily. "Come, boy."

The shadow had once again filled the doorway. The dog jumped down and padded silently out of the room. It was deathly still. I couldn't move. Tears filled my eyes. I swallowed a sob before I sat up in bed and turned on the lamp. The clock read 2:00 A.M. I sneezed.

"It was probably a bad dream," Roger said as he sipped the cup of coffee I had put in front of him.

"Dream, shit. I know what I saw." My hands were still shaking. "By the way, I really do appreciate you coming over."

"No problem." He yawned. "There's nothing missing, VCR, television, typewriter, your keys, they're all here."

"Damn you, Roger. Don't treat me like some hysterical idiot," I screamed. He looked startled. "I didn't mean that. I . . ."

"What the hell is going on with you?" Roger had stood up, walked around the table, and pulled me to my feet. "Phoebe, this last week has been . . . I don't even know how to approach you on this. You just haven't been acting . . . I don't know, you just haven't been right or something."

"It's . . . it's this whole Jennifer Kuntz thing. It doesn't make sense. Now, this dog . . ."

"Let's not deal with, uh . . . the dog right this minute. Let's take care of Jennifer Kuntz. What doesn't make sense?"

"You don't believe me about the dog, do you?"

"I believe you. Now what about this Jennifer Kuntz thing?"

"It's like a rock thrown into a pond, and the ripples stretch out in every direction. Mary Kuntz thinks someone has damaged her psycho daughter to the point of no return. There's something weird as hell going on up at Whispering Pines. Two kids are dead. John's on my ass to stay out of trouble. I've been damn near killed by a horse, and now a dog invades my room."

"Coincidence."

"Get real, damn it. Are you forgetting someone ransacking my fucking office? Are you forgetting that my sister is freaked out because my brother asked some of the same questions I did about the damn center?" I felt myself getting hysterical. "Are you forgetting about . . . about Ben?" I tried not to break down. I told him about the allegation, the letter, and the bracelet. "It all ties together, Roger. Somehow, it all ties together."

"Phoebe, how many times have you told me that March played with your mind? Maybe you're creating all of this out of some, I don't know, out of some need. If I didn't know better, I'd think you were getting paranoid."

I stepped back and looked into his eyes. "The cops are following me."

"Shit." Roger threw his hands up in the air and walked into the living room.

"Listen to me," I said as I followed him and told him about the allegation made by Jennifer Kuntz shortly before Ben's death and the letter and how John had handled it. He said nothing as he walked over and grabbed my shoulders.

"I would have done the same thing, Phoebe. I would have dropped it. Hell, the guy was dead. He killed—"

I reached up and touched his lips with my index finger. "Don't. Don't say that. I didn't believe it then, and I sure as hell don't believe it now. He knew something." My voice was choking up. "Every time I turn around, I catch a glimpse of a police cruiser. I might be a lot of things, but paranoid isn't one of them."

He walked to the couch and sat down. I followed and sat down beside him. He was leaning forward, holding his head in his hands.

"Roger, put everything you know about me, personally, aside for a minute."

He looked up at me, shook his head, and went back to cradling his head in his hands.

"Just listen to me," I pleaded. "Then you make sense out of it for me."

I spilled my guts, from my first encounter with Mary down to the information I had gotten at the courthouse about Malcolm Gage owning the land and signing it over to Frank, who in turn sold out to Stroud. It caught his attention.

"How the hell did you find all of this out?"

"It doesn't matter. Doesn't it sound like a buy-off? Like Frank Kuntz was trying to appease Stroud?"

"Only if you take it to its furthest possible conclusion."

"How about via Cutter Gage? Doesn't that strike you as a little odd?"

Roger just looked at me.

"Roger, will you help me? Please?"

"No, I won't. I told you that this whole damn thing could blow up in my face, not yours. Subject closed. Do you understand?"

"If I can prove to you that more is going on up there than meets the eye, will you help me?"

"No, Phoebe. Call the cops. Or, better yet, turn around and flag down the cruiser that's following you. I've got to get home. I've got a meeting first thing."

Roger stood up and looked down at me like I was nuts. I could tell he thought I was two steps away from heavy medication and confinement.

"Are you going to be all right?" he asked.

"According to you or according to me?"

He said nothing. In a few moments I heard the door close as he left. I checked all the windows, left the light on in the kitchen, and lay down on the couch. In the dull glow of the living room, I turned on my side and looked at the row of family pictures I kept on a table nearby. Mama, Daddy, and all of us when we were kids. Ben and Charlene in happier times, Sam in uniform, Michael the day God claimed him. I sat up and went back through the pictures. Something was wrong. Missing. It hit me like a hammer right between the eyes and knotted up my stomach.

The only picture I had of Kehly was gone, frame and all. The space where it had stood was now ominously vacant. I frantically searched the apartment; it was nowhere to be found. Then I remembered the letter I had taken from Stroud's office. I jerked open the desk drawer I had tucked it in. It wasn't there. It wasn't anywhere. On both counts, whoever had invaded my sleep knew exactly what they were after.

By ten the next morning I was feeling like shit. It had taken me all night to go through every conceivable place I might have put Kehly's picture or the letter from Jeffrey Lord. I didn't find either of them. I knew I wouldn't. Inside, I had to take every precaution to prove to myself I wasn't losing it. An abject terror kept bludgeoning me.

Now there was a new twist. A new name. Kehly. I had tried calling her but couldn't get an answer. I called the department store and had them ring her department.

"I'm in the middle of something, Phoebe," she whispered. "Can I catch you later?"

"Sure. I . . . I just wanted to see how you were."

"Fine," she said and paused. "Are you all right?"

"Why wouldn't I be? I'll get you at home tonight. You will be home, won't you?"

"Of course I'll be . . . wait a minute. . . . I'm going to hit an AA meeting, but I'll be home after nine or nine thirty. What's wrong, Phoebe?"

"Nothing. Nothing is wrong. Take care of yourself."

Neither of us spoke for a minute.

"Call me?" she asked.

"You bet. Kehly?"

"What?"

"I . . . there's . . ." I knew anything I said would sound insane, so I opted for nothing. "Never mind. I'll call you tonight. I've got to go to dinner at Charlene's. It'll be after that."

"I'm glad, Phoebe. It's about time. I'll talk to you tonight."

"Sure. Tonight."

The line went dead.

It didn't take long to find Jeffrey Lord's phone number in Tymer, Wisconsin. They had several listings at Lord Manufacturing and two at his residence. I dialed the first residential number and waited.

"Hello?" The voice sounded ultrafeminine and very young.

"I'm . . . I'm calling for Mrs. Lord. Is she available?"

There was a dead silence.

"Hello?" I asked.

"There is no Mrs. Lord. She's been dead for years. Who's calling, please?"

"This is, uh . . . Helen Jenkins. I'm a writer and uh, we're, the state historical society that is, we're doing a story on families that have been in business for generations in Wisconsin. Lord's definitely fits our profile." Thank God for a quick mind.

The voice on the other end relaxed. "Oh. I'm sure if you call the office and ask for my father's secretary, her name is Gwen, she'll be more than happy to supply you with whatever information you need."

"Your father? Then you must be—"

"Dinah. I'm Dinah Lord," she said with a surge of pride.

"I've heard a little about you, Dinah." I figured I'd go for broke. "I would have asked for you, but I thought you'd be at school."

"This is my break. I like to be near my father when I can, so I come home as often as possible. It's just the two of us . . ."

"No brothers?"

"No, I'm afraid not. I'm just on my way into town. If you'll call Gwen at the plant . . . Do you need the number?"

"No. I have it. Maybe you could give me a quick profile on your father. Just to make it a little more of a human interest piece. Father, daughter, that sort of thing."

"What did you say your name was?"

"Helen . . . Helen Jenkins."

"Miss Jenkins, my father is in his seventies and not up to doing a publicity piece of any kind. So, if you'll excuse—"

"Wait," I panicked. "I lied."

"Pardon me?" The offensiveness in her voice was obvious.

"I got your name from a girl . . . a girl you met in treatment."

There was nothing but silence from the other end.

"She ran away from Whispering Pines," I continued cautiously.

I heard a deep sigh. "If she's away from that place, she'll be fine. What is it you want?"

"I need to know about your experience up there."

"My experience with Whispering Pines practically destroyed me and my father. If my father had bought the lies from Dr. Stroud, I'd probably still be there."

"How so?"

"Stroud played a little game working my father and me against each other. Granted, I had a drug problem, which by the way was hardly dealt with there. Who gave you my name?"

"Jennifer Kuntz."

"You're lying. Jennifer Kuntz is Stroud's personal psycho. I'm surprised she hasn't killed someone yet. I don't know what you're after, but don't ever call here again."

The line went dead. I hung up the phone and stared at the receiver.

Water pulsated from the shower head against my face and body, but failed to wash the exhaustion from my muscles and the haunting voices of Gina and Shawna Unger from my mind.

By noon I'd gained a second wind that at least allowed me to think straight. I tried reaching Mary Kuntz. No one answered. Just as I hung up the phone, Roger called.

"Where are you?" I asked. "I thought your calls were being monitored." I justified my sarcasm in my voice as a counter to his disbelief about the dog in my bedroom.

"Look, I'm sorry about this morning, and I am in a phone booth. Something about this whole thing doesn't jibe. Someone has been on my computer."

"What makes you think—"

"I don't have much time. Just listen. All my files are time-dated.

Some are old, some are more recent. I called up something this morning, and the date was yesterday, the time was around ten last night."

"I thought you were on a terminal?"

"We are, but this was my appointment record. Just a crap file that I keep junk in. I checked some other files, and the same thing. Between ten and midnight last night someone had gone through most of my files. Something *is* up."

"I've been trying to tell you that. By the way, have you seen that picture I keep of Kehly around?"

"No. Why?"

"It's missing. I can't find it—"

"Why would you be looking for it in the first place?"

"Because"—I caught myself articulating slowly—"it's missing. . . . Never mind, Roger."

"You've probably just misplaced it. I've got to get back. We'll talk tonight."

"Right."

"Phoebe? Be careful. Catch you later."

It didn't take much to track down the counselor, Jean Dillard, whose name Mary had given me. The high school informed me that she was on an extended leave of absence for medical reasons and that I could probably reach her at home.

I dialed the number the school secretary had given me and let it ring. Just as I was about to hang up, Jean Dillard answered. All it took was mentioning Jennifer Kuntz's name and I had directions to her house. Beneath the distraught voice, she sounded almost eager to talk to someone. In twenty minutes I was on Poly Drive ringing her doorbell.

She was a tall, large-boned woman, thin in the face and broad in the shoulders. Her hair was short, dark, and streaked with silver, and she had an air cast on the lower part of her left arm. She exuded strength not only through her size but through her rich, commanding voice.

Smiling, she led me into a tidy, plant-filled living room and directed me with her hand to sit down on a futon, one of two arranged around a low glass coffee table. A thick, squat candle burned in the middle of it. The scent of vanilla wafted wonderfully through the room.

The soft, mellow sound of Kenny G was barely audible throughout the house. The atmosphere reached out and stroked me, putting me immediately at ease. She was prepared for me. She reached out, picked up a tall glass of iced tea from a tray on the coffee table in front of the couch, and handed it to me.

"We get silly the longer we live alone, and hang on to old habits. I'm afraid I've never been much of a coffee drinker, so I drink iced tea all year round. Myself, I'm having a noon Scotch. Do you mind?"

"Of course not," I answered and caught a whiff of booze on her breath. "I appreciate your letting me intrude on you like this. If this is a bad time . . . ," I said, looking toward her cast.

"Carpal tunnel syndrome. I've lived with it for years and decided to get it taken care of. It's no big deal," she said and raised her glass toward me. "I don't do pain pills well, so I've prescribed myself this in small doses. It works. I'm curious . . . what did you say your name was?"

"Phoebe, Phoebe Siegel."

"What line of work are you in, Phoebe?"

"I'm an investigator."

"How does this relate to Jennifer Kuntz?"

I briefly told her about being approached by Mary, left out the part about Ben, and gave her my rap about how any information she shared with me would be held in the strictest confidence. She sipped and watched me intently.

"If you had approached me one year ago, I more than likely would not have talked with you, Phoebe. Now," she said and paused. "Things change. People change."

She smiled but didn't try to hide the look of sadness in her eyes.

"I don't under—"

"What do you need to know about Jennifer? How can I help?"

"You worked with her at the school?"

"Yes, I did. For nearly six months. Jennifer, how shall I say it, became very important to me. I don't have children, regretfully, but there was something in her, and in me, that just clicked."

"Did she approach you?"

"No, she was having problems—I'm sure her mother has filled you in on them. At the time, she was referred by the dean of girls. I work throughout the school system, and one day a week I hit the high school. Jennifer is bright, Phoebe. Extremely bright. How's she doing with the drug thing?"

"That's why I'm here. I had an encounter with her out at their farm," I said and told her about the incident. "She seems a little off her rocker."

"There were always underlying problems with Jennifer. I'm not sure I'd use the term *off her rocker*, but she was definitely a very angry and disturbed young woman. I talked with Dr. Drummond about Jennifer. He told me that . . . I really can't betray any confidences."

"This is urgent, Miss Dillard." There must have been a tone to my voice that convinced her. Maybe it was my own controlled hysteria.

"Jennifer encompassed about every personality disorder you could imagine. In spite of this, Dr. Drummond felt that she could learn to live a productive life under the right circumstances, and with continued therapy and medication, of course. I've tried to keep tabs on her, but there were extenuating circumstances," she said and drifted off somewhere.

"Like what?" I urged.

She fell silent and studied me for a moment. Her eyes scanned my face. She sighed, took a swallow of Scotch, and leaned back on the futon. When she didn't say anything, I wondered if she had been hitting the booze long before noon.

"Like what?" I asked again. "What extenuating circumstances were there?"

She rolled her head toward me and opened her eyes. "How much do you know about the family?"

"I've met Mary, and have seen the father. I've never talked with him."

"I've talked with both of them. Mary several times, the father only once. I thought that because of Jennifer's, uh, problems, her dysfunction, that I would find her mother a battered woman, either emotionally or physically."

"I didn't pick up on that with—"

"You wouldn't. It's not there. Jennifer pretty much tied my hands with the confidentiality thing, so it was impossible to share much with Mary. I knew it was frustrating for her."

"Look—"

"Be patient. I've always known I'd have this conversation with someone eventually. I never kidded myself that it would be easy."

"I'm sorry, go ahead," I apologized, not knowing what was coming.

"Like I said, I clicked with Jennifer immediately. It didn't take long to establish a bond between us. The poor damn kid was ready to burst. She had a problem with trust, but between us it worked somehow, and it only took three, maybe four meetings before she poured out the whole sad story."

She looked away from me quickly, wiped a tear from the corner of her eye, and stood up. I watched her walk to the bay window at the far end of the room. For the first time, I was doubting not only her sobriety but her stability.

"Listen, I need some background on this kid. I'm—" I stopped and considered the ramifications. "It's become a personal thing with me."

"Every kid I've ever counseled has become a *personal thing* with me. With Jennifer it was even more so." She came back and sat down.

"Jennifer has more than likely always had some psychotic episodes. I tested her and didn't find any surprises. At first I thought it might be a familial thing, but, like I said, I found Mary, other than being distraught over her daughter, fairly well balanced. With Jennifer, it was like asking what came first, the chicken or the egg. The underlying behavioral problems or the acting out."

"Then she *is* off her . . . uh, she isn't functional."

"Let me put it to you this way. Jennifer came into this world with problems; her environment added to them and created what you no doubt ran into out at the farm."

"Would it cause her to have hallucinations? Would she lie?"

"Jennifer's reality was more bizarre than any lie she could come up with, although she could have—" Jean stopped and looked at me. "What's the personal thing in here for you?"

"Her mother told me that Jennifer had made an allegation against a local policeman. Did you know about that?"

"No," she answered, laughed, and shook her head in what I took to be disbelief. An unseen hand loosened its grip on my heart. "I did know about her involvement with the policeman. We spent a lot of time on that one."

I opened my mouth but couldn't formulate any words. She watched me. Her eyes never left mine. "Did you believe it?" I gasped.

"Yes, I did. He was her knight in shining armor. She honestly felt that he could protect her from—"

"Jesus." Nausea swept over me. "Are you sure?"

"What is it?" she asked and came over and sat down beside me.

"Nothing. It's all right. What did she think he could protect her from?"

"Life. You have to understand that Jennifer medicated herself with drugs. She couldn't understand her emotions, her feelings, or her guilt. She was a prime target for a little adult male affection," she said and sneered. "God, how we screw up these kids."

It wasn't hard to tell she was getting tipsy. "You're sure about the policeman? Did she ever tell you his name?"

"No. That's the one name she didn't give me."

"There were others?"

"Do you know why I'm breaking every code of ethics to tell you these things?" she asked, slurring her words.

She stood, walked to a table near the bay window, picked up a decanter, and filled her glass. I said nothing; the booze would keep her talking until she passed out.

"I lost someone I loved very much. It made me take a look at my life. It would have been easy to say I had gotten my just desserts."

"How do you figure?" I asked, wondering how coherent an answer I would receive.

"I made a choice with Jennifer Kuntz that has haunted me every single hour for the past three years. It was a choice made out of self-preservation, fear, and probably, if I got honest with myself, shame. Are you involved with anyone?"

She walked back to the futon, a little less sure on her feet than when I had first gotten there, and sat down.

"Yes I am, but what has that got to do with—"

"I'm close to fifty, Phoebe. I had the same lover for nearly twenty-five years. We met at the University of Minnesota when I was getting my master's in psychology. I chose to come home and work here; my lover chose to teach at a private college back in Minnesota. Even with the distance between us, we managed to maintain a committed, monogamous relationship."

"You said that you recently lost someone. Was it—"

"Yes," she said and took another drink. "To breast cancer."

Why not? The past hour had been full of revelations. There probably was something appropriate to say. Something better than I'm sorry. When something better didn't come, I sat silently.

"It was a well-kept secret. No one on my job, no one in my family, ever suspected. I even had a few dinner dates with a couple of guys just to keep appearances up. Only a few close friends in Minnesota know about my relationship. I spent three months a year living in Minnesota, and the rest of the year I commuted. That's why I was so shocked when . . ."

"So shocked about what?"

"Jennifer Kuntz finally let it all out that last week we worked together. She told me she had been sexually abused for as long as she could remember. Her drug problems started when she discovered that maybe, just maybe, what had been happening to her was wrong."

"Jesus. Who—"

"I was making a move to have her pulled out of her home. There was someone I had been in contact with who was willing to take her in. It took a lot to get Jennifer to agree to go to the authorities with this. She was scared to death."

"And did you?"

"I had set up an appointment with Mary Kuntz. The day before she was to come in, someone else paid me a little visit. God, I must have looked like a fool."

"What do you mean?"

"I figured I had the upper hand. After all, I had Jennifer's file on my desk, and I was *loaded for bear*, as they say. I was in such a rage that I couldn't wait to sit across from the son of a bitch."

Jean reached up and wiped her mouth with the sleeve of her shirt. I had visions of Frank Kuntz attempting to cow her.

"What happened then?"

"He didn't show up. Someone else came. I had my file, he had his. He didn't beat around the bush. It was all there, twenty-four years of my life and it was all there. In essence, if my file on Jennifer was opened to anyone, he'd open his on me. You think I'm pretty low by now, don't you?" Tears filled her eyes, and her trembling hand brought the Scotch back up to her lips.

"That's why you stopped seeing Jennifer?"

"Right. You see, Phoebe, my parents are in their eighties, and I have a brother teaching in this same system. It would have destroyed them. And, as I understood it, Beth's—" She paused and looked toward me. "Did I mention that was her name?" She muffled a sob. "That her name was Beth?"

"No, no you didn't." Instinctively I reached over and touched her arm. "God . . . I don't know what to say to you."

"It would have destroyed Beth's career. I made a choice. I weighed Jennifer against all those other lives, and I made a choice. God help me."

"I need this information, Jean. You've gone this far. Please, take a quantum leap and give me all you've got."

"I kept extensive notes and had prepared my own statement that I had intended to give to the authorities," she said, tears streaming down her face. "It will take me a day or two to go through my things. I'll call you when I have it together. I need to get a pencil and paper," she said as she rose and walked out of the room. When she returned, she walked unsteadily to the table. "What's your num—"

"Let me give you my card." I pulled one out of my purse and put it on the table.

She picked up the card and read it through bleary eyes.

"Jean, who brought the file in to you? Do you remember?"

Her laugh was bitter. Her mood shifted. "I did try to contact Jennifer recently," she said apologetically and ignored my question.

"Did you get hold of her?"

"Yes. I did. I asked her how . . . uh, how she was dealing with things. I wanted to tell her that I would stand behind her now. I . . . I need to do that, you know?"

"I understand. What did she say?"

She picked up her Scotch and raised it dramatically into the air. "She told me to fuck off."

"Who brought the file to you, Jean? Do you remember his name?"

"I'll never forget it," she said and turned toward me. "John, John Flannery."

My hand dropped the glass of iced tea I was holding. It crashed down onto the glass-topped coffee table and shattered into a million shards. I reached for the napkin that was lying on the table. I didn't even feel the splinter that penetrated my palm.

▽

15

M Y MIND SLAMMED SHUT on Jean Dillard's revelations. I mentally flipped down a list of insanities that she, or I, could be inflicted with. Nothing seemed to fit. What I'd hoped would be the missing link that would provide me with sufficient information to pull the plug on Whispering Pines turned out to be a diabolical fact I wasn't equipped to deal with.

I had to get to John. Jesus, I didn't know what I was even going to say to him. I had no sooner parked in the lot behind City Hall than a shadow fell through the truck window and scared the hell out of me. I jumped practically over to the passenger side of the truck and turned toward my would-be attacker.

"Policemen are our friends. Didn't anyone ever tell you that?"

I looked up into a pair of reflective sunglasses and a broad, toothy smile. Lanny took off the glasses and leaned into the truck.

"Shit," I said, half-smiling, half-glaring. "You may as well have hit your siren. Aren't you supposed to be out fighting crime in the city?"

"Every day. What are you doing down here?"

"I thought I'd stop in and see Uncle John."

"He's not in."

"How do you know that?"

"I was just there myself. His secretary told me he was upstairs talking to the chief. Anything I can help you with? You look a little stressed."

"It shows?"

"Yup. It's been one of those mornings all the way around."

"What do you mean, Lanny? Haven't met your quota of tickets this month?"

"Now you don't really believe that old myth, do you?" he said and laughed as he opened the truck door. "Come on, I'll buy you a cup of coffee."

Lanny called in on his remote and told Dispatch that he'd be taking twenty minutes, and before long we were sitting in a booth in the cafe around the corner from City Hall. It's tough to sit across a table from someone you know as well as I knew him. There were moments when conversation and camaraderie came easy to us, even after all these years. But then, there were the other times, like right then, when the air between us seemed charged with feeling, not all good.

"You look a little pale. Anything I can help with?" he asked.

"Maybe," I said and tossed it around in my mind. "Maybe you can. What do you know about Whispering Pines?"

"Whispering what?"

"Whispering Pines. It's that holistic institute on top of Rims that passes itself off as a drug rehabilitation center."

The waitress approached the booth and took our orders. Lanny poured on the charm. By the time the blushing brunette left, she was stumbling over her words.

"Still the magic touch."

"I keep in practice," he said and grinned.

"I bet you do." Again that cutting edge slipped into my voice. "Anyway, do you know about that place?"

"Wasn't the kid they pulled out of the river connected up there?"

"Yeah, she was."

"Can't help you much. It's the first one I've heard of from there. They must run a pretty tight ship." He picked up on my silence. "Do you know something I don't?"

"No, not really. Just snooping around. It's complicated."

"I can deal with complicated."

"There's something going on up there."

Lanny leaned forward. "Like what?"

"I don't know . . . something. I've got a client who thinks they screwed up her kid." Conveniently, I left out everything else. "I've been running around in circles and keep ending up back at the same place. "Whispering Pines."

"Give me a few names, and I'll check them out for you."

I hesitated. "It wouldn't help, Lanny. But thanks for the offer."

"You don't know that. I can run them and see what I come up with."

I figured, what the hell? "Victor Stroud," I said as Lanny took a small notebook from his pocket and started writing. "And Frank Kuntz. I want to know if he's got a sheet on anything, domestic abuse, anything. Jean Dillard . . . no, forget that. She'd draw a blank."

"Who is she?" he asked and looked up.

"A school counselor. It's nothing." If anything, I wanted to ask him how far Cutter Gage's fingers reached into the police department, the whole damn community.

"What's all this have to do with what you're working on?"

"I don't know, yet. But I'm getting close. All these people tie in and . . ."

"And what?"

Anyone who has ever experienced a panic attack knows how fast they come on. My breath caught in my chest, my pulse raced, and I felt like the finger of doom was digging into my psyche.

"Forget it . . . forget I said anything. I've got to get out of here." The air thickened around me. I stood and started to leave.

"Whoa," he said and reached for my arm. "Look at your hands. You're shaking. Sit back down, Phoebe."

There wasn't much of a choice; my knees were buckling.

"Look, Lanny. I can't get into this right now. I need to figure a few things out . . ."

"Who knows you better than I do?"

I compiled a quick mental list and stopped at the fiftieth name. I took a deep breath and made my break. "I'll catch you later."

"What about the coffee?"

"Enjoy it. I'm out of here."

He wrote something down, tore a page out of his notebook, and shoved it in my hand. His hands felt rough as he folded my fingers closed over the piece of paper. "This is my home phone. If you change your mind, call me. We were a pretty good team once. Remember?"

My memory served me well. Too well. I got outside the cafe and took a couple of deep breaths. Just as I stepped off the curb, someone hit their car horn and slammed on their brakes. The hair stood up on my head.

"Watch the damned light, ya bimbo," someone screamed from a truck three feet from me.

I looked up at the traffic light and back at the mottled-faced guy driving the truck. In a burst of dramatic arm stiffening, he flipped me off with more enthusiasm than he looked capable of and pulled on through the intersection.

"The light's changed now, lady," a voice from beside me said.

I looked down into the smiling, if somewhat smug, cherubic face that was looking up at me. "Thanks. Where were you a minute ago?"

The smile left. "I . . . uh . . ." was all I heard as I ran across the intersection.

Lanny had been right. John wasn't in, but Tillie was. And more agitated than I could remember ever seeing her.

"He's been trying to get ahold of you, honey. Where will you be in the next hour or so? I'll get back to him when I—"

I looked over her shoulder out into the squad room. Kyle Old Wolf looked at me and motioned with his head toward the hallway.

"Tell him I'll come back around three this afternoon. You sure you don't know what he wants?"

"I'll give him the message."

There was something going on with just about everyone I had run into that day. I walked out into the hall, leaned against the wall, and waited for Kyle. The coldness of the marble soaked through my lightweight jacket and tensed the muscles in my back. I twisted my head from left to right, trying to loosen my neck and not notice the creep in handcuffs sitting on a bench beside the elevator.

The two deputies sitting on either side of him were talking with each other, totally unaware of the greasy little man running his tongue over his lips as he tried to make eye contact with me.

"Where are you parked?" Kyle walked by, spoke without looking at me, and kept moving toward the stairs.

"Out back."

I followed. Our footsteps echoed through the stairwell. He said nothing else until we'd walked out of the courthouse and toward the city parking lot. It took me a halfhearted run to keep up with him.

"Kyle, I'm not into this jogging crap. What's on you mind?"

I stopped and leaned against the truck.

"How's the beast running?" he asked.

"This is about my truck?"

He scowled, looked around, and leaned toward me. "You didn't hear this from me."

"I haven't heard anything."

"I've been trying to call your place. I didn't want to leave anything on your machine. Remember that kid they fished out of the river?"

"Shawna Unger?"

"Right. I was up at the hospital and ran into the coroner. The kid didn't drown."

"Impossible. John said that—"

"No matter. They're really keeping a lid on this. Now get this."

I just stood there and stared at him.

"They figure she crawled out and somebody bashed her head and rolled her back in. She was dead when she hit the water the second time."

"Go on, Kyle."

"Joss asks me to have a cup of coffee with him, and I figure a little inside information is good for the soul, so I agree. I follow him down to the cafeteria. He's shook, Phoebe. Really shook. Kids get to him."

"What the hell did he find?"

"First of all, there wasn't a drop of water in her lungs. At first I figured it was working on a kid that had him rattled. Then we got talking, or rather I was doing the talking. He was so distracted . . ." Kyle took his hat off and swung it across his thigh, and then placed it back on his head. "My first instinct was that those two kids she was with knew damned well she was dead when they phoned it in."

"Kyle, for God's sake, what the hell did he find?"

He hesitated, took a deep breath, and moved closer.

"It wasn't what he found, it was the scene. We were there within minutes after she took a dive off the bridge. We had cops everywhere, and the whole place was cordoned off. You know how fucking thorough he is . . ."

"Keep going, Kyle."

A cruiser pulled up next to us. A deputy got out, walked around his car, and approached us.

"I've got a report to go over with this guy. Get ahold of Joss. I told him you had some interest in the girl," Kyle whispered.

"He's not going to tell me a damn thing, Kyle." I smiled at the approaching deputy and tried talking under my breath and gritting my teeth. "Don't leave me hanging like this."

We stood there like grinning fools, trying to carry on a hushed conversation while the deputy got closer and closer.

"You're right, meet me at the morgue tonight. Ten o'clock. I'll set it up," Kyle whispered; he looked down at the ground and then back up toward the deputy. "Hey, Vanada. You ready to go over that report?"

"That's what I'm here for. Don't want to cut into your . . ." The guy grinned and eyed me.

"No problem. Phoebe, great talking to you. Catch you later," Kyle said and strode off.

I got into the truck and sat there. The city bus drove by, leaving a trail of diesel stink in its wake, and the lunch crowd was bouncing up at the intersection waiting for the light to change. Business as usual. That is, except for Jimmy Padilla and Shawna Unger.

My cryptic conversation with Kyle only served to confuse the names and the issues, bond the living and the dead into a macabre cast of characters, all with something in common; they were all connected with Whispering Pines. I turned the key, pumped the starter, and backed out of the lot.

Donna Jo Johnson was alone in the office when I walked through the door. She looked up when she saw me approaching the counter.

"Repossessed any hearing aids today?" I said and forced myself to smile.

"That hurts. You know I hate this job." She feigned insult and threw a file on the counter. "I did my best. You're not going to like this, but the guy you're looking for, I had to run a skip trace on him."

"And what did you get?"

"Triple A credit rating. He could buy the state of Texas if he wanted to. It wasn't always like that. Five years ago he had a practice outside of D.C. and was in real financial straits. He wasn't out here very long when things took a sudden turn for the better and he cleaned up all his debts in one fell swoop."

I turned away from the counter, dug a quarter out of my pocket, stuck it in the M&M's machine, and turned the knob. It made sense to keep my mouth busy.

"Are you sure?"

"I'm sure."

There wasn't anything else to say. I turned around and started to leave.

"Phoebe, I think you just got a ticket. A cop just pulled away from in back of your truck."

By the time I made it outside, the cruiser had disappeared into traffic up the hill. There was a single driver behind the wheel, that much I could tell. There wasn't a ticket on my car. I didn't figure there would be. My paranoia was so rampant by that time, I crawled under the truck to see if my brake line was intact. It was. I wasn't.

When I opened the door and got in, a piece of paper fluttered down from the dashboard and landed on the floor. I picked it up. One side was blank. I turned it over. It was a bad photocopy, grainy with almost no contrast. It didn't matter. Kehly looked back at me, smiling, her mortarboard tipped slightly to the side.

I'd challenged the Ides, and they were coming back at me with all they had. Hard. I drove out to Ascension Cemetery.

The temperature had thrown ten degrees to the wind. The sky had turned angry and threatening. The tops of the pine trees above my head swayed back and forth as the wind picked up. Maybe there was thunder or lightning. I don't remember.

I could feel the stone hardness of the bench, the rigid steeliness of my spine, and the cool, wet rain as it ran down my face.

"Talk to me, please talk to me. You said you'd always be there for me, Ben. Well . . ." I tried swallowing the lump in my throat. "Well . . . the fact of the matter is, I know you figure in this somehow. Somewhere. I'm in trouble, Ben . . ."

A raven screamed above my head in the trees. I looked up and saw it as it spread its black wings and craned its neck down toward me. It cocked its head to one side and stared at me with its orange-ringed black eyes. With one lunge it flew off the branch, swooped down toward me and off into the rain.

". . . You've got to help me. Someone, a cop, is following me. And I don't know why." I reached into my pocket and took out the folded picture of Kehly. As I opened it, drops of rain hit it, joined others, and ran down the front of the paper.

"Somebody has Kehly's picture and . . . and I don't know what they're trying to tell me."

I waved the paper out in front of me. "If you know, then tell me. Help me, please help . . ."

Thunder resounded above my head and drowned out my words. I covered my mouth with my hand and choked back the storm that was rising in my throat. A flood of emotions battered against my will as I stood, dropped the wet paper to the ground, and left. The dead weren't talking.

16

THE RAIN HADN'T LET UP. I pulled the thick terry-cloth robe closer around my body, leaned against the wooden edge of the window, and stared out at the street. The apartment had darkened without my even noticing. Somewhere, a phone was ringing. Persistently.

I turned away from the window and made my way toward the sound, picked up the receiver, and mutely listened for someone to speak. It was the fifth such ritual I had performed in the last two hours. And, for the fifth time, there was no one on the other end of the line.

Eventually, someone would speak. If not today, maybe a day from now, a week from now. It would come. The Ides always delivered, but on their own terms. All I had to do was wait, and prepare.

I depressed the disconnect button for a couple of seconds, let it up, and dialed Kehly's number. I took a deep breath when she answered and hoped my voice wouldn't betray my feelings.

"What's up?" she asked.

"I told you I'd call . . . so, I'm calling. Rudy around?"

"Nope. He's got Guards this weekend. A couple of the gals at work wanted to run up to Chico Hot Springs, but the weather sucks. What do you think?"

"Sounds good to me. What's a little weather?"

My motives were purely selfish. It didn't take a psychic to figure out that whoever had taken her picture from my apartment was capable of using her as a pawn in a game yet to be played. The rules weren't out on the table yet.

"You're right. But I do have an option. Mama called a little while ago and wanted me to come spend the weekend with her. It's a tough choice." She giggled. "On the other hand, I could just as easily curl up on the couch with a good book, or someone who's read one."

"Kehly . . . someone broke into my apartment last night."

"Jesus. Did they take anything?"

"Your graduation picture. I—"

"My what?"

"I'm working on this . . . uh, this case, and some of the people involved are a little off side. You know what I mean?"

"No, I don't know what you mean. Why don't you make it a little clearer? Why the hell would someone want *my* picture?"

"I don't know. It's got me a little concerned . . ."

"Shit, Phoebe. Does this have anything to do with all those damned questions you were asking me about the treatment center? Does it? God . . . it's just like when Ben . . ."

"No," I lied, thinking that she'd freak out if I told her the truth. "Don't get yourself all worked up. Some punk probably thought the frame was expensive. No big deal. It's just good to cover all the angles."

"Are you sure?"

"No, but the odds are that it's nothing. Nothing at all."

"And that's why you've called me more in the last two weeks than you have in six months. Right?"

"I gotta run. Charlene's tonight, remember?"

"I hope it goes well. It's going to mean a lot to her, Phoebe. Is George going to be there?"

"With any luck at all, no."

"Be nice. She's family."

"I'll call you later if it's not too late. If you don't answer I'll check at Mama's. Take care, Kehly."

For a minute, she said nothing.

"Phoebe?"

"Yeah?"

"I love you."

"Me too."

"I want you to say it, Phoebe."

"I just did."

"No, you didn't. Say it. You'll feel better."

"Christ, I love you too. So?"

"So . . . good-bye. Good luck tonight. I know how hard it is for you to go out there."

The line went dead. I didn't feel any better.

* * *

Emerald Hills sits in the foothills above Lockwood, Billings's step-child. People pay big bucks for unpaved roads, a few scrub pines on a couple of acres, and a good view of the city lights at night.

Prickly pear cactus and yucca plants thrive in the sandy soil, as do diamondback rattlesnakes, which sun themselves on sandstone cliffs in the summer and hibernate in colonies beneath the Great Plains in winter. It's a stark place, one I would never opt to live in, but Ben loved it.

I was thankful for the darkness, the soft sound of rain beating against the top of the truck, and the mesmerizing sound of the wipers as they fanned across the windshield. It reminded me of another time, another trip to Ben's house.

For that brief time I drove the winding road through the pitch-black night, I had nothing on my mind except the rain and the wipers. Looking back, I can see that it was the lull before the storm. I turned onto the road that led to Charlene's, stopped at the crest of the hill, and looked down at the house. It was ablaze with lights and life.

I wanted to turn around, leave, drive back through the night, but I needed what memories were left inside that house. I drove down the hill and pulled up beside Charlene's Volkswagen Bug, turned off the ignition, and got out.

My legs were shaking as I pushed the doorbell. Charlene opened the door, stood there for just a minute, then reached out and grabbed my hand.

"I was worried you wouldn't come," she said. "It's good to have you, Phoebe. George was going to grill something, but look at it outside." She waved her hand toward the yard and rattled on, talking faster than usual. "Jeez, I'm not nervous or anything. I always make my dinner guests, I don't mean you're a guest, Phoebe . . . you're family . . . what I'm trying to say is . . ."

"Why not try 'come in'?" I couldn't help smiling. I'd loved her for as long as I had known her.

"Right," she said and blushed. "Come in. Dinner's ready. And it just happens to be your favorite."

I walked through the door past her and sniffed the air.

"Venison roast?"

"Right. You've still got a good nose." Charlene guided me through the living room and into the dining room. "Sit down, I'll get you a cup of coffee. George is down in the garage. I'll yell at him."

"Slow down, Charlene." I turned and looked at her. "I'd love a cup of coffee. Just slow down."

I sat down at the dining room table and smiled at her.

"I'm nervous. More than I thought I'd be. If you think I'm bad, you should see George. He's cleaned the same shelf at least ten times in the last hour."

"Let's just get through this. . . ." I said it before I even realized what I had said. The smile left her face, her shoulders sagged. "I didn't mean it like that. I'm a little uptight myself. It's been a long time, Charlene. This is hard . . ."

"Hard on all of us." George's voice startled me. "How you doin', Fee?"

He was leaning against the kitchen door, wiping his hands on a towel. It could just as well have been Ben standing there, coming up from the garage after working on the truck. We looked at each other until I couldn't hold the gaze anymore. I rested my elbow on the table, leaned my forehead onto my hand, and shook my head.

"Fuck," I said, again reaching for great articulate heights.

"No, just dinner. You should have brought a date," he said, walked over to Charlene, and put his arm around her. "Venison will have to do. It's a little whitetail I got last fall, and she'd been feeding on wild plums. It should be just as satisfying as . . ."

"Bambi's mother, no doubt?" I looked at them both. "Enough . . . I'm not up to any mental fencing. How are you, George?"

He walked over and grabbed my shoulder. "It's good to see you. You didn't bring that killer cat of yours, did you?"

"Cat?" Charlene asked.

"Remember the third degree you gave me over those scratches on my back? Phoebe can back up my story. She keeps a bobcat in her apartment."

"True?" Charlene looked at me and grinned.

"Exaggerated, but true. My cat did attack him. Must have been his after-shave."

We all laughed, still ill at ease but making the most of the situation. We maintained that level for the next two hours. They were happy together. I hated it. He was considerate with Charlene to the point of being sappy. Charlene, as she always had, mothered the hell out of him, and waited on him hand and foot.

She insisted I sit and watch her do the supper dishes. George disappeared back out to the garage, leaving us alone. It was time to exhume whatever she could remember about the weeks before Ben's death.

"More coffee?" she asked and sat down at the table.

"No. Not for me," I said and covered my cup with my hand. "I'm glad we have some time."

"Me too. It means more to me than you know. I've missed you." Her eyes teared as she reached out and clasped my cup with her hand. "You're my little sis. You always will be."

I choked back the rock-hard lump in my throat and squeezed her hand. "I'm glad I came. Charlene?"

"What?"

"I need to talk to you. I need to ask you . . ."

"Anything, you know that. What's on your mind?"

"Ben . . ."

Charlene stood up from the table and walked to the sink. "I hate these stainless steel sinks," she said as she picked up a can of Comet and started shaking cleanser into the sink. "They take more work than you realize."

"Charlene, please."

She turned around and glared at me. Her hands were placed protectively over her stomach. "I'm pregnant, Phoebe. Three months. We're thrilled about it. Please, I'm begging you, leave this alone. I loved Ben. You loved Ben. But I was his wife. He was what I lived for, and when he died, I died. My life with him was buried with him. Christ . . ."

"I'm not trying to—"

"Then don't. My life is with George now. He's a good man, Phoebe. We both cherish Ben's memory."

"This isn't about George and it isn't about you, it's about Ben, and the time right before he—"

"Phoebe . . ." She looked suddenly tired, strained. "What do you want from me? Wasn't treating me like some pariah for three years enough for you? Punishment enough for me?"

She was right. I had punished her. "I don't want anything. Something, uh . . . this could be critical, Charlene."

"Critical to what?" She leaned back against the counter.

"Just let me talk with you about this. Just this one time. Please?"

She walked to the table, sat down, and stared at me. When she didn't say anything, didn't protest, I took the leap. It was hard to guess what her reaction would be.

"Did Ben seem . . ." I searched for the word. "Did he seem all right?"

"Are you asking me if he was stable? Depressed? Suicidal?"

She wasn't going to make it easy.

"I guess that is what I'm asking."

158

She leaned back in the chair and closed her eyes. I heard George rattling around in the garage. *God, don't let him come in now*, I thought. Charlene opened her eyes, looked at me, and slumped in the chair.

"There was a time when I asked myself those questions a million times a day. So much of what happened is a blur; I walked through it like a zombie. Now it's in the past somewhere. Now when I remember, sometimes I feel happy and sometimes it still feels like I have a cat inside me, trying to claw its way out."

"Charlene, believe me, I wouldn't put you or myself through this if it could be avoided. Was he suicidal?"

Her answer was blunt. Confident. "No. He wasn't."

"But?" I sensed more.

"Things hadn't been easy for Ben for a couple of months. He was, I don't know, different. You know how easygoing he was."

I nodded, remembering his easy smile, the laughter that came so quickly.

"He was on edge. Depressed? Maybe. Right before, the week before in fact, he had a hard time sleeping."

"Did you ever ask him what was going on?"

"Of course I did," she snapped defensively. "He always sloughed it off, though. You know how he was; he carried the ball for the rest of the world. In the beginning, I figured it was the job. You know how that goes. They're under incredible strain. But then, later on . . ."

"When later on?"

"A couple of weeks before he, before *it* happened. Some kid, a girl kept calling the house. It unnerved him. I even confronted him one time and asked him if he was having an affair."

"What did he say?"

She looked at me curiously. "You know what he'd say, Phoebe. He said no. Christ, Ben wasn't the fooling around kind. You know that. I was just having an insecure moment."

"Yeah, I do know that."

"He could have, you know. He was . . ." Her voice cracked. "Then I was cleaning the garage one day, and I lifted this box down. It started a big fight between us."

"Why?"

"There was a book in this particular box under some other junk, old rags, that kind of thing. I thought it was odd that the book was in with those kinds of things."

"Charlene, what kind of book was it?"

"One of those blank ones that you write in. A journal of sorts. I was curious, so I started paging through it."

"What did it say?"

"Something silly. Something like a young girl would write. Kinda dramatic. Let me think."

"Please, Charlene."

"Book of Shadows. That was it. High drama."

"Are you sure?"

She grimaced. "I'm sure."

"Did you ask Ben about it?"

"I didn't have to. He walked into the garage when I was going through it, Phoebe. He went into a rage. I'd never seen him like that before. It was the first time he ever really scared me."

"I don't buy that Ben could have ever gotten violent with you, Charlene."

"I never said that. I said he was in a rage, and he was. He threw everything back into the box, put it on the shelf, and told me never to go through his stuff again. Two weeks later he was dead."

"Did you ever talk to anyone about it?"

"I may have mentioned the incident to Michael. It was during the time that Ben was having a rough go of it, and I was worried. As I recall, he told me Ben had been trying to get ahold of him, but Michael had been busy and hadn't gotten back to him. But he did promise me he would."

"That figures. Did Ben ever say anything else?"

"About the book? No. Not until later. But his moods started getting worse. He looked terrible, Phoebe. He wasn't sleeping, and even when he was on days he wouldn't come home until late, sometimes not until early morning. Two days before he—" She stopped, wiped a tear from her cheek, and continued. "He insisted I stay with his mother when he worked nights. He didn't want me alone in the house and even went so far as to buy me a gun. You know how I hate them."

"I don't believe you didn't push for some answers."

"For Christ's sake, Fee. I didn't know what the hell to think. The morning it . . . it happened, he called. Something had changed. He was more up than he had been for months. He kept telling me over and over that things were going to be okay. He even said he was going to put the lawn in."

"The lawn?"

"He hadn't talked about doing anything to the house for months. That one little statement gave me more hope than you can imagine."

"Did he ever mention a place, Whispering Pines?"

"Whispering Pines . . . maybe, maybe he did. That sure sounds familiar. Or maybe I just saw it written somewhere. But, yeah, I do know that name. Why?"

"Just wondering. Charlene, what happened to the bracelet, the Medic Alert bracelet that you had made for Ben? Do you have it?"

"Phoebe," she said and giggled nervously. "Why are you asking about that bracelet?"

"Is it around? It's critical that I know what happened to it. Was it buried with—"

"Stop it, Phoebe. I don't know what happened to it. Jesus. Do you think I was checking him for jewelry, for Christ's sake?"

She looked hurt, and it made me feel like a heel. "Forget it."

She covered her face with her hands, mumbled something I couldn't understand, and then looked back up at me. "I think he lost it."

"What?" I asked.

"The bracelet. Now that you brought it up, I don't remember seeing it. Isn't that odd? And I can't remember the last time I saw it."

"Do you have that book?"

"I doubt it. George cleaned all those shelves off last year. We'd had some tough spring rains, and the garage had leaked. I suppose it just got thrown out. Should I ask him if—"

"No," I blurted out so fast, she looked shocked.

"What's this all about?" Charlene leaned forward. Her expression demanded an answer. Any answer.

"Charlene, I can't say anything right now. But promise me you'll keep this between us. Only us."

"George is my husband, Phoebe. We have no secrets."

"There was a time you and I had secrets. Please."

She studied my face, struggling with her loyalty to her husband and a memory of a time when we did have secrets and ultimate trust between us.

"I won't say anything. I'm uncomfortable with it, but I give you my word."

I rested my head on the table and then looked back up toward her. "Thank you. Hopefully, I'll be able to explain all of this to you very soon."

"I've saved something for you, Phoebe. There was so much going on during that week after . . . after the funeral, I totally spaced it out." She started to rise from the table and stopped midway. "That was something else that was curious. He kept telling me that if anything were to happen to him, that you should . . . no, he was more emphatic than that. He said you had to have this. That you'd know what to do with it."

"With what?"

She finished standing and looked toward me. "It might take me a minute to find it. Wait here. Okay?"

"Sure."

She got up and left the room. I stood, walked to the picture window in the living room, and looked out into the night. The rain was still falling. The phone rang behind me. I turned, and George was standing in the doorway watching me. The phone kept ringing.

"Would you get that, Phoebe? George must not hear it." Charlene yelled from somewhere down the hall.

Without taking his eyes off me, George reached to the wall, took the phone off the hook, and answered it. He walked around the corner. I couldn't make out what he was saying; his voice was low, secretive. Charlene walked back into the room.

"Who was that?" she asked as he hung up the phone.

"I've got to go in."

"Now?"

"Right," he answered. "Do I have any clean shirts?"

"Sure. They're hanging up in the laundry room. Did someone call in sick?"

George looked at me for a second more and then turned to Charlene and smiled. "Yeah, someone called in sick." He kissed her on the forehead and walked off down the hall.

"Here it is," she said and handed me a small brown sack.

I reached into the sack and pulled out a small zippered book. My eyes filled with tears. "Ben's missal. My God, we got these when we were kids. Did we get in trouble with these things. Are you sure this is for me?"

"I'm sure."

"I probably need to brush up on my prayers." I looked at my watch and smiled up at her. "I've got an appointment at ten. Guess I better hit the road. Thanks for dinner, Charlene. I really did enjoy being here with you."

We hugged each other. I wanted to hold on to her forever. It felt good, like coming home. She walked me to the front door and watched me until I got into the truck. I waved and pulled out of the driveway and up the road. I gripped the steering wheel and tried to keep my hands from shaking.

▽

17

THE TRUCK STARTED CHOKING at the top of the driveway. I'd barely made it over the crest of the hill when it sputtered and died. Maybe it hated leaving home; maybe it felt Ben's presence the same way I did.

I hit the steering wheel a couple of times, knowing damn well it wouldn't do any good. I reached under the seat, grabbed a flashlight I kept there, and shined it into the glove compartment. What I needed was there: a pair of pliers and a piece of coat hanger wire bent into an L-shape.

I set the emergency brake, got out, and crawled under the truck. I clutched the flashlight in my armpit and directed it up to the plug at the bottom of the gas line. I've always been a little claustrophobic, so my strategy was consistent: get in and get out.

Gasoline started dripping slowly from the hole and onto the ground. I crammed the end of the wire up the hole and rodded it out the best I could. The plug rolled off my chest and onto the ground, and it took me a minute to locate it and put it back in the hole.

As I started to scoot out from under the truck, I heard footsteps on the gravel and someone step up onto the running board. I looked toward the rear of the truck and saw nothing. The truck sagged just a little as someone sat down behind the steering wheel.

Every muscle in my body froze. "Hey! What's going—" I said and tried to scoot out from under the truck.

A heavily booted foot came down on my shin. "Don't move, Phoebe." The voice was low, threatening. "I just took the brake off. It'd be a damn shame if this heavy old truck started rolling."

I tried to move my leg under the grinding weight. "George? What the fuck are you doing? Get your foot off my—"

"Shut up and listen," he yelled. I knew he wasn't kidding

around. "You're snooping around and asking questions about shit that isn't any of your damned business. What's it going to take to back you off?"

"Look, you son of a bitch—"

"You're not in a bargaining position, Phoebe. This is my best shot. Keep the fuck away from Whispering Pines. Have you got that? No more questions. No more *nothing*. Clear?"

"You think I'm afraid of you, George? You're wrong." I struggled against his foot.

The pressure let up. I was debating trying to scoot out the other side just as he grabbed both my ankles and jerked me from underneath the truck. My head hit the edge of the frame and bounced back down on the gravel. The smell of gasoline was strong. The door of the truck slammed shut. In one smooth movement he leaned down, picked me up under my arms, and lifted me off the ground.

My head was reeling and throbbing in pain. The smell of gasoline fumes didn't help any. George slammed me against the side of the truck and held me there by pressing his forearm against the top of my chest just shy of my throat.

"If I didn't know better," I gurgled as he pushed his arm up toward my throat, "I'd think you were coming on to me. I have to tell you, this kind of foreplay is a real turnoff."

"I told you to shut the fuck up. This isn't kiddy shit, Phoebe. You don't have a big brother coming around to save you. This is for real."

I struggled against him. My throat burned under his arm. I couldn't breathe.

"In a breath," he whispered as he brought his face close to mine. I could feel warm bursts of breath as he spit the words at me. "All I have to do is hold my arm where it is, just exerting a little more pressure, until you pass out. Somebody would find you, maybe it would be me, tomorrow morning with your fucking skull crushed under the back tire. It wouldn't take much, just this much more . . ."

Helplessly, I hung there, my breath cut off. A low buzzing sound started drilling through my head as I neared unconsciousness. I had no control over my eyes as they rolled upward, pleading, submitting, under his grip. My shoulders were numb, my hands tingled.

I crashed to the ground, gagging, gasping, and puking bile into the dirt.

"I'll know if you talk to anyone, ask any more questions, or dig any deeper. Have you got the message? It wouldn't take much. No more warnings, Phoebe. No more."

The only thing I was aware of was being on all fours, trying to stop the spasms that were wrenching my stomach and the dull throb that hammered my brain. Gravel flew into my face as he pulled his truck around mine and sped off down the road into the night.

I reached the apartment, parked the truck in back, shoved Ben's missal into my jacket pocket, and crawled over the back fence. Once inside, I headed for the bathroom and emptied my stomach of dinner. I closed the door to the bathroom before I turned on the bathroom light and looked at myself in the mirror.

There was a dent in my forehead from the truck frame and a small cut above my eye where a piece of gravel had flown up and hit me when George pulled away. There wasn't one square inch of my body that wasn't vibrating with anger. The bastard. The dirty low-down bastard was in on all of it.

My paranoia at being followed by the cops melted away and became high-octane fuel for my rage and determination. I put the lid down on the toilet and sat on it. The missal felt bulky in my pocket. I pulled it out and held it. Instinctively I grasped the small brass cross hanging from the zipper and unzipped it. It opened naturally to the middle.

I scanned the pages. At the bottom Ben had underlined a Latin passage. At one time Latin was important in the Mass; it kept the Latinless confused and in awe. I followed the lines and tried to make sense of them.

Sanguis Domini nostri Jesu Christi custodiat animam meam in vitam aeternam. Amen. The words were clumsy on my tongue. I could have saved a little time by reading the translation on the opposing page. "May the blood of our Lord Jesus Christ preserve my soul for everlasting life. Amen."

It was out of character. We both hated Latin and had avoided it at each and every turn of our Catholic upbringing. To write in one's missal with anything permanent had to fall under some category of sin. This was more Michael's style. God would forgive someone like Michael. I looked in the front of the missal to make sure it even belonged to Ben. It did.

Missals, for Ben and me, were for passing notes back and forth in mass or for hiding our most secret thoughts. Mama and Dad would never have thought of searching our missals like they did our dresser drawers or beneath our mattresses or in the depths of our pockets.

I searched the corners of the pages for any that were earmarked.

Toward the back I spied one and turned to the page. Tucked inside was a small receipt from a Rapid Mart store dated March 22, 1986, the day Ben died. On the right-hand page was the prayer to obtain proper disposition for death. My eyes scanned through it.

"God rewards the good, and punishes the wicked . . . that he died also for me . . . I have committed many sins . . . I turn away from them and hate them . . . I love you, O my God, forgive me . . . My God, have mercy on me!"

I sat back and balanced the missal on my lap. He knew he was going to die. He knew. It didn't make sense that he would read the prayer and then blow his brains out. It did make sense if he thought someone else might do it for him. And why was the Rapid Mart receipt in it in the first place? Unless he had it with him at the time.

My fingers clasped the small cross. I started to zip the missal closed when I noticed it still bulged slightly in the middle. I opened it back up and shook it, hoping anything tucked inside would fall to the floor. Nothing did. I turned it over in my hand and checked the front and back covers. Nothing was there.

I checked the ribbon bookmarks; they marked nothing that had any significance. I pulled the faded ribbons tight to stretch the length of the missal. One came loose. Without thinking I tried to tuck it back in the spine of the book.

I grabbed my toothbrush from the shelf above the sink and used the flat end to push the tip of the ribbon down in the spine. A piece of paper dropped to the floor from the bottom. At first I thought it was part of the lining; then I reached down and picked it up.

It was folded several times and was about an inch wide and five or so inches long. All my senses focused on that skinny piece of folded paper. I laid the missal down on the edge of the tub and slowly opened the paper.

The names were there. Most of them. No dates, no phone numbers, just names that had become familiar to me three years after they had become familiar to Ben. Malcolm Gage, Victor Stroud, Jennifer Kuntz, and Whispering Pines. At the bottom, scrawled almost illegibly, were the lines

Never let a man imagine that he can pursue a good end by evil means, without sinning against his own soul. The evil effect on himself is certain.

Someone had underlined and circled three words with such pressure that it carved a pencil-wide groove into the paper and tore a small hole at one end of the line. The words *by evil means* stood out from all the rest. I had asked for a sign, anything. Now I had one. All I had to do was figure out what the hell it meant.

Kyle Old Wolf was sitting on the flagstone wall that fronted St. Joseph's Hospital. I was fifteen minutes late.

"I wondered if you'd show." He jumped off the wall and started walking down the sidewalk.

"I thought we were going in."

"We are. We've got to go through the emergency room. Security and all of that. You ready for this?"

"Probably not. How grossed out am I going to be?"

"Depends on you. I come from a long line of scalpers, remember? Nothing grosses me out."

Kyle talked briefly with a private security guard and motioned me toward the elevator. We got on, and he pushed the B button. Again my claustrophobic tendencies took over. I took a deep breath and let it out a second later when the door opened on the opposite side. We stepped out.

"Kyle, I want you to look at something for me and tell me if it means anything to you." I dug the quotation out of my pocket and handed it to him.

"Do I win a prize?" he asked and grinned as he unfolded it.

He read it and said nothing as he handed it back to me. "Well, does it?"

"Where did you come onto this?"

"It doesn't matter. Have you heard it before or not?"

"The whole damn state has heard it, Phoebe."

"What do you mean?"

"When the MIB was formed, and Cutter Gage got the top seat, Gage went after this guy that tried his best to block his appointment. Gage sicked his hounds on him and dug up enough to smear the guy pretty badly. And he held the information until the time was right."

"Go on."

"The guy was running for a congressional seat, and sure enough—"

"Gage pulled the plug."

"Right. The guy had been taking a few kickbacks from some out-of-state interests that were trying to bring something in, I think it was a meat-packing outfit, and Gage got him."

"Why am I not surprised?"

"The guy tried defending his actions saying that he had done it to bring some jobs into the state and that anything he did, he did for a good end. God knows where Gage found this," Kyle said and handed me the small piece of paper, "but he did, and it was on every damn television and radio station, and plastered in print all over the state."

"How long ago?" I asked and tucked it back in my pocket.

"Two and a half, maybe three years ago. Where'd you come across it?"

"It doesn't matter. I just needed to connect a name with it."

The long, badly lit tunnel stretched before us. There were no frills down here. A maze of pipes ran over our heads. There was a deathly chill in the air that made sense to me.

"This place gives me the creeps. Are you sure he's down here?"

"Doc Joss? He said he would be. No reason to question it."

"I really do appreciate this, Kyle. Maybe . . ."

He laughed, stopped in front of a benign-looking door, and pushed a buzzer.

"I've been doing a little digging myself. We'll talk about it when we get out of here." As we waited for the door to open, he shuffled his boot on the tile floor.

"Long line of scalpers, huh?"

"So they tell me."

The door opened. A short, white-coated, graying man in his late fifties looked up at us. He removed his glasses and placed them on top of his balding head, rubbed the bridge of his nose with his thumb and index finger, and said nothing as he stepped aside and allowed us passage into the morgue.

It was a lot colder than the hallway. It definitely wasn't a big-city morgue with walls of stainless steel lined with doors. In fact, it resembled a lab more than anything, with the exception of three steel surgical tables anchored to the floor with drains underneath them. There wasn't a body to be seen.

"This is the woman I told you about, Doc. Can you tell her what you told me?"

He eyed me for a minute and then shrugged. "Kyle told me you knew the girl. That you had an interest in her somehow."

"Yes, I do . . . I mean I did. I do have an interest in how she died," I said, sounding like an idiot.

"There's no reason to be nervous, young lady. The dead can't hurt anyone. Only the living. Ask your friend here, the sheriff—"

"Deputy," Kyle gently corrected him.

"Whatever. Maybe you should be sheriff." He laughed.

"I've just completed my report. I'll be giving it to your boss tomorrow. I would appreciate it if neither of you would say—"

"You've got our word on that," Kyle broke in.

The coroner studied me for a moment, then walked toward a door at the far end of the room, opened it, and disappeared inside. I heard the wheels of the gurney before I saw it. It entered with him pushing from behind. Unceremoniously, he kicked the door closed behind him.

My eyes were riveted on the form hidden inside the white plastic bag on top of the gurney. He pushed it close to one of the tables underneath a high-intensity light and positioned the gleaming globe so that it illuminated the immediate area.

I could hear my breath draw in. So could the coroner.

"She's been on refrigeration, my dear. Decomposition is at a minimum," he said as he started unzipping the bag.

The sound tore through the room, magnified by my own fear and repulsion. Kyle walked up beside me as I moved toward the plastic shroud.

"Sure you're up to this?" he whispered in my ear.

"Just catch me if I fall," I whispered back.

I don't know what I expected, but without warning of any kind, the Doc, as Kyle referred to him, threw back the top of the white bag. I didn't know what I was looking at. I didn't gasp. I couldn't. I leaned closer and tried to figure out what the hell was in front of me.

An apron of white tissue looked back at me from where a face should have been. Long trails of caramel-colored hair hung obscenely from under the glistening mask and ended just above her bare breasts. I must have gasped or wavered. Kyle reached out and held my arm.

The older man looked toward me as he placed his hand under her neck and lifted her head. In one swift but gentle motion, he turned Shawna Unger's scalp right side out and tucked her hair behind her neck. He had peeled the entire top of her head off and had left it hanging over her face.

"Shit," I said. It was all I managed to squeeze from my larynx. I felt a surge of blood to my stomach as my knees started to give way.

"Sorry about that," he said offhandedly. "I have some minor things to put back together. I did get her skull stuffed and the lid back on, but that damn phone ringing all day would distract anyone."

"Get to it, Doc," Kyle murmured. I could tell the Frankenstein-ish floor show had gotten to him also.

"When they brought this young lady to me, it was assumed she had drowned. I didn't question that," he said and moved around to the top of the table. "I assumed the postmortem would be routine, so I opened her up and was curious to find she didn't have any water in her lungs. I noted that on my report. There were some bruises on her upper arms, sustained before death, some superficial scrapes on her chest that I concluded were from the bank when she crawled out or was pulled—"

"Pulled or crawled out of the water?" I asked.

"What'd I tell you?" Kyle whispered under his breath.

I pulled my arm free from Kyle's grasp and stepped closer to the table.

"This young woman was not a drowning victim. Her heart did show some clinical manifestations of a myocardial infarction—"

"A what?"

"A heart attack. Her age threw me on that one, but I've been in this business long enough not to rule anything else out. There was no trauma to the chest indicating a blow of any kind, nor was there any degeneration of the heart tissue to indicate some congenital condition that had just never been caught. For all intents and purposes, she was a well-developed, healthy young woman around . . . I guess seventeen to eighteen years old. A real puzzle."

I looked down Shawna's nude, pallid body. A large, neatly sutured scar ran the entire length of her chest. Her hands were flat against her hips, as though she were lying at attention. Her face was garish and swollen, but peaceful. Her eyelids were parted just enough to allow me to see the dullness of her once light-filled eyes.

"We ran a standard check on her urine for drugs. There was a heavy concentration of tranquilizer. Thorazine to be exact. I'd say she had it during the past week of her life at least. I did draw some blood so that I could run a complete screen."

"What are you looking for?" Kyle asked.

"Anything I can find. If she's had anything in the not-so-distant past, that's where I'll find it, and I'm taking a wild guess that she has."

I was in a state of cadaver shock.

"Come over here," he said, left Shawna, and walked to a counter on the far side of the room. He leaned over, opened a small refrigerator, lifted out a large covered receptacle, and placed it on top of the counter.

He threw the cloth off the top. Gleaming and easily identifiable was a perfect gray mass of brain, Shawna Unger's brain.

"This is interesting."

He turned the bowl around. The top back of the brain, an expanse of convoluted matter about four inches long, looked red and angry.

"Do you see this area?" He spoke low, leaning close to the bowl, probing the bloody tissue with his finger. "Do you know what it is?"

"Is it a tumor of some kind?" Kyle, again in charge of questions, moved closer for a better look. I kept my distance.

"No. It's the result of a very professional blow to the back of the head." Without warning he raised his hand and brought it down on the stainless steel counter. I jumped a foot off the floor.

He removed his glasses and rubbed the bridge of his nose. "My guess is that this young woman did in fact jump off the bridge and somehow made her way to shore. She coughed up a certain amount of water that she would have ingested when she hit the river. There were traces of that in her esophagus."

He stood and walked back to Shawna's lifeless body.

"Then something scared her enough that she went into an arrhythmia. At the same time, someone delivered a blow to the back of her neck with such force that it crushed two vertebrae and ruptured her cerebellum. Death was instantaneous."

"Shit." I gasped.

Kyle turned to me, grabbed me by the arm, and led me toward the door. "Let's get out of here," he whispered.

When we got into the elevator, I leaned over and put my head between my legs to keep from passing out.

"Are you game for a midnight run?" he asked.

"To where?"

"Whispering Pines."

$\triangledown$

18

I HAD BARELY GOTTEN into Kyle's Blazer, had turned to lean against the passenger-side door so that I could look directly at him when, suddenly, there was no door. Strong hands gripped my shoulder as I fell backward. I grabbed for the edge of the Blazer and held on. It didn't take much to rip my hand away.

Before I knew it I was slammed up against the vehicle, my arms pulled behind my back. Pain shot up my arm as someone I hadn't even seen yet hit a handcuff against my wrist and snapped it shut. Kyle, in turn, was pressed up against the other side. I could see the left edge of his body, his left arm disappearing behind his back.

A strong, insistent hand pressed my face up against the cold metal; another hand patted me down. Without a word, the same strength that had pulled me out spun me around. I didn't recognize the face. The don't-give-me-any-shit-or-I'll-hurt-you expression, I recognized.

They didn't bring Kyle in with me. I tried to see where the other unmarked car went but missed it when my own driver whipped a U-turn and headed downtown. Neither man in the front seat said a word, not even when we pulled up to the side door of City Hall. Unceremoniously, they got out; one came around, opened my door, and pulled me out.

We walked into the building in silence, rode up the elevator in silence, and walked right into Uncle John's office, in silence. John's silence screamed at me, reached out for me, and grabbed me by the throat. My not-so-gentle escort shoved me down into a chair, cuffs still on, and walked over and sat down in a chair on the far side of the office.

John swiveled his chair around. I knew he'd been looking at the row of pictures on the sill. When he turned around, he leaned back, rested his chin on his folded hands, and shook his head.

"Phoebe, Phoebe, Phoebe . . . I tried to tell you to stay out of trouble, stay on your side of the fence, within the law, and you wouldn't listen."

What could I say? "Can you take these cuffs off?"

John raised his eyebrows and looked toward the guy in the chair. He shrugged, got up, reached behind my back, and released my aching wrists. I heard the door open behind me, but John's eyes held me. I can't remember a more uncomfortable moment in my life.

"What the hell have you been doing?" His fist came down so hard on the top of the desk, I jumped a foot off the chair. "Didn't I make it clear? Didn't I give you every goddamned edge? And why . . . why didn't you come to me?" He hit the desk again. I jumped again. "Why?" he screamed.

"I . . . it . . . I was . . ."

"Don't." He raised his hand to silence me. "Don't say a word."

Double messages have never been my forte, but by this time I figured I would be better off following his lead.

"The gentlemen who brought you in are with the FBI. They've had an agent working on, uh . . ." He hemmed and hawed and looked over my head and behind me. Some unseen presence gave him permission to continue. "Working on a situation up there for some time now. Damn near a year. You came close to blowing his cover. You put the agent in an untenable position . . ."

"I—"

"For once in your life, shut up." His voice boomed. "Now, this is what I want from you. I want to know what you were doing at Whispering Pines, both times. And I want to know right now."

It was now a game of roulette, a game of chance. I needed to stall for time, for more information. My best bet was to get him to blow what little restraint he had left. I had two things going for me. He wouldn't hit me, and he wouldn't shoot me . . . or would he?

"I don't know what you're talking—"

"Maybe I can refresh your memory." The voice came from behind me. It was hauntingly familiar.

I turned toward the voice. The face looking back at me was handsome in a rough sort of way. He was a big guy, dressed in dark pants, a white shirt, and tie. An identification badge was clipped to his shirt pocket. I tried to read the name as he came around me and sat down on the edge of John's desk.

There was so much tension in the room I couldn't believe this jerk was half-smiling. It was one of those slow recognitions that kind of creep up on you and make you feel like the biggest fool in the world. I knew my mouth was hanging open. The name formed on the tip of my tongue and tried to manifest itself into a coherent sound.

"Crank?" I asked in utter disbelief.

There was little activity in the restaurant at that late hour. A couple of the waitresses sat at the far end of the counter talking quietly. I looked in their direction, trying to find the vilest, most obnoxious thing to say.

All I could come up with was "Ya know, Crank . . ."

"Maybe all of that animosity will disappear if you call me Robert."

Animosity? I had spent two hours being grilled by this guy and his cronies, and he had the balls to think that a different name could change things. Fat chance.

"If I'd met you as Robert . . ." I shrugged and looked him right in the eye. "It doesn't matter. You pulled a good scam. Hurray for your side."

I clapped softly, my hands held deliberately high, in front of my face, for added effect.

Robert, or Crank—whoever the hell he was—laughed, shook his head, and took another sip of his coffee. He wasn't that bad looking all cleaned up. He wasn't bad at all. If I hadn't been feeling so duped and so . . . caught, my mood would have been much better and his company more appreciated.

"I'm sorry we brought you in like that. There wasn't much of a choice. We didn't want you going back up to Whispering Pines."

"What about Kyle? What happens to him?"

"It's not up to us. His supervisor will handle it. What were you two looking for in the morgue?"

"You're bright guys. Figure it out."

"You know what, Ms. Siegel—"

"Oh, please, *Robert*, call me Phoebe."

He grinned at me and laughed. "Jeez . . . I walked into that, didn't I?" The smile faded. "The bottom line is I worked at a damned job I hated for eight months hauling frozen food all over this damned town. This isn't child's play. This is for real, and your constant stream of bullshit doesn't help a fucking thing," he said and leaned toward me. "I sat in that office for two hours watching you cover your ass and clam up. I don't have time for this shit. If you've got anything, anything at all that will help us, lay it out."

It could have been me sitting where he was. Coming on hard, coming on soft, growing more frustrated minute by minute. He was around my age, probably with the same goal of blind service I'd had all through . . .

"I hear you were at the academy," he said.

For one quick minute I thought he was reading my mind. I gave him all the silence he needed urging him to do just that.

"And I hear you lost a brother."

"I didn't lose him. I know right where he is," I said, trying my own game of hardball. "You lose at cards, Robert . . . you lose at—"

"Games like the one we're playing now. Only the stakes are higher this time. We have a pretty good idea that the kid they fished out of the river stumbled onto something, fed the information to her old man, and he made a move on Stroud."

That caught my attention.

"Anything you say will stay between me"—he poked his finger in his chest—"and you. It'll go no further. You have my word on that."

It reminded me of the way Ben always talked with his hands. It was a family trait. If we sat on our hands we were mute, unable to speak. Sitting there, staring into his index finger, made me smile.

He leaned back and started tapping his finger on the table. Exhaustion covered his face. I felt sorry for the guy.

"Christ, I'd like to know how you find any humor in this."

"I don't, it's just that"—I shifted in my seat—"for a minute there you reminded more of someone. Like I'm tired, right? If I had something, anything, that would help you guys out, I'd tell you."

"The night you rode up with me, what were you after?"

"Uh . . . a file. Just like I told my uncle. I've been working on a case for a client who had a kid in there for treatment. The girl has been involved with Whispering Pines for three or four years on and off again, and the results have been less than satisfactory. I wanted to see what she had in her file. That simple."

"I doubt that anything is that *simple* with you. Why would you set yourself up for a breaking and entering rap?"

"That'd make you an accomplice."

He shook his head, smiled, and looked back at me. "Who's the kid?"

"Confidential, sorry," I shrugged. "Can't help you out on that."

"What do you know about the guy that's in charge? Stroud."

"Not much. I told John everything. What do you know about him?"

"He's a con artist, but he's kept the place legitimate. He operated a private practice outside of D.C. Most of his clients were kids, usually from wealthy mainline families with heavy political connections. Desperate people in a desperate situation will listen to anyone who says they have answers. Stroud had them. A little manipulation on his part with the kids, who were basically dysfunctional in the first place—"

"He kept them sick."

"Right. Plus, we think he's been shaking down a few of the parents. The kids spill their guts to Stroud, and then Stroud uses the information to his advantage."

"Extortion?"

"Probably. Insurance fraud more than likely. He's been hanging on to the kids longer than necessary. We've got volumes from professionals who have been involved with his clients after release. Seems they're more fucked up than when they went in. We've had a file on him since D.C. We were ready to nail his ass when he up and moved. We've been close to him out here, but the SOB stays one step ahead of us."

Jennifer Kuntz flashed through my mind. Shawna Unger, split open and minus a brain, flashed on a bigger screen. I shuddered.

"Are you okay?" His concern seemed genuine.

"Fine. I'm fine. Why the cover? A delivery boy?" I tried to laugh.

"There's been a lot going on up there. For the last couple of months he's been cutting back on his staff and lightening the load of in-resident patients. Then last week we got a call from the Padilla kid at the local office—"

"Jimmy?" I asked incredulously. "He . . . called the FBI office?"

"Yeah. He said he had some information about a law enforcement official that was being blackmailed. Seemed he thought his girlfriend was involved somehow."

"What happened?"

"The agent that answered the phone knew I was involved and told this kid that he'd set up a meeting with me."

"And?" I knew what was coming.

"Seems he had a change of mind, got strung out, and hung himself in jail."

"Shit. What about the officer? Do you know who he is?"

"We thought it might be some beat cop, but from the conversation, the kid hinted that it was someone bigger. Who knows? We do think that Stroud is ready to jump. We just don't know which way."

He looked bad enough that I knew I must look half dead. I ached everywhere. My hand went up to my throat; George popped into my mind.

"I've had a cop tailing me all over town."

"Guess it's my turn. Do you know who it is?" he asked.

I hesitated, thought about Charlene, and the ache in my throat where George had tried to make me one with the truck. "Yes. I do. . . . George Shanklin."

"Christ, why didn't you say something when we were in your uncle's office?"

"I figured you guys already knew. Maybe you're slipping."

"I'll check him out. Cutter hasn't mentioned the name."

"Gage?"

"Good man. Do you know him?"

"Everybody does. I'd really like to stay and chat, but I'm fading." I stood and looked down at him and wondered how anyone could associate the word *good* with Cutter Gage. "It is all right if I leave, isn't it? Or . . ."

"Cuffs are off. Be my guest," he said. Then he reached out and held my arm as I started to walk away. "Stay away from Stroud. We're about to reel him in."

"Right. Gotcha." I drew on what energy I had and winked at him. "Check Shanklin out."

I walked out of the restaurant and stood on the sidewalk. There wasn't a part of me that wasn't screaming for sleep. I looked up at City Hall and saw the lights on in John's office. There was no way I was ever going to hear the end of this.

The truck was twelve blocks away. There wasn't anybody on the streets. Up Twenty-seventh Street I could hear a street sweeper scraping and sucking debris from the gutters as it moved downtown. A cop car pulled up across the street, parked, and turned out its lights. I watched the officer as he got out, walked to the back door, and opened it. A pair of feet flashed out and started kicking wildly.

Within seconds a couple of other cars pulled up, and the boys in blue got out and tried to assist. Their voices carried easily across the empty street.

"Jesus, you stink, Jones," one of the cops said and started laughing.

"He puked on me, and he puked all over the car. You guys get him out of there, or I'll bust the dumb fuck's ass."

Amid the laughter, the feet seemed to calm down under the threat. A head emerged, then a whole body, docile and quiet.

"You guys got a beer?" a drunk slurred.

"Shit," one of the cops yelled and jumped back from the door. "He's pissing all over himself. Shit."

I started walking toward the truck. My steps echoed in the dark.

I don't like the dark. Never have. Things breathe when you can't see them. Refrigerators, furnaces, walls, even furniture, all take on lives of their own. Anybody foolish enough to chalk up those noises and things that go bump in the night to expansion and contraction has never really listened.

Tonight I was listening. Stud was curled up beside me. It was the only time I can remember hanging on to that cat and enjoying it. A warm body is a warm body, and even Stud would do in a pinch.

When the phone rang, it startled me enough that my hold tightened on Stud. He let out a howl and used my thighs as a springboard to leap across the room. His claws dug deep through my jeans into my flesh. I reached for the phone.

"Hello?" I growled, rubbing my wounds.

"Is this Phoebe Siegel?"

"Maybe. Who's this?"

"Maureen Sandler. Jean Dillard called me this afternoon. I debated calling you. Sorry for the late hour, but I had to wait until my husband was asleep."

I perked up.

"Right. What can I do for you?"

"I was surprised to hear from Jean. It's been years. Three at least." Her voice was soft, uneasy, barely audible.

"You'll have to speak up, uh . . ."

"If my husband knew I was calling, he'd . . . We talked about it, and he didn't think I should get involved. It's not that he doesn't care, he just . . ."

"Maybe we should start over. Why would Jean Dillard have you call me?"

"My married name is Sandler. I've been married for several years."

"Congratulations. Is this like some kind of a survey or something?"

"My maiden name was Kuntz. Jennifer Kuntz is my sister."

The human mind has no limit to the amount of information it is capable of processing. Any other time, my mind would have immediately processed this revelation and reacted accordingly. The problem was that I was overloaded; this was the proverbial straw.

"Then Mary is—"

"Mary is my mother," she said slowly.

"Frank?"

"My father," she answered.

"You have to forgive me, I had no idea . . ." Or did I? My mind went back to the slides I had watched of Jennifer. There had been another girl, a look-alike, only older. "Mary didn't—"

"She wouldn't. I haven't had any contact with my family for years. I have a good life, a daughter of my own, and a husband."

"How did Jean Dillard know about you?"

"Jenny told her. I had kept in contact with a friend in Joliet. Jenny had given Dillard her name, and my friend contacted me. I considered trying to have Jenny placed with me, but"—she paused "but Jenny has always been fragile. We, my husband and myself, didn't know what kind of effect it would have on our daughter, so we decided against it. I've never been sure about what happened. Miss Dillard had promised me that she wouldn't reveal my whereabouts, and I figured that she could best deal with doing what was right by Jenny."

"Why did you run? I've met your mother. I like her."

"I'm an incest survivor, Miss Siegel. I didn't want to destroy my mother or myself."

"Then . . ."

"Jennifer's circumstances are no different than mine were. The difference between us is that I left, ran away, when Jenny was six. I had to. . . . You have to understand that if there had been any way, any way at all . . ." Her voice quivered with emotion. "I was a kid myself. There's no way I could have taken her with me."

For the next twenty minutes she filled me in on the years since she had left. Her story was similar to Jennifer's. A problem with drugs, a walk on the wild side, and life in the streets. There was one big difference. She was a fighter, a survivor.

Ending up in Missoula, she fell in with a group of people who worked with street kids. They must have seen in her the same things I heard in her voice. She met and married a student at the university and moved to Sheridan, Wyoming, where she had lived for the past five years.

"I can't believe you haven't had any contact with your mother."

"I couldn't," she said and took a deep breath. "My only satisfaction has been that he knows I'm out here somewhere. I'm happy, we're happy. I've even felt guilty about that. But I can't let anything jeopardize what I have now."

"Does Mary know about your child?"

"No. Jenny doesn't even know. Is she . . . is she all right?"

"Your mother?"

"Both of them, Mama and Jenny."

"There's . . . a lot is going on right now. Jennifer is, well . . ." How the hell do you tell someone that her sister has turned psycho? "Is there any way you could come up here and—"

"It's out of the question. I . . . my husband would never allow it. I . . ."

"Listen, Jean Dillard is willing to come forth and blow the lid off this thing. It would take too long to go over it on the phone, but this involves more than your sister," I said firmly. "If you can't come here, then I'll come—"

"No," she answered hysterically. "That's impossible. I'm sorry. It took me years to deal with my past. I can't throw that away." Her voice changed and became charged with pain and anger. "Years, Miss Siegel. I had to come to grips with the fact that what happened to me wasn't my fault. That I had stepped into someone's shadow, someone's sickness, and that it wasn't who I was, it was simply something that had happened. No one, not you, not Jenny, no one will pull me back into that."

"Don't you think Frank, I mean your father, should pay for what—"

"Pardon me?" she asked.

"There's not one shred of hope for your sister if your father isn't brought to justice."

"My father?" Her voice was incredulous.

"Are we on the same track here?"

"It wasn't my father, Miss Siegel." She laughed bitterly. "It was my grandfather. If my *father* should be tried for anything, it would be for the fact that he sacrificed his own kids in order to hang on to the few crumbs my grandfather threw him."

"Jesus!" A wave of nausea spread over me. That was what Stroud had on Cutter Gage, and that was what Jimmy Padilla knew.

"Don't get me wrong. As far as I'm concerned, my father is just as guilty as my grandfather. I was ten years old when my father found out."

"He knew?"

"You bet he knew. We were moving horses for my grandfather one time and I got to ride with him. We stayed out overnight and the weather turned. I got cold so I climbed into my father's sleeping bag."

"Look, you don't have to go into this with me."

"Everyone is horrified, but no one wants to hear it. Right?" She laughed cynically.

I said nothing, and she continued. I steeled myself against the sickness that coiled in my stomach.

"I loved my father. I trusted him. I snuggled up against him and started fondling him. It was the natural thing to do. It was what I had been *taught* to believe was natural. Loving."

"Shit . . ."

"That was his reaction. He was shocked and started asking me questions. I told him about Bompy," she said and took a deep breath. "That's what *Cutter* insisted Jenny and I call him. I guess it made him feel more benevolent somehow. He went into this rage. We went back in the middle of the night, and he confronted my grandfather. I only heard part of the argument before they realized I was listening and sent me away."

"Then he quit? He stopped?" I knew asking that was like hoping for a happy ending in *Sophie's Choice*.

"No. My grandfather got to me the next day and told me that if I ever shared our *special secret* with anyone, my mother and father would have to leave and that they would leave me with him. Have you ever met him?"

"Yes, I have."

"Then you know how persuasive he can be. I stayed as long as I could. My father avoided me, couldn't even look me in the eyes. I look back now and figure he saw himself, his grubbing worthlessness, every time he looked at me."

"Your mother . . ." I felt myself losing it. "What about her?"

"Mama? I doubt that to this day she had any idea. I've . . . I've wanted to call her so many times . . . I . . ."

"Hang up the phone, Maureen." A voice sounded from the other end of the line. "Hang up the damned phone."

Maureen covered the mouthpiece for a second and then came back on. "I have to hang up now," she said quietly.

"Wait," I said in a panic. "You've got to come up here. Please . . ."

The line went dead. I wanted to call Roger, but I knew the hour was ridiculous. I wanted to go home to Mama and crawl in beside her like I had so many years ago and have her tell me everything was going to be okay.

The digital clock beside my bed glowed crimson in the night, each minute, each second, passing, melting into the next. I didn't even bother to turn the scanner on. My mind was in a state of confused suspension. Sleep was impossible. Stroud found out. It became his payola. Ben, poor Ben found out. It became his death sentence. And George, George somehow milked it for all it was worth.

I tossed and turned until the clock read four thirty, and then I reached into the drawer of my nightstand, found the paper I was looking for, and dialed the number written on it.

It seemed to ring into eternity. Finally, a not-so-coherent voice answered.

"Lanny," I whispered. "It's me. Phoebe."

He paused and then spoke. "Phoebe. . . . What time is it?"

"Early. You told me I could call if—"

"Sure. Sure. What's up?"

"I need some help . . . I, uh . . . I wouldn't call like this if it wasn't urgent. I need help, Lanny. George . . . he . . ."

"What about George?" he asked sleepily.

"I had a run-in with him last night. I think, no, I know he's mixed up in something up at that treatment center I told you about. Remember the kid they pulled out of the river?"

"Sure. What about her?"

"She didn't drown, and there's more."

He didn't say anything.

"It's Cutter Gage. He's . . . Kyle Old Wolf and I—"

"Kyle? How the hell did he get in on this?" His voice was louder for a minute, then he started whispering again. "I'll be over. Give me time to get dressed, and make sure you've got some coffee."

"Thanks, Lanny. Prepare yourself. It's all damn unbelievable."

I put on a pot of coffee, sat down at the kitchen table, and waited. By the time he arrived, I had formulated the entire story in my mind. I was determined not to leave anything out.

When I finished, he had his chair pulled close to mine and was holding both of my hands in his. He didn't say a word, didn't ask a question through the entire thing. He just watched me, shook his head now and then in disbelief, and held my hands.

"That's it. The head of the highest law enforcement agency in the state, and they've got Kehly's picture, and I know it was George that put it on the truck seat. They're trying to tell me that the wrong move, any move on my part, and Kehly—" I couldn't even say the words.

"I've got to have time to think about this. It's hard to believe that old George—"

"He's not the benign jolly giant that you think he is."

"He's a little hotheaded, but, Phoebe, how the hell long have we known this guy?"

"Long before you and I got married. . . . Lanny, I'm sorry, I didn't mean to—"

"Mean to what? Remember? I do it all the time." His grip tightened on my hands. "I've never forgotten, Phoebe. I won't."

"I . . ." Something formed in my stomach, twisted it in a knot, and started to squeeze. "Don't do this, Lanny. Not now."

He let go of my hands and stood up. The moment, no matter how tense, disappeared quickly.

"Listen, I'm off until tonight. It's almost seven. I'll give you a call around six tonight. In the meantime, don't say a thing to anyone. You just don't know who's in on this with George. Shit," he said and shook his head. "That's damned hard to swallow."

"Lanny, I thought about going to John and telling him the whole story, but then something came up, and now this sick shit with Cutter Gage . . ."

"I wouldn't go to John, not yet anyway. Let me have some time before you, or we, do anything. Taking on Gage is like sticking your hand in a fan. We have to move carefully on this."

"You're right. I'm just not thinking straight." I started to move toward the door.

His arm shot up and blocked my way. He reached out, touched the tip of my chin, and tilted my face up. I couldn't move. He put his head down close to mine, and I could feel his breath, warm and moist, on my face.

It's funny what the mind and body do in a moment of remembrance. It was the most natural thing in the world, something we had done hundreds, maybe thousands of times before. I responded, maybe more out of need than anything. All I know is I needed the closeness, and he was there, close, kissing me.

"What the fuck is going on?" Roger's voice burst into the room.

He was standing inside the door, just staring at me. There wasn't a lot I could say. Lanny looked at him briefly, then smiled at me, reached out, and touched the side of my face.

"I'll call you around six tonight. Okay?"

"Sure . . . I . . . Roger, this is Lanny Wilson."

"I don't give a shit who he is," he said, and then it dawned on him. "Lanny . . . your . . . you don't waste much time, do you?"

"Right," Lanny said and stuck out his hand. Roger ignored it. "I'll talk to you tonight. Good to meet you . . . uh . . ."

Roger just stared at him, and then at me, with a look of total horror. "I don't believe this," he said. His entire head, down to his shoulders, was bobbing up and down.

"Roger, I called Lanny and asked him—"

"You called him?" His voice broke. His face turned deep red. "*You* called *him*?"

"I'm taking off now," Lanny said and walked out the door.

"Roger . . ."

"Don't . . . don't say a damned word. Shit, Phoebe." His eyes filled with tears. "What the hell did you take me for? This guy . . . he's married, isn't he?"

"Roger, it isn't what it looks—"

He burst into a low, cynical laughter. "Christ, try something original." He turned and started out the back door.

"Roger, wait . . . let me tell—"

"I've waited," he said and turned around to look at me. "No more. You're stone cold. It's always been your way or no way. We're different, you and I." He reached up and placed his hand on my face. Instinctively my hand encircled his wrist. "Jesus, you're all I've ever wanted. I even figured that by letting you go, you'd come back. Shit! Did you have a good laugh with that guy afterward?"

"Get out, Roger. Get the fuck out of here! Now!" I threw his hand away from my face. "If that's all the better you know me, then get the hell out."

"I don't know you," he said, spitting the words out of his mouth. "How the hell could I, you don't even know yourself."

The entire wall shook when he slammed the door. I turned toward the table. My head buzzed, my eardrums were pounding. I fell into something black.

I woke up on the couch late Saturday afternoon with Stud curled up on my chest and listened to the wind blow outside for a long time. Exhaustion had pulled me into an emotionally bankrupt sleep. There were no feelings. No problems. Nothing.

It didn't take long for reality to set back in once I was awake. My entire body was on a pain alert. I got up, opened one of the front room windows, and listened to the rain that the wind beat against the side of the building.

I knew that I had to pull it together and that a shower would help. I turned the shower head to the hardest pulsating flow I could. The stinging bursts of water felt good against my skin. I let them hammer my body past the hot water and into the tepid and then the cold.

I could feel my mind coming back to life. As I stepped from the shower, I heard the phone ringing. My heart caught in my throat. It had to be Roger. If it wasn't, I was going to call him. If he wouldn't talk to me over the phone, then I'd find him. It was as simple as that.

By the time I reached it, the answering machine had attempted taking the call, but the caller had already hung up.

When the phone rang again, my heart jumped. I'd go to any length, short of groveling, to explain to Roger what had happened between Lanny and me. It rang again. I needed a couple of seconds more. My hands were sweating like crazy. I reached out, grabbed the receiver, and interrupted the third ring.

"Roger, before you say anything, you have to listen . . ." No one answered. "Roger?"

The silence that came through the phone crawled into my ear like an invisible, hungry predator, reached out, and filled me with knowing. I tried to take the phone from my ear. My hand wouldn't work. My arm stiffened.

"Roger?" I said in something below a whisper.

"I'm calling for Helen Jenkins."

Relief flooded me for one teasing and torturous second. I giggled in hysterical relief. "Sorry, you've got the wrong num—"

The word hung there, suspended in my mind. Helen Jenkins . . . the name I'd used on Stroud and on Dinah Lord. My mouth dried up. I struggled to speak. I didn't have to.

"Helen . . . it is all right if I call you Helen, isn't it? I hope I'm not calling during the dinner hour."

Stroud's voice rendered me speechless, nonfunctional.

"My, my. I would have thought you'd been waiting for this call."

I sat down on the couch, dropped the phone to my lap for a moment, and braced myself. When I put it back to my ear, I was prepared to do battle. It was the first time in my life I felt unarmed.

"What do you want, Stroud?"

"Victor, please call me Victor. Let's keep this informal. It's not like we don't know each other, is it, Miss Jenkins?" I could hear him quietly laughing, mocking me.

"I asked you, what do you want?" The strength in my voice surprised me.

"I'm calling with good news."

"You've got a gun to your head. Well, go for it."

"No, actually, I've decided to take your sister into the program. Let's call it a refresher program. We've been through our initial interview, and she has agreed that . . ."

He couldn't have her, there was no way she would have . . . My mind was tripping out. *But she would go with George. Anywhere.*

"Let me talk to her," I said, trying not to let the panic show in my voice. "Now!" I commanded.

"That's not really possible. I'm afraid she was, how shall I say it, a little resistant at first, which necessitated my sedating her."

"You bastard."

"I wouldn't worry about her. She's quite relaxed at this moment. We did have a harder time with the gentleman, though."

"What are you talking about? Who—" It hit me like a brick to the temple. Would Roger have gone to Kehly after he left here? Probably. And he, in turn, would have listened to or gone anywhere with George. "If you've hurt either—"

"Quite the contrary. Kehly is fine. Sleeping like a baby. Of course, like I told you, we had a tougher time with the attorney. He was worried we were going to hurt the young lady. A wasted concern, actually."

"I'm coming up there—"

"Most assuredly. It's totally against our policy, but, taking all things into consideration, I agree with you. Of course, we have to have our customary consultation before you see them. What time would be good for you?"

"Now . . . I'm coming now."

"How about ten this evening? By that time, Kehly will have had another treatment—"

"If anything happens to either of them, you prick, I'll see you burn in hell." Rage had replaced fear.

"It's in your hands. You're an intelligent young woman. Because of that, I know that I don't need to tell, I mean ask, you to keep this little, uh, situation between us. Ten. I would recommend that you're not a minute late. The gates will be open. I believe you can find your way to my office."

The line went dead, as did every nerve in my body.

$\triangledown$

19

ACCORDING TO MAMA, SHE had talked to Kehly shortly before three o'clock that afternoon. Kehly had passed up the opportunity to go to Chico Hot Springs. Roger had answered Kehly's phone when Mama had called.

With a mother's instinct, she knew immediately that Roger was in the midst of some crisis that no doubt involved me. There was no way I could answer any of her questions. What would I have said? Your daughter's been kidnapped, along with Roger, but don't worry, it only involves a former state senator who now happens to be the head of the MIB and this psychiatrist who's probably a sociopath and one of his demented patients. I've got it under control. No way. So I lied. By the time we got off the phone, she was convinced that all was well, on every level.

I called information for Sandler in Sheridan, Wyoming. There was only one listing. I was beginning to understand about choices. Mine was simple. Two people I loved were in jeopardy. That was all that mattered. Maureen Sandler had to come through for me. I didn't have anything else. The phone rang a good ten times before a deep male voice answered.

"Yeah?"

"I need to speak with Maureen."

"Who's calling?"

Something exploded in my head. "Put her on the damn phone. I don't have time—"

"She isn't here."

"Then where is she? Who is this?"

"This is Miles Sandler. I'm Maureen's husband."

I knew I wouldn't get anyplace bullying this guy, so I took a deep breath and hoped for the best.

"Your wife called me last night. I've got big trouble up here, and I need her help."

"I know about her call to you. Why didn't you just leave things alone? She's been through enough." I hated the pleading in his voice.

"I don't have a choice here. I—"

"Maureen isn't here. She's in Hardin."

I knew the town, sixty miles east of Billings, nearly halfway between here and Sheridan.

"She's on her way here?"

"No, she's on her way home. She drove up early this morning after she talked with some Joan . . . Jean, it was Jean, she talked to her and took off. She called me a few minutes ago."

"She's already been here?"

"Yeah, it didn't go well."

"Go well where?"

"With her mother. She saw her."

"Oh God."

"She told me to tell you that this Jean had the information ready that you needed. What the hell is going on up there? Is Maureen in any danger?"

"Not if she's on her way home, she isn't."

I didn't even bother to say good-bye.

I tried calling Lanny at home but hung up when his wife answered. For an hour I sat and stared at the telephone, willing it to ring, dreading that it would. When it finally did, it sounded like an alarm going off inside the apartment.

"Phoebe . . ."

"Lanny, shit. I've been going half nuts. Stroud called. . . . He's got Kehly and he's got Roger . . . God . . ."

"Slow down. Just tell me what he said."

I gave him a blow-by-blow play of my conversation. He listened, silently. When I was through, he still said nothing.

"Say something, damn it. Christ, what am I going to do? Ten o'clock, Lanny. That's all the time I have. Until ten."

"Let me think a minute. He said the gates would be open. Right?"

"Right."

"Okay. I've got to cover someone on shift tonight. It's too late to get out of it, but this is what I'll do . . ."

We agreed that Lanny would be on the grounds by the time I got there. I was to do whatever Stroud wanted of me, but I would stall for time. I didn't remember that the dogs would also be on the grounds until after we had hung up. There was no way I could call him back. He'd have to deal with them.

I went into the bedroom and dug through the top of my closet until I found what I needed. I took the box down from the shelf, set it on the bed, opened the lid, and lifted the bundle out: last year's Christmas present to myself, a Model 1006 10-mm Smith & Wesson. It had cost me over seven hundred dollars, and I'd only fired one clip-full of rounds in the basement of the dealer I had purchased it from.

I took the loaded clip from the box and slammed it in. There's something about a gun in your hand. If you hate them, it's like holding a rattlesnake by the neck. But right now, for me, the thirty-eight ounces in my hand was all I had between myself and God only knew what. I didn't know what I'd be up against.

I grabbed a jacket with deep pockets, pulled it on, and put the 10 mm in the right-hand pocket. The phone rang.

"Hello?" There wasn't a sound from the other end of the line. "Hello?"

"Phoebe, this is Mary Kuntz. I found a book, Jennifer's book. It's called the Book of Shadows. I think you might want to look—"

"Look, Mary, I've got a lot going on right now. Hang on to it. I'll get back to you. Okay?" Something clicked in my mind. I needed an edge, a bargaining point, and Jennifer just may have chronicled that edge in her diary.

"Mary?" She didn't answer. "Mary, talk to me."

"I . . . I'm here, Phoebe. I'm sorry to have bothered you like this. It's not important . . ."

There was a quality to her voice that was giving me the creeps. I didn't have time to figure it out. It had to be coming from her surprise visit from Maureen. "Mary, I'm on my way. I'll be there"— I looked at my watch. It was 7:00 P.M.—"I'll be there in twenty, twenty-five minutes. Thirty tops."

She didn't respond. "For God's sake, Mary. Do you hear me?"

"I'll be waiting." She hung up.

By the time I turned south on the narrow two-lane highway toward the Kuntzes', the rain had let up, the clouds had cleared, and the temperature was dropping. I could see my breath inside the truck.

The engine sputtered. "Don't fail me now," I said and patted the dash. "Please."

I turned left onto the gravel road and took it slow over the ruts.

I definitely didn't need to shake any rust loose in the gas tank. If the truck stalled now, it would be deadly, in more ways than one.

When I reached the Kuntzes' mailbox, I turned off the road and stopped, expecting that I would have to open the gate. It was open. I drove down the lane into the yard. Jennifer's car was gone. Only two were parked by the house. One I knew to be Mary's and the pickup I assumed was Frank's.

The yard light wasn't on. The house was dark. I left the truck running and the headlights on, put it in neutral, pushed on the emergency brake, and got out. There was a ghostly stillness, a dead calm that replaced the cold night breeze.

My feet felt like lead weights as I started toward the back door. I stayed in the headlight beams. My shadow raced out in front of me and touched the door before I did. In six more steps, I caught up. My shadow crawled up the side of the house and hung there like a black-skinned mime towering above me.

Nothing moved, nothing made a sound as I reached out to knock on the door. It opened slowly toward me, pushed by some unseen, unhurried hand. I took a step backward and reached inside my jacket.

"I saw your lights, Phoebe," Mary said as she stepped aside and held the door open.

"What are you doing in the dark, Mary? Let's get some lights on in here," I said and stepped past her into the house. "Where's the switch?" She didn't answer.

I turned around. She stood there, looking out into the dark yard. "Where's the light switch, Mary? Let's get them on and—"

"They aren't working, Phoebe. I have some candles in the cupboard." She turned and walked around me into the dark kitchen.

I stood there, trying to follow her sounds as she rummaged around. I heard doors open and close, a drawer slide open, and then she reappeared near the table. The pungent smell of sulfur filled the air as she struck a match and lit a candle she had placed on a plate in the center of the table.

"Jennifer made this for me one Christmas a few years back. It's so beautiful I just never had the heart to light it. Don't you think it's beautiful?"

She straightened up, the match still burning in her fingers. I walked over to her and blew it out.

"It's a Christmas candle. All the kids made them that year. Look at it, Phoebe. Don't you think she did a nice—"

"Mary." I held her by her shoulders and turned her toward me. "What's going on out here? Are you alone?"

"I, uh . . . no, no I'm not alone."

"Who's here with you?"

"Frank is here. We've been talking, Phoebe. About the girls, about my little girls and about the book."

"Where is he, Mary? Where's Frank?"

"Who?" She shook her head.

"Frank. Where is Frank?" My hands tightened on her shoulder. "What the fuck is going on out here?"

"He's down at the barn, Phoebe. My daughter came home today. She has a little girl," she said and raised her hand to her hair and stroked it. "She looks just like Maureen did. Blond curls all over her head. She called me . . . she called me Grandma."

"I know Maureen was here, Mary." She brought her other hand up and stiffened as she held something close to her chest. "What's in your hand?"

"It's the book. I . . . I . . . found it."

"Hang on to it." She held it so tight there was no way she was going to let it go. "Take me down there . . ." I stopped. I didn't need a rematch with her daughter. "Where's Jennifer?"

I looked over her shoulder toward the doorway behind her, fully expecting a knife-wielding blond to leap from the darkness.

"I don't know. We had an argument this morning, and she walked out. I begged Frank to stop her. She stood there and laughed at him, at me. He did nothing. He just left for his sale."

"Mary, we need a flashlight, anything. Then I want you to take me to Frank."

"He isn't much of a talker. Never has been, but I thought he'd try—"

"A flashlight, Mary. Where is one?"

She walked toward the refrigerator, reached up on top, and took down a small flashlight. "Will this do?"

"That's fine. Now let's go."

She walked through the door and out into the beams of the truck. I followed. Our shadows melted into each other as we walked around the edge of the house. It was pitch black. Mary walked without faltering in a straight line. As my eyes adjusted to the dark, I could see the defined edges of the barn. There was no light, no hint that anyone was there. If they were, they were sitting in the dark.

Mary stopped when we reached the corral. I turned the flashlight toward her. She brought her arm up and shielded her eyes from the light. I moved the beam away. Her arm dropped back to her chest. She still clutched the diary.

"Where is he, Mary?" My voiced sounded alien.

"We talked for the first time in so long, it was hard to remember." She turned and looked off into the night. "I was upset that Jennifer had left . . . upset with him for not stopping her."

"God damn it, Mary." She was so out of it that any cooperation from her was going to be minimal at best. "Frank," I called out.

"He was crying, Phoebe."

"Frank!" I yelled as loudly as I could. Still no answer.

"I left him down here and went back to the house. I just wanted to sit in her room for a while. I knew we had lost her, I knew that, Phoebe. But a child . . ." Her voice broke; a heart-wrenching sob stabbed through the night. "You never really lose a child. Not one that you've had inside you. No one can ever take that, or the memories, away."

I walked to her and put my arms around her shoulders. As soon as I touched her, she stiffened. "We have to find your husband. I don't have the time to stand out here—"

"Then I saw it, just a corner of it sticking out from under her dresser. I've never snooped. It's not my way. But I picked it up and I read it anyway. They were her words," she said in a quivering, mewing voice. "Her thoughts . . . and I needed them."

I looked around through the darkness. A breeze came up and pulled a strand of hair over my face. I turned and brushed it away. Something sparked down toward the ground inside the corral. In a split second it was gone. Then it reappeared, sparked, and disappeared again as the breeze stopped.

A shrill whinny split the air. I jumped back and looked toward the rail of the fence. Blacky's head reared over the top rail. The moisture from his nostrils was white, vaporous in the moonlight.

"Frank! Frank Kuntz!" I screamed.

"When I had finished reading it, I just sat there for the longest time. Then . . . I came down here . . ."

The great black stallion had disappeared, swallowed by the darkness.

"Mary." I grabbed her by the shoulders again. "We're getting out of here."

I could feel the breeze again. She looked beyond me, toward the corral. This time a buzz accompanied the spark. Mary stared, the sharp white light reflected in her eyes.

"Frank." My throat ached I yelled so hard.

"He was in the corral with Blacky. He poured some grain in the trough and set the bucket under the fence. I showed him the diary—"

"Mary, we're leaving." The buzzing behind me started again, borne on the breeze that was now steady. "Come on."

"He missed seeing Maureen, Phoebe. He'd gone to a sale, and when he got home, I told him Maureen had been here. Then I showed him," she said and held the diary up. "He knew as soon as he saw it, that I knew what he had done. My God." She clamped her hand over her mouth.

"We're out of here." I released my hold on her shoulders and grabbed her hand. "Let's go."

"He touched her, hurt her. How could he do that?"

I stopped and turned to her. She still stared toward the corral. The impact of her pain tore through my chest and settled in my stomach. And then I knew. "What?" I asked incredulously. "What have you done?"

"He's there, Phoebe."

I turned and looked toward the corral. Down low to the ground, a wire swayed, touched something, and sparked again. I stepped closer and scanned the top rail of the fence with the flashlight. My back was to Mary, but I heard her move behind me, follow me.

"Frank?" My voice was weak, barely above a whisper. "Frank . . . we need to talk . . . okay?"

I directed the beam down toward the sparking wire. It took me a moment to figure out what I was seeing. Frank's face, or what was left of it, was turned toward me.

"I asked him why . . . why he had hurt her, but he didn't answer me. He just stood there."

The wire swayed and landed erratically on his cheek, sparking on the dead, blackened flesh. I moved the flashlight beam over his crushed skull and down the length of his broken body.

"I begged him to answer me, to tell me why." She whined behind me. "But he wouldn't."

I couldn't move. I couldn't take the flashlight beam from his battered face. I couldn't breathe. "Jesus," I said, more a wheeze than a word.

I dropped the flashlight to the ground. It rolled and turned back behind me. I saw the shadow of her hand held high in the air gripping something, something long. My mouth dropped open as the black silhouette swung down in an arch toward my head.

"Mary! No!" I screamed and dodged sideways, my arms up to block her blow.

"I had to!" she yelled. "My babies! My little girls! He knew! He knew and he didn't help them!"

Her hand came down a foot away from me and crashed onto the metal bucket by my feet. The blows rang through the night, assaulting my senses as she hit again and again.

The horse reared high and screamed as his hooves slashed through the air. I could hear them crushing the lifeless body beneath them.

"I kept hitting and hitting until he was down, until he was still." The rod dropped from her hand as she followed it to the damp earth. The only sound was Mary's sobs as they tore from her grief-stricken body. "He didn't help them, and I had to hurt him for that . . . I had to . . . my God, I had to . . . ," she sobbed.

I crawled over to where she huddled on the ground. Her shoulders convulsed as racking cries tore from her soul. My arms encircled her. I shuddered and held her close.

When I finally got her into the house, she was back in the protective shield of her delusion. There were no more tears. She just sat across from me at the table and watched me page through the book by candlelight. Each line, each paragraph, screamed with the pain and the anger and the bizarre fate of Jennifer Kuntz. I closed the book and looked across the table toward a smiling Mary.

"She walked early, you know. She did everything early."

"Mary, we have to call the police." I stood and started toward the phone.

"They kept trying to tell me something was not right with Jennifer, but I didn't believe them. They were wrong, weren't they, Phoebe?" She smiled toward me. "He was hurting her, and she didn't think she had anyone to turn to."

"The police, Mary," I said, convinced now that I couldn't handle this alone.

"No, dear, we don't need to call them. An officer was already here. I told him . . ."

"What do you mean, a police officer was here?"

"I sat and tried to talk to Frank, but he was so still. I picked up the book, I had dropped it, and when I turned to come back up to the house he was standing there."

"Who?"

"The officer. I stopped and talked to him for a moment and invited him in for coffee. He told me he couldn't right then, but that he would be back shortly."

"Shit." I reached out for her and grabbed her arm. "We've got to get out of here. Now!"

"I have to get my purse, Phoebe." She stood, walked through

the dark doorway, and then returned with her purse. "Shouldn't we wait for—"

"Not a good idea, Mary. Trust me on this."

Within seconds we were in the truck and I was backing out of the driveway. I could see car lights coming from the main highway.

If you're coming here, you're going to have to hit me head-on to stop me, I thought. I mashed my foot down on the gas pedal and backed through the gate, swung the truck around, and surged forward. The lights neared.

"Hang on, Mary," I said as I headed straight for the oncoming car. It swerved and hit the ditch. I could tell it wasn't a cop car.

We rode in silence until we hit the interstate. I pulled off the exit and headed into Billings. I had to take her someplace, but where? There was no way she was going with me. I wouldn't dare take her to Mama's, and I was running out of time.

Sharon, the massage therapist, wouldn't be open on a weekend, and I had no idea of where she lived anyway. Then the name I needed popped into my mind. Jean Dillard. Christ, why hadn't I thought of it before? I pulled into the Easy Mart store on Shiloh Road, left Mary in the truck, and ran to the public phone mounted on the outside of the building. Someone had torn the phone book out. I dialed information, got Jean's number, and dialed again. She answered after the first ring.

"This is Phoebe. I need a favor, Jean. I—"

"Jennifer's sister stopped by and saw me. She had been at her mother's place. Is Mary all right?"

"She's with me."

"I got the papers together that you needed. Maureen wanted to make sure they would end up with the proper authorities. I'm trusting that you'll do that."

Her words came out slurred. With Mary on my hands, this was all I needed. "Right, they'll get there. Jean, I need a place for Mary Kuntz to stay for a while. Just for a couple of hours."

"Is there something wrong?" she asked.

"I can't get into anything right now. I'm about ten minutes away from your place. Can I bring her by?"

"That's fine. I'll have the papers waiting for you. Someone is at my door. I have to go. See you shortly."

"Wait! Don't let anyone in!"

She'd already hung up. I got back in the truck, patted the dashboard for luck, and put my foot on the gas pedal. The engine died as soon as I pushed on the accelerator.

"Shit," I yelled and pounded on the steering wheel.

By the time I finished emptying the sediment bowl and got back on the highway, twenty minutes had elapsed.

Any car coming toward me, any car behind me, could mean trouble. Big trouble. I took the Shiloh Road exit and decided the best thing I could do was come into Billings on the back road. It would give me a clear shot at Poly Drive and a better view of anyone on my tail.

By the time I reached Poly Drive, I was swerving at every shadow. I drove slowly past Jean's house. The lights were on in the front room. My first instinct was to pull in the driveway, yank Mary out of the car, and deposit her with Jean with little or no explanation.

Instead, I drove down the street, found the entrance to the alley, pulled into it, and parked the truck at the far end.

"Mary, this is important. You have to understand precisely what I'm going to tell you."

I spoke deliberately, trying to get the message across that my sister and Roger were in danger, and that she and I were as well.

"Jean Dillard, you know who she is, Mary? She lives near here. I'm going to talk to her now, and I want you to stay in the truck. I'll be back for you. Okay? Don't leave the truck."

"I won't, dear. How long should I wait?" she said as she reached over and patted my hand.

Fuck, this wasn't going to be easy. "Wait until I come back for you. Do you even understand what I'm saying?"

"I'm all right," she said and continued to pat my hand. "You just go on and do whatever it is you have to do. I'll stay right here. I'm fine, dear, really I am."

I hesitated and then got out of the truck. I didn't have a lot of choice. I ran down the alley and back onto Poly Drive. It's hard to look casual when you're stressed as hell and running out of time. I walked up the sidewalk to Jean's front door and rang the doorbell. No one answered.

I knocked and leaned past the door to look into the front room. I could hear music coming from inside. I knocked harder on the door. Still no response. I turned the knob. The door was unlocked. I looked around; when I was sure no one was watching, I opened the door and walked in.

"Jean?" I called out.

I walked from room to room calling her name. Each room was as orderly and neat as the last. The house was big and spread out.

Toward the back, I finally entered the kitchen. It was spotless and would have looked like something out of a model house, if it hadn't been for the persistent drip from the faucet. The only thing it lacked was plastic fruit in a wicker basket on the table.

Music continued to drift through the house, following me, or maybe leading me, from room to room. To the right of sliding glass doors that I assumed led out to the backyard, a door stood ajar. I walked over to it and pushed it open. Light spilled into the garage. The music was instantly louder.

I reached my hand around the edge of the doorjamb and felt up and down the wall for a light switch. There wasn't one. I stepped down the first stair and was met by a blast of cooler air. I moved my hand up above my head and felt for a cord, anything that would activate light. I stepped farther into the garage.

My hand brushed a hanging cord. I grabbed it and yanked. Light flooded the area. Jean's car was parked on the far side.

"Shit, she's probably one of those nightwalkers or something," I muttered and turned.

Her feet hit me in the face. I stumbled backward and fell to the cold cement. One shoe on, one off, Jean Dillard's body swayed from our collision. Her head lobbed to one side. One hand was caught under the cord that cut deep into her neck, the swollen tips of her fingers curled outward, spread garishly apart in her last attempt to save herself.

I crawled crab style toward the door leading back into the kitchen. With strength from somewhere, I pulled myself up by the doorjamb. Nausea rose in my throat. Two in one night was more than I had the stomach for. My mouth filled with water. I reached for the sliding glass doors, fumbled with the lock. They slid open, and I fell out onto the patio.

Sirens tore through the night as I sucked in the cool outdoor air. I could hear the cars as they sped down Poly. With a burst of fear, I ran back toward the alley. I scaled the high wooden fence and dropped into the darkness on the other side just as footsteps rounded the edge of the house. I could hear the harried voices of the cops.

I waited only a second before I ran to the truck. My feet didn't even seem to hit the ground. I opened the door and got in.

"Did you see your friend, dear?" Mary asked.

I didn't answer. I pumped the pedal, put the truck in gear, and pulled out of the alley with my lights off. I stopped at the corner and looked down the street. Three squad cars had pulled up onto the sidewalk. I pulled the truck across the street and up toward Rimrock Road just as neighbors started coming out of their houses and gathering in front of Jean's.

George was up ahead somewhere, in the dark, and he was headed for the same place I was. Whispering Pines. Mary sat beside me, staring out as I drove down Rimrock. She just sat there, clutching that damn book and her purse.

$\triangledown$

20

I HELD MY WATCH up to the dull light of the gas gauge on the dashboard. It was exactly nine fifty-five. Mary had been silent until I pulled off the highway and onto the road that led to Whispering Pines.

"We're going to Whispering Pines, aren't we?"

"Yes. You have to stay in the truck again."

I pulled up next to a black Chrysler with state plates and turned off the truck engine. Gage would be inside.

"We shouldn't be here."

"Don't worry," I said. "I have a friend on his way."

"Jennifer needs help. Miss Dillard tried once. Maybe she'd try again . . ."

"Shit," I mumbled.

"I was thinking about God on the way up here, Phoebe. If there was a God, he wouldn't have let this happen to my girls. He wouldn't—" She stopped, looked out the side window, and back toward me. "Do you think there's a God?"

"Beats me, Mary."

All the sympathy in the world, all the understanding, wasn't going to undo what had already happened. I had to be brutally realistic; her presence could blow it for Kehly and Roger. The thought crossed my mind that I should tie her up, but I didn't have anything to do it with. I sure as hell wasn't going to knock her out.

I turned toward her. "I've got one minute to meet Stroud. If you leave the truck . . ."

A cold, hard look crossed her eyes. "I'll wait here. You have my word."

"My friend is a policeman. Tall. Redheaded—"

"I . . ."

"Mary, if you see him, tell him I'm inside. He'll recognize the truck. Okay?"

"Phoebe . . ."

"Understand?" I asked harshly.

She lapsed into a hurt silence. I just couldn't give a shit right then.

I took the gun out of my jacket pocket and slid it under the front seat. Stroud was nobody's fool. I got out of the truck and looked around. The place was dark, dead still. The only sounds in the night were my footsteps as I climbed the stairs toward the front door. The hall stretched before me. A single lamp on a table at the end of the hall illuminated my way.

When I reached the doors to Stroud's office, I took a deep breath and entered. The lights were low. The highly polished wood paneling and the opulent furniture glowed in the dim light. All of the masks, dead eyed and silent, stared down at me. It struck me as odd that so luxurious a room would smell so heavily of cheap lemon-scented furniture polish.

I was alone. Whatever confidence I'd had when I walked through the doors was vanishing. I heard movement on the stone porch beyond the French doors. Stroud walked into the room. He was taller than I had remembered, more imposing. He smiled, walked around the desk without speaking, and reached out to shake my hand.

"Welcome."

"Cut the shit, Victor." I wanted to lunge toward him, claw his eyes out, tear his throat with my bare hands, and that was the gentle stuff.

"Sit down. I'm hoping this situation hasn't gotten so far out of hand that we can't come to some mutual, shall we say, understanding."

"I want to see my sister."

"Soon," he cooed. "Please, have a seat." He extended his hand toward the chair I had sat in on my first visit.

Stall for time and hope like hell Lanny is where he said he'd be. I'll have to be ready, I thought. I sat down.

"Whose car was that parked outside?"

"Malcolm Gage has decided to join us. He'll be here in a moment. He's feeling a deep sense of regret that you've, uh, heard some disturbing information about—"

"Bullshit."

"I find that offensive, particularly from a lady."

Lady? This guy was really deluded. He leaned forward and looked at me intently.

"I need to ask you a few questions before we go any further."

"Is this a pass-or-fail test, Stroud?"

He hung his head and laughed softly. "No, this is no test."

The door opened behind me. The hair stood up on my neck, but I didn't turn around. Cutter Gage didn't just enter a room, he electrically charged it.

"There's not a problem in the world that can't be solved through mutual agreement and intelligence." Stroud's voice was as arrogant as ever.

"Shawna Unger. Was she a problem that you solved through mutual agreement?"

"I had nothing to do with Miss Unger's death," Stroud answered as Gage walked past me and sat on the edge of Stroud's desk.

"No one meant for that young woman to die," Gage added. "A moment of panic. A mistake. Victor let his guard down." He turned toward Stroud and sneered. "Did I ever tell you how disappointed I was with that, Victor?"

Stroud stirred uneasily in his chair. "During one of her several attempts to flee," he continued, "she ran onto some information—"

"Let me guess. Could it be—" I brought both hands up to my temples and closed my eyes. I had to go for broke until Lanny showed up—"I've got it. She found out what pricks you are. Am I warm?"

Stroud sat up straight in his chair. His entire expression changed. I felt myself pushing my body back into the chair. Then he relaxed, returned to the facade of icy smoothness, and smiled at me.

"Shawna delved into areas that she had no right inquiring about. The information she came up with was sensitive and potentially embarrassing."

"To whom? You?"

"Oh no. I'm sure by now that you're aware of the special relationship Cutter had with Jennifer."

"Don't push me, Stroud," Gage said and stepped toward him.

"Of course, Jennifer suffered from a histrionic personality disorder that easily justified her rather dramatic behavior. There were other, deeper problems, of course—"

"That you took advantage of. Right?"

"Wrong. I'm not a monster. I care deeply about my involvement with adolescents. That's why I kept Jennifer near me here at the center. From the moment I discovered what—"

"Stroud." Gage's voice was shaky.

"He's right. It's enough to say that I protected the girl. Gave her sanctuary from the harsher realities of her life."

"Let's get this over with. What are we going to do with her?" Gage asked bluntly.

"Did you see that, Phoebe? Did you see how he asked me that? Cutter and I have become quite dependent on each other."

"Shut up, Stroud," Gage said. His voice was deep, menacing. "You've said too much already."

"The rich, Miss Siegel, and the powerful. . . . Society hasn't been all that fair to them. We not only use them as role models for our material success, but in the process we ascribe to them standards of morality that aren't always there," Stroud said. He stood and walked over to where I was sitting. He laughed and kneeled down beside me. "In fact, if the truth be known, and I'm speaking from experience here," he continued and looked toward Gage, "the wealthy and the powermongers may be less moral, because their power can protect them from the consequences of their acts."

"And you make a financial killing by using the threat of those consequences to your best advantage. Am I right?" Being this close to the guy made my skin crawl.

"Didn't I tell you she was bright, Cutter?" Stroud stood and walked back over to Gage. "She's got the whole picture. It's over. We've got one choice and one choice alone."

"It's looking that way," Gage offered. "It really is looking that way."

In the time it took for me to look down at the floor in disgust and back up again, it was over. The sound was nothing more than a muffled pop. Stroud looked into Gage's face with curious shock as his hand reached out for something to steady himself on. He was dead before he hit the floor. I felt the front legs of the chair I was sitting in lift as I pushed myself back into the soft leather.

"We'll find *another* way, won't we, Phoebe?"

"Sure," I answered breathlessly. "What's the choice here? My throat slit or a gut shot?"

The next thing I knew, Gage had tossed the gun through the ten feet of air separating us. I caught it.

"There was only one bullet in it. I only need your prints."

I was aghast, looking down at my hand curled around the gun's grip and then back to Gage's face.

"I've just ridded the world of the lowest kind of vermin. A blackmailer," he said as he pulled a black leather glove from one of his hands and then the other. His voice was hollow.

This guy was insane. Gage looked at me. Beads of sweat stood out on his forehead.

"You son of a bitch," I said and started to get up out of the chair.

Gage shook his head and motioned me to sit back down. "I'm a strategist. I don't see problems, I concentrate on solutions. Now, I'm going to need your help, Phoebe. Maybe . . . just maybe, between the both of us, we can find an equitable solution here."

"God, you are one crazy—"

"Do we destroy a career, a lifetime of public service, a family, when there are options? I've made mistakes, but what is paramount is what I've done in this state politically." His eyes looked frenzied.

I had to keep him talking. "How did it happen, Cutter? How did you let a slimeball like Stroud put the squeeze on you?"

"I underestimated him. Stroud became a force to be reckoned with. The FBI notified me when he moved into Montana. By that time I was director of the MIB. It was a fluke that Jennifer ended up with him. By the time I got around to talking with him, he already had information about . . . uh . . . ."

A slight twitch in his cheek gave him away. His facade was crumbling. Jennifer *was* my ace in the hole.

"Things became complicated. A local policeman took an interest in her," he said as he walked toward me and stopped in front of me. He was in control again. "Once this officer took advantage of her, slept with her, it was Stroud who manipulated and directed her fantasy about him. Stroud was very, very adept at that. But, again, we underestimated someone. Jennifer. Jennifer trusted him, opened up to him, and before we knew it, both Stroud and I had someone to reckon with."

The muscles were knotting up in the back of my neck.

"Victor felt that it would be to his advantage to have a liaison on the police force. He thought he'd have some leverage with her paramour. According to Jennifer, they had been intimate. Lovers. As it turned out, it was with another police officer."

"George Shanklin?" I asked. My heart was racing; the palms of my hands were soaking wet. I needed time. More time. "Was that who did it?" He didn't answer.

"My brother, Cutter? Did Stroud kill him? Or did Shanklin?"

"Another time, another time," he said and waved his hand in the air, erasing my question from his reality. "And now, here we are in a very similar position. Do I have leverage with you, Phoebe? Or is this a no-win proposition?"

"I'd say you had the upper hand, Cutter."

"As for your brother? I was told, later, that he had begged for his life. Sad. Sad state of events. And all because we had no leverage. No bargaining power."

Something, someone, picked me up out of the chair. There were no hands on me, no one around me. I wanted to run, cry, scream. My emotions fought my rational self for control. I couldn't blow it. Not now. I steeled myself, walked around behind the chair, and placed my hands on the top of the back. Lying on the shelf beside me was Stroud's prize petrified penis. I picked it up and turned, holding it innocently down by my side.

"What about Jennifer? Where is she now? Someone could walk into this room at any time, Cutter. There must be at least twenty, maybe thirty people up here."

He laughed.

"Yell if you want to. Scream your head off. I've had to keep Stroud informed of the investigation around him. He's been preparing for this moment for months. The last of Stroud's patients left this morning. Employees have been cut back slowly over a month or so. Stroud was leaving the country. With my help, of course. I had no choice but to keep him ten steps ahead. The only matter we had to clear up is the one involving you."

He stood and waved me toward the door in the paneled wall. "Don't blow it, Phoebe. I'm no one's fool. If you'd feel more comfortable, you may follow me. Your young man is just two doors away. Make up your mind."

The arrogant creep walked ahead of me. He knew he held all the cards. We reached a door; he stopped and pushed it open. We entered what looked like a small but well-equipped examination room. On the south wall, swinging doors with glass windows stood closed.

Someone else was here. No one I could see, but I felt it. Gage was too confident, too cocky. I turned to my right and saw Earl, Gage's right-hand man, leaning against a wall. He stiffened as our eyes met. The shoulder holster he was wearing knocked against a metal file cabinet. I looked away.

On my right, a stainless steel counter stretched the length of the room. Gage paced back and forth, twirling something he had pulled out of his pocket. It glinted under the fluorescent lighting. Why shouldn't it? It was Ben's silver Medic Alert bracelet.

"You've met Claire?" Cutter asked absentmindedly.

I hadn't heard her enter the room and jumped when Gage spoke.

"Miss Siegel is concerned for a couple of our guests. Take her to the one in there."

Gage immediately huddled with Earl in the corner. Their voices were inaudible. Without a word, Claire turned and walked toward the swinging doors, pushed one open, and waited for me to pass through. The room was dark. The door closed behind me. I stood still and waited for my eyes to adjust.

When they did, I could tell I was in a small ward of some kind. Curtains were pulled closed around what looked like separate cubicles. A gooseneck floor lamp stood a few feet from me. I walked to it and turned the light on.

Green curtains hung to the floor, obscuring whatever was behind them. At the far end of the room was a small waiting room, with glass doors leading out onto the same stone porch that was accessible from Stroud's office.

I dropped the walking stick and threw the first curtain back. The curtain rings clattered over my head. I was prepared for anything. There was nothing. I grasped the second curtain open and hung on to it, unaware that it was tearing down from the rings that held it to the rail.

I threw the curtain back and gasped. Vomit worked its way up my throat. The curtain tore free and fell to the floor; I almost followed it. My knees buckled. Roger turned his head slowly and looked at me. His lips were dry; his mouth moved without sound as his eyes rolled back in his head. I stumbled toward him. He was naked except for the sheet that covered him from his waist to his knees.

"My God!" I don't know if I spoke or if the words were still formless and just echoing in my mind.

"Are you all right? Talk to me, damn it. Say something."

I tried to translate the *argh* that was coming out of his mouth into something I could understand. "What, what are you trying to say?"

"I don't . . . I don't know where we are . . ." The words came slowly. His lips stuck together each time he formed a word. "My m-m-mouth, I need . . ." He raised a hand and touched his lips. His arm fell limply back to his side.

I looked around and saw a sink and paper cups hanging nearby. I turned on the faucet, filled one of the cups, and carried it back to him. The cold water spilled over my hand. I cradled his head and raised it enough to pour water into his mouth. He struggled to raise his hand to help me.

"Jesus . . . Jesus . . ." I couldn't say anything else. "You've got to help me, Roger. . . . Where's Kehly? Where is she?"

He raised a feeble hand and pointed toward the curtain on the other side of his gurney. "There . . . she's there . . ." The words gurgled from his mouth; water trickled down his chin.

I let his head back down, walked to the next curtain, and threw it back. She was there. Silent. Her eyes were closed. I reached out and took her hand in mine. It was warm. I could feel her breath against my hand as I stroked her cheek. Tears filled my eyes. I looked up from her face. The doors leading outside were in my direct line of vision. A shadow moved across the lawn.

My body and mind were numb. I had to get those doors open. If it was Lanny . . . if I could just reach them in time . . . let him know where we were. Voices were coming from the outer room. I ran around the table Kehly was lying on and lunged for the doors. I found the lock and clicked it up. The shadow was gone. I saw no one.

The swinging doors opened behind me. Jennifer Kuntz walked into the room, smiling. She said nothing as she walked toward Roger. Roger raised his head, a wild look in his eyes. He was too weak to fight her as she touched his forehead.

"He's very good looking." She stroked the hair back from his forehead.

I moved toward her. "Jennifer, I need your help—"

As soon as I looked into her eyes, I knew it was a lost cause. Over Jennifer's shoulder I could see Claire through one of the windows. She looked and then disappeared. I didn't want to do anything that would bring them in there.

The walking stick was at Jennifer's feet. I leaned down and picked it up.

"Do I know you?" She smiled and started walking toward me. "I'm—" She stopped and turned toward the noise behind her. Cutter Gage walked into the room. Jennifer smiled only for a moment. The change came within seconds. The muscles in her face relaxed as the haunted look moved through her eyes. She was gone. A younger, more pitiful reality had taken over.

"Bompy?" she said and held her arms out to him in a voice so childish, I cringed.

He swung his hand toward her outstretched arms and moved them aside. "Get the hell away from me," he said cruelly. Jennifer recoiled and let her arms fall to her sides. Her lips pouted as she brought her brows down to hood the pain in her eyes.

Gage came toward me. "I need to talk to you myself," he said to me breathlessly. "I can make you understand. We can work this out." He nervously swung the bracelet around and around on his index finger.

Jennifer looked beyond us both and toward the back door. Something deep within her fought for control, and shadows of delusion and pain and reality cloaked her face. In a kaleidoscope of emotion, she struggled for some semblance of understanding of what was happening around her.

"Jennifer?" a voice called from behind me.

I couldn't believe my ears. I turned slowly. Jennifer stood anchored where she was. Mary drifted into the room, both hands held straight out in front of her. The barrel of the 10-mm pistol she was holding pointed directly at her daughter.

"I found the book, baby. I understand now. I'm so sorry . . ." Tears ran down her face. Her hands were rock steady.

I looked at Jennifer. A single tear coursed down her face. Her eyes rolled and focused. Gage froze in his tracks, Ben's bracelet hanging limp from his finger.

Everything went silent. Jennifer lowered her head and stared at Mary. "Mama . . ." The voice was soft, young, full of fear. "Mama, I . . ." She opened her arms. "I want to go home."

Gage dropped the bracelet. Jennifer looked down at it just as Gage leaned over and picked it up.

"That's mine," she said and moved toward him.

"I love you, Jennifer. You're my life. My baby." Mary smiled, but she didn't lower her arms. "Move away from him, honey."

I looked quickly at Gage. His face was ashen, frozen in terror. He couldn't take his eyes off the gun, my gun, that Mary held.

"Give me that," Jennifer's childish voice pleaded. Jennifer took another step toward Gage.

She attempted to reach out and touch the hand with which Gage grasped the bracelet. Again, mercilessly, he shoved her out of the way. She staggered backward and steadied herself on the counter.

"What the hell are you doing, Mary? Put that damned thing down," Gage said, unable to move.

"You bastard," Mary said softly. She smiled and shook her head. "My life . . . you've destroyed my life. My babies . . . my little girls . . . how the hell could you . . ."

"I can explain, Mary baby. . . . I was sick, I was . . ." Gage stepped toward her.

I was trying to watch all three simultaneously. Time slowed down. Frame by frame, they all moved at once. I saw Jennifer out of the corner of my eye lunge for the hand that held the bracelet. She moved in front of Gage just as Mary squeezed off the first shot.

Cloth exploded from Jennifer's back. Bone and blood flew in the air as the bullet ripped through her. Jennifer's hands reached up and grasped Gage's shoulders. She hung there. Gage's eyes never left Mary's. Jennifer looked toward Gage's face. A deep-throated gurgling sound followed the blood from her mouth as she slid down the front of him.

Gage reached down, held the girl's wrists, and followed her slowly to the floor. Claire pushed open one of the swinging doors, looked in, and ran away. The door swung back and forth, its arch becoming smaller and smaller until it was still.

The muscles in Gage's cheeks twitched. His body jerked. His hands still held Jennifer's wrists as she crumpled and lay prone on the floor. He wasn't even aware that the bullet had passed through Jennifer and entered him.

Mary squeezed the trigger a second time. Gage's body flew backward as another bullet tore through his upper torso. Jennifer crawled toward me, one hand stretching out, reaching for me. Her body jerked. She reached out for the curtain, pulled herself up, and then fell toward me. I could feel the warm blood flowing from her as it soaked through the front of my shirt. My hands caught her.

"Mama." The girl screamed. "Mama-a-a-a-a." The word stretched into eternity as another shot rang out.

Mary walked toward Gage, her arms steadily held out in front of her. "You'll never hurt my children again. Never. Never again." Her words were little more than menacing growls from her throat.

Sound exploded around me. The round tore Gage's chest open. His glazed eyes stared into space. Blood gushed down the front of his shirt. He crumbled to the floor. Ben's bracelet fell from his hand. His eyes never left Mary's face.

$\triangledown$

21

I LOWERED JENNIFER TO the floor, my hands covered with her blood. Looking up, I saw Claire's face, distorted in horror, framed by the glass window in the swinging door. The only movable object near me was a large metal cabinet on rollers. I pushed it in front of the doors to block Claire, who disappeared, and to keep Earl from entering.

I turned to face Mary. Her arms were hanging by her sides. The gun fell to the floor with a dull thud. She dropped to her knees and crawled toward her daughter. Jennifer reached out to her. Mary grasped her hand and inched closer. When she reached her, she cradled Jennifer's head in her arms. Jennifer reached up and touched Mary's lips. Mary closed her eyes and started a lullaby, slow, gentle, barely audible.

Jennifer's hand slipped from Mary's face, leaving a crimson smear of blood on her mother's cheek. Jennifer smiled, raised her hand again, and touched her mother's face. Mary, oblivious, did not hear the words.

"I love you, Mama . . . I—"

Jennifer's hand fell a final time. Mary rocked back and forth, her lost child in her arms. She was smiling. Damn!

The cabinet I had barricaded the door with was sliding away. I pushed against it but couldn't hold it. Within seconds they were in the room. Claire rushed me, her hand coming down across my face with such strength it sent me to my knees.

"You stupid, stupid bitch!" Claire screamed.

I was within feet of Mary. My mind reeled. I could smell the strong scent of musk and death, could hear moans coming from above me, and the drone of Mary's humming. The side of Earl's pant leg brushed my face as he edged around me.

"Oh shit, oh shit," he said and continued to mumble in a hoarse, low voice. "What are we going to do? What the hell are we going to do?"

"Shut up!" Claire boomed. "We've got to think. Think this through . . ."

"It's over. Christ, it's all—" Earl's voice rose from a whisper to a high-pitched whine.

"You stupid idiot. If you don't get it together . . . we've got to get them out of here. Somehow . . ." Claire paced back and forth. "Take that one."

"Which one?" Earl's voice neared hysteria.

"That one. The one up there. Get him out to the car, take him somewhere, and dump him. Then get your ass back here." Her words were clipped, direct. "I've got to wait for—"

"How the hell do you think I can move him by myself?"

"Drag the son of a bitch. I've got to take care of the girl."

By this time I was on all fours. I looked at Earl as he moved toward Roger.

"No." I screamed and lunged for Roger. My head exploded. My body collapsed as I slipped into a black, bottomless pit.

I felt the coldness of the tile floor against my cheek. Someone was whispering to me, pulling me up from the darkness. My head throbbed in blinding pain. My eyes wouldn't focus.

"Phoebe. . . . Get up." It was a rasping, urgent whisper.

I felt the hands under my arms, felt myself being lifted, steadied. I squinted and tried to focus. Roger was gone. Mary still held her daughter. I was confused. I had no idea where I was or what had happened. Slowly the room became defined. Lanny was holding me under the arms against the wall.

"Lanny . . ."

"Don't talk . . . don't say a word. Stay right here."

He left me propped and walked to the sink. He returned with a towel and held it over my face, wiping down again and again.

"Lanny . . . they've taken Kehly and Roger. . . . They were going to throw him off the—"

"Kehly's in the other room. I saw them with her. Keep your voice down." Lanny stroked my forehead. "Christ, it's gone too far. Too fucking far."

"What . . . what are you talking about?"

He was behind Lanny before I knew it. I screamed. Lanny turned. George's fist hit him in the face and slammed him to the floor. I dove for the walking stick. Lanny was struggling to his feet.

George's back was to me. I grasped the stick. The steel rod inside felt like two tons in my shaking, weak hands.

I took a step back and swung it with everything I had at George's head. He dropped like a rock onto Lanny. Lanny shoved him aside and stood up. I ran toward the back doors and slid them open. The wind carried a sheet of rain into the room and across my face.

I turned toward Lanny. "We've got to get help. My God . . . we've got to get help."

I looked out over the lawn. The city lights were visible through the rain in the distance. My mind was clear, determined. You've got to get out of here, call Uncle John.

"Phoebe . . ." I could hear the groan but for a moment couldn't figure out where it was coming from. "Phoebe . . . it's him."

I looked at George. He was on his hands and knees, his head hanging down, practically touching the floor.

"He's getting up. Do something."

"It's him, Phoebe . . . ," George whispered.

"I know you, don't I?" Mary asked in a daze, looking up at Lanny. "You're the young man that was out at the farm. The policeman."

I knelt beside her, held her chin, and turned her face up to mine. "What are you saying, Mary?"

She smiled. "The policeman I told you about that was standing on the hill above the barn." She turned and looked at Lanny again. "I bet you came back and we had already left. Didn't you?"

"Lanny?" I looked toward him.

"She's out of her mind, for God's sake. Shanklin, keep your fucking mouth closed or I'll close it for you."

Lanny had his gun out of his holster and was holding it on the back of George's head.

George didn't shut up. "It was him. Phoebe . . . ask him about the kid in the river. I heard him. I heard the girl. I thought he had found her, but when I got to him, no one was there."

"Shut up, Shanklin."

"Ben. Ask him about Ben," George pushed.

"I told you to shut up," Lanny said as he swung the barrel of the gun against George's head.

George fell to the floor. His face was turned toward me. I saw him grimace and bring his hand up over his head.

"For God's sake, Phoebe, you told me yourself George roughed you up. Right?"

"I did tell you that, Lanny. But I told you some other things. Things you were going to check out for me." It was all coming together. "What's he talking about? What about the girl? What about Ben?"

Lanny looked panicked, troubled. There were tears running down his face. "It went too far. Too far . . . before I realized what was happening. That damned Dillard woman. Why the hell did you go to her? Why, Phoebe?"

I started to stand. "What the hell . . . Lanny?" I asked in disbelief.

"Stay down there, Phoebe." He looked wild and pointed the gun toward me. "I gotta think this through. I gotta . . ."

He rubbed his forehead. Sweat trickled down to his brows even in the chill of the room.

"Lanny," I said again.

"They told me they wouldn't hurt him. They said they . . . no, they *promised* me all they wanted to do was talk to him. That's all. Just talk."

"Who, Lanny? Who are you talking about?"

"It was the kid. That damn sick kid." Lanny tensed his jaw. The muscles contracted and relaxed in rapid succession. "Ben knew I was in trouble. He knew I was in trouble, and I begged him. One damned mistake. Just one. . . . Shit. . . . I begged him not to go to John."

"You?" I asked in utter disbelief. "I don't believe this," I mumbled. "God, I don't—"

"I didn't have any choice. They made me."

"You killed . . . you couldn't have. Not Ben," I said and felt the sobs ripping, straining to break free from my throat.

"Earl did it for Gage. They lied to me. They said they just wanted to talk to him. I believed them, God . . . I believed them . . ."

Earl entered the room, kneading his hands in front of him. "We got a mess, Wilson. A real mess going on here. We gotta get out of here."

"You son of a bitch." I started to move toward him.

He flinched and backed up. "I wouldn't do something dumb like that. That's why we're all here right now. Dumb mistakes. Right, Lanny?"

"Shut up!" Lanny screamed. "It's through. It ends right here." Lanny turned the gun toward him.

"Hey, it's all of us out of here or none of us out of here." I could tell Earl was playing all his cards. "Ask him the truth about your brother. I wasn't in that one alone. Or the Padilla kid. That was his baby. His and his alone. He set it up, the whole damn thing." Earl's voice kept rising.

"You pitiful bastard." I started toward Earl. Lanny swung the gun back toward me.

"Don't push. Begging would be better." Earl tried to stiffen his jellied backbone. "Your brother did. God, it was great." Earl sneered. "Atta boy, Wilson. You know what we have to do. Right? Shoot her. Shoot!"

"Phoebe, if I had known . . . they lied to me . . . Ben was going to turn me in for . . . he caught me with the Kuntz kid. Shit," he screamed and stamped the floor with his foot. "They lied."

"And John? He's in on this too?" I asked.

"Oh, that one," Earl said. He turned toward Lanny. "She's referring to the counselor that you paid a little visit to." Earl was pacing like a caged rat. "Lanny used Flannery's name that time."

"Lanny," I pleaded. "You? All along it's been you?"

"She was a dyke, for Christ's sake, Phoebe. And working with kids," he answered and shifted the gun from his right hand to his left. "She was nothing. She wouldn't have ever found out it wasn't John. Shit, the kid spilled her guts about me. I didn't have a choice." He ran the fingers of his free hand through his hair.

I covered my ears with my hands and screamed. "N-o-o-o-o!"

The word spiraled from my mouth in agony and disbelief. The sound just kept coming. Inch by inch, every nerve in my body vibrated and sang. My head buzzed. I looked toward George; he was conscious, staring at me. He moved his forehead, moved his lips, trying to form a word, a message.

"Are you with us, George?" Earl said, looking down. Without warning Earl pulled his foot back and kicked George in the back. George groaned but never uttered a word. "Guess he's not," he said and laughed again.

My eyes went to George's face and back to Lanny's. It flashed through my mind what George was trying to tell me. I looked to my left. The gun Mary had used was lying within reach, out of Lanny's sight. It was my best bet.

"Let's get this over with," Earl said. "Now. Or we don't stand a chance. I shoved Roger's ass into the river, and we've got to roll."

"Where's Kehly?" Lanny asked Earl without taking his eyes from mine.

"Claire's taking care of that," Earl answered. "Now do what you know you have to do and let's get out of here."

"I'm not going to kill her. I can't . . ." Lanny sounded shaky, confused.

"Then give me the goddamned gun and I—"

I lunged for the 10 mm. Lanny looked surprised. The tip of his barrel followed me. I could see his finger start to squeeze the trigger. My hand tightened around the grip.

I was in total control. Everything in me was on high. He pulled off a shot directly to where I had been. I saw George get up off the floor. It was fast. Lanny was swinging the gun toward me. I opened my mouth and released three years of rage, and grief, and every shell left in the clip.

I remember the rain. I remember the ride down the hill and how the lights of the city seemed to swallow the darkness as we neared. We passed the spot on the Rims where they had found Ben. Just for a moment I thought I saw someone standing there, a blur, an outline. I touched the glass with my hand and it was gone, behind me somewhere. Forever.

It's cold in here. I can't quit shaking, even under the blanket that someone wrapped around my shoulders. I think it was George. Mary's still there, tapping that mindless tune on her purse with her finger. She won't look at me. I need to get Jennifer off my hands. No matter how hard I try, the dried brown blood won't flake away.

"Somebody, get her a wet cloth. . . . What the hell is wrong with you guys?" John's voice breaks through my concentration. "Phoebe, Michael is here. George went to get him."

"Fee . . . are you okay?" I feel the softness of the palm of his hand slide down the side of my face.

"I'm fine." My voice is hoarse. My eyes are heavy and dry.

"You're tough; just hang on a little while longer and we'll get you out of here." Michael's voice caresses my anguish.

I nod yes and lean back against the wall. Someone hands me a warm, wet towel.

"Let me do that." I look up and let Michael take the towel from my hand.

There are tears running down his face. His hand holds mine while the other gently strokes the caked blood from my hands. I don't take my eyes from his face.

"He didn't kill himself, Michael," I say softly. I don't want to hurt him. I don't want to hurt anybody. "He didn't do it."

"I know, Fee. George told me the whole story. For years he'd been digging around. He never believed it is a suicide."

"He attacked me, Michael." My mouth is so dry it is hard to form the words. "He . . ."

"I heard. He was terrified you were headed for a confrontation."

"I got them both killed. Kehly and Roger. I killed them."

"Kehly's at the hospital . . . she's going to be—" He stops and hangs his head. "I saw her before I came here. Mama is with her."

"You're lying to me, Michael."

"I talked to her, she's worried as hell about you."

"Oh, God," I say and lean back against the wall. Pressure is building in my chest, pushing against my throat. I try to swallow and can't. I look at Michael again. "Roger?"

"It doesn't look good, baby. Do you remember what happened?"

"No . . . I . . . he took Roger . . ."

"Maureen Sandler called John as soon as she got home and told him the whole story. John tried to find you, Phoebe. He finally tried Charlene. By that time George had filled Charlene in on what he suspected. John was just minutes behind George."

"Jesus." My mind fought to comprehend it all.

"They've got a bunch of guys down at the river, but . . ."

The pressure continues to build. I can barely breathe. Someone walks behind Michael and speaks to Mary. She stands and follows him from the room. She doesn't look at me as she walks by.

"Phoebe, I want to take you to Mama's. John said you could leave in a few minutes."

"Michael . . ."

"What, baby?"

"Please take me to Kehly," I say and stand up. He pulls the blanket up over my shoulders. I start walking toward the door. Uncle John looks up from two uniformed cops he is talking with and walks over to us.

"Are you leaving?" he asks.

"Yes. I need to see Kehly . . . Will you call me . . . call me when they find Roger?"

"You know I will. He was a good man . . ."

"Hey, Captain," someone yells.

"Can't you see I'm busy here? Hold your horses," John shouts back.

"They've got a guy down at the river."

Michael's arm tightens around my shoulders.

John shakes his head toward me and scowls at the cop. "Not now."

"Look . . . there's some crazy running nude through the trees right where they're dragging the river. Says he's an attorney and he won't come out until someone gives him some clothes . . ."

My knees give out. Michael grabs under my arms and holds on.

"We need a couple of more guys if you've got 'em. We gotta do something with him or he'll freeze his balls off," the cop says and laughs out loud.

The pressure bursts from my lungs, expanding everything on its journey up my throat, seeking demanding release. Tears build in my eyes and flood in a constant stream down my face. The sobs come one after another, unstoppable, unrelenting. They echo through the room. I sit down on the floor, wrap my arms around myself, rocking back and forth, moaning. Releasing. God, I'm crying. I'm really crying.